PEACE RIVER

PEACE RIVER

Chip Ballard

To order additional copies of this book, contact:
Xlibris Corporation
1-888-795-4274
www.Xlibris.com
Orders@Xlibris.com
58157

For my loving mother.

Acknowledgement

Thanks to former Hardee County sheriff, Newton Murdock for his help with police procedure in early stages of the manuscript; Dr. Carolyn Pinkard for her uncanny wisdom and literary insight; Saundra Woodward and Noreen Cullen for their valuable editorial assistance.

Prologue

Sandy rolled out of bed, picked her jeans from a crumpled pile of clothes on the floor, and wriggled into them. She pulled her wrinkled sweater over her head, not bothering with a bra.

She thought of her dad and mom asleep a few doors down the hall and wished she could go and crawl into bed with them, just curl up in a nice safe ball under the covers as she had when she was a child—not that long ago, she realized.

In her bathroom, she brushed her teeth and then her hair. She set the hairbrush on the countertop and studied herself in the mirror. Everyone raved about her beauty, but the face staring back at her didn't strike her as particularly pretty now. She was too pale. Her eyes looked sunken. The black hair that framed her face and lay in dark swirls upon her shoulders made her appear ghostly.

She looked into her eyes, which she believed to be her most striking feature. Strangers young and old stared at her eyes wherever she went. Some suspected her of wearing special contacts. Everyone who saw her agreed that she had the most incredible eyes they'd ever seen. They were large eyes, deep green, like winter rye grass, and dotted with flecks of gold the color of summer hay.

Looking into the mirror, Sandy thought of Elvis; her heartbeat quickened. Elvis adored her eyes. "Honey," he'd said, "I could sit back and look at your eyes all night long. Just lookin' at those eyes, that's enough for me."

Thinking of Elvis, Sandy became excited. This feeling was new to her, even if she was sixteen years old and a senior in high school. No other boy had ever affected her this way.

She couldn't wait to tell her friends. But Elvis didn't want her to tell anyone because he didn't want to tarnish her reputation. Sandy moved away from the mirror.

Maybe she'd tell Kara. Kara would be the first to know that Sandy Carlton was finally across-the-river-and-into-the-trees in love—with a boy most of Pinewood County believed was a loser.

Actually, Kara would be the second person to know. In a moment of unbearable excitement, she'd told one other friend. Sandy regretted that now but believed her secret was safe as long as her friend didn't get too high and blab.

Thinking of her meeting with Kara made her think of the meeting after that, the one on the Peace River she'd lain awake all night worrying about. She didn't want to think of that now. She didn't want to think about anything but Elvis.

*   *   *

As she turned into the Mendel's driveway, Sandy's headlights swept across the lawn. To Sandy, the sparkling dewdrops looked like sprinkles of tiny shards of cracked glass.

She saw Kara through the screen of the porch, sitting in her wicker chair, holding a steaming mug with both hands. Kara stood up and smiled as Sandy walked through the door.

"Have some coffee," Kara chirped in a little-girl, singsong voice that Sandy hadn't heard in a while.

"You sound awfully chipper this morning, Kara. How are you?"

Kara shot her a glance. She was quiet as she fixed Sandy's coffee. Handing Sandy the mug, she pursed out her bottom lip and puffed at a wispy strand of blonde hair that had fallen down on her forehead.

"I know that tone," she said. "What you mean is, I sound awfully off my meds, right?"

Sandy laughed.

"Maybe I mean that."

Kara set her mug on the table, wrapped her arms around herself, and smiled. She closed her eyes and rocked side to side, as if swaying to music only she could hear.

"Well, I feel great." She sighed, rocking, her eyes shut. "I've been on cloud nine since I first laid eyes on Jim, you know that. He's my soul mate, the love of my life."

Sandy tasted the coffee and sat down in the plastic chair opposite Kara's wicker. Kara stayed on her feet.

"You mean Mr. Pratt?"

Kara opened her eyes and stopped rocking. She sat down too and turned to Sandy. "You're such a prude. No, I don't mean Mr. Pratt. I mean just what I said. Jim. So he's a little older than me. Who cares?"

"Your mom and dad would care plenty."

"Jim's the most gorgeous man I've ever laid eyes on, and he likes me. I know he does. You see how he looks at me in class."

"Mr. Pratt looks at all the girls, Kara."

"He's a man, isn't he? But he doesn't look at other girls like he looks at me. He's in love with me."

"He looks at Diana like that."

Kara banged her mug down on the Formica tabletop so hard the mug cracked, and coffee sloshed across the table and spilled down on to the porch floor.

"Shit!" Kara looked at Sandy. "Are you all right? Did I get any on you?"

"You missed me."

Kara eyeballed the door to the kitchen, hoping her dad wouldn't come barreling through it, bellowing about the racket the girls were making. She tiptoed into the house for some rags.

"Sorry," she said, sopping up the coffee on the tabletop.

"Kara, you know how you get when you go off your meds. It isn't worth it. Why do you do it?"

"How would you know if it's worth it? You've never lived in my head."

Kara toed open the screen door, squeezed the coffee-soaked rags out into the yard. "Diana used to be my friend. Now she's trying to take Jim away from me. Damn her!" She wiped over the tabletop once more, then squatted down and went to work on the floor.

Sandy let moments pass before she spoke. She was bursting to tell Kara about Elvis.

"Listen, Kara, we've been best friends since we played bluebirds in our kindergarten play and whistled the bluebird song and—"

"In perfect harmony!"

Sandy grinned.

"Think we've still got it?"

They puckered up, blew air, and began to giggle. Then they started laughing and laughed until their sides ached; when they got themselves under control, they whistled a few bars of their bluebird song, in perfectly awful harmony. That got them laughing again.

Sandy looked at her watch. It read 6:55. Her next meeting was at seven thirty at a remote spot on the Peace River. Sandy knew the place but hadn't been there since her sophomore year when she'd eaten Thanksgiving dinner there with her parents, Mr. and Mrs. Mathews, and Diana.

"Kara, I have to go. Listen, forget about Mr. Pratt. Don't get involved with a schoolteacher. Think what a mess you'd be getting into. Will you do that for me, just think about it?"

"I have thought about it. It's all I think about. If Diana steals Jim away from me, I'll kill her!"

"Don't say that."

"I mean it."

Sandy set her mug on the table and stood up.

"Kara, get back on your meds."

"Don't go."

"I have to."

Kara stood up. The girls embraced.

"Forget him, Kara. You're too good for him."

"Jim's in love with Kaaaara." That singsong voice again. "Jim's in—"

"No."

"Love with Kaaaara."

Sandy got in her car and put down the window.

"Bye, Kara."

She backed out of the driveway, drove up Dove Lane to the highway and turned south. A heavy gray overcast wrapped the sky, blocking the rising sun and making it so dark that cars drove with their headlights on.

As she passed Uncle Buck's Blue Duck Café, Sandy saw Deputy Mike Evers stumble up the front steps to the front door. *Hung over again*, she thought.

Sandy drove a little farther, brightened her lights, and watched carefully for her turnoff. Suddenly it was there, and she made a quick turn off the highway onto a grassy lane between rows of orange trees. When she exited the grove, she drove across rugged pastureland toward an oak hammock that bordered the Peace River.

She did not notice the vehicle with its headlights off that nosed out of the orange grove and rolled into the pasture behind her.

Chapter 1

Pinewood County Sheriff Charlie Morris knew he was dreaming but could neither wake himself up nor fully convince himself it was only a dream; thus, the nightmarish terror did not diminish. In his dream, he was in his office, looking out the window, when sheets of paper from the pile of paperwork on his desk, which reached the ceiling, began to fly off the pile and zoom around the room like small flying carpets. One by one, the pages joined the paper parade until the room was thick with them, and on each one, a smiley face appeared, and they all began to wink and leer. They dove at him, spun around his face, slashed his neck, arms, and hands—making paper cuts that stung like wasp bites. He opened his mouth to scream, but no scream came; it was like the scream was stuck in his gut. He strained harder and harder until the scream almost came, but it stuck again, this time in his throat. He began to gag and choke, and he was certain that the scream must escape, or he would die.

His eyes popped open. He was slick with sweat; he felt it on his face, in his hair, and on the sheet beneath him. Although he was awake, the terror of the nightmare stayed with him—it would linger until the light of day burned it away.

He knew what prompted the nightmare. Although the paperwork on his desk didn't reach the ceiling, it was just as overwhelming and never seemed to be done.

Charlie looked at the red numbers of the clock on the dresser. It was 6:02, much earlier than he wanted to be up this morning. He had plans, all right, but they didn't include getting up before the chickens or going to his office. But now that he was awake, and pretty sure he couldn't get back to sleep, he figured he'd make use of the time and get some of that paperwork done before it really did reach the ceiling, begin to fly and start taking swipes at him.

Charlie swung his long legs off the bed and felt the coolness of the hardwood floor on his bare feet. He stood up, all six-foot-three inches of him, and looked down at his wife, Sally. Over the years, she hadn't complained much about the odd hours his job demanded; and in his first year, every time he'd gotten out of bed, no matter what the hour or how quiet he tried to be, she'd wake up. Now he couldn't wake her if he tried.

Still he tiptoed across the room to the closet. Ignoring his uniforms, he put on jeans and a sweatshirt and slid his bare feet into a pair of old loafers. *Good enough for fishing.*

On his way out of the bedroom, he touched his wife's hair with his fingertips. She moved under his touch but did not awaken. He smiled, amazed that he still loved her so much after fifteen years of marriage. In the bathroom, he closed the door and reached for his toothbrush with one hand as the other turned on the water in the sink. He decided a quick shower might help wash away remnants of his hellish nightmare.

*   *   *

Charlie walked to the boat that was hooked to his pickup, ready to roll. Using his flashlight, he looked beneath the tarp at the big Igloo cooler that was packed with ice, water, and beer. On a blanket beside it was a thermos of coffee. He had everything ready: tackle box, fishing rods, cane poles, extra packs of cigarettes, worms. In a smaller cooler, there was a pound of chicken liver and a pound of beef liver. He was ready, all right. *Those catfish might as well just jump out of the water and give themselves up.*

*   *   *

Driving the short distance to the office, Charlie wondered if Tom had gotten back from Tallahassee in time to get some sleep. They'd had this fishing trip planned for a month; he didn't want anything to interfere with it.

Charlie parked his squad car in the parking lot across the street from his office. He climbed out of the car and stood beside it for a moment and looked up at the sky. It was 6:35 but so overcast it was still dark outside. He hoped it wouldn't rain, and he made up his mind, right then, that he was going fishing even if it did. Nothing was going to keep him off the river today.

Usually he or Tom worked Saturdays, but he'd arranged for them both to be off today. For a month, he'd listened to Tom brag about a catfish hole he'd discovered before Charlie began to believe him. Tom said he caught so many fish in that hole, his cooler began to overflow, and he had to start throwing them back. It sounded fishy, but Tom told it with enough likely details that Charlie's curiosity was sparked, and the more he tried to forget it, the more he thought about it. Now that he was finally going to try it himself, he couldn't wait to get on the river.

Charlie walked through the empty parking lot and across the street to his office building. He climbed a short flight of stairs and heard the telephone ringing as soon as he opened his office door.

Hurrying to answer it, he kicked over a trashcan the janitor had left in the way, again. He flicked the wall switch, sat down in his brown leather chair behind his desk, and snatched up the phone.

"Sheriff Morris."

A staccato blast of high-pitched words tumbled from the receiver so fast Charlie couldn't understand any of them.

"Whoa, whoa, wait a minute. Slow down, who is this?"

"She's dead, Sheriff. You hear me? She's dead! Me and—"

"Who—"

"Me and Billy got up early to go fishing, and we—"

"Who is this? Who's dead?"

There was moment of silence. Charlie could hear fast breathing.

"I'm trying to tell you, if you'll let me. As soon as we got there, we saw her lying right on the edge of the river and her face was down in the grass and there was blood on the back of her head and . . ."

Charlie groaned inwardly, held the phone away from his ear and scowled as the caller's words raced on. In spite of the hysteria and machine gun delivery, Charlie now recognized the voice.

Jimmy "Jumbo" Jones and his cohort, Billy "Bozo" Bradley, the town clowns, were at it again. Charlie had dubbed them the "dynamic duo of disaster," and they seemed to think it was a compliment and tried hard to live up to it. Neither was actually malicious, but the practical jokes they pulled bordered on criminal; if they were older, their pranks could warrant time in the slammer.

Last week, on his twelfth birthday, Jumbo stood five-foot-six and tipped the scales at one hundred and eighty pounds. The week before that, he'd called 911 and reported a house on fire at 329 North Elm Street, which was Charlie's address. The report was passed on to Charlie, and he'd sped home, arriving right behind the town's only fire truck.

There was no fire, no smoke—nothing but two pranksters playing hooky from school, hiding in the azalea bushes that bordered the house across the street from where they watched the fun. Charlie hoped he had frightened them with the severity of his anger and the dressing down he gave them. When he drove them home, he reminded their mothers there was a juvenile detention center in Bartow full of kids just like them.

And they're already at it again.

"Listen, Jumbo, I told you that—"

"Sheriff, listen, please, I swear this is no joke! Not this time. I'm telling you—"

"No. I'm telling *you*! I'm fed up with—"

Jumbo's voice went up two octaves. "Shut up, goddamn it! She's dead! You hear me? She's *dead*!"

Charlie yanked the receiver away from his ear and stared at it. Had he heard right? Jumbo was the town clown, Flowing Wells' Tom Sawyer, but Charlie had never heard him swear, let alone at an adult. He sounded shaken all right. Charlie put the receiver back to his ear.

"Jumbo, if this is more of your bull, I will personally drive you to Bartow and help them lock you up, and then I'll recommend they throw the key away. You understand me?"

After a moment of silence, Jumbo began to sob, which startled Charlie more than the swearing. The boy had risen to new heights of mischievousness and had become an accomplished actor, or—Charlie could not believe it—he was telling the truth.

Charlie glanced at the pile of paperwork that had prompted his nightmare and lured him to his office. He looked at the coffee pot. It stood cold and empty on the counter by the window that overlooked the parking lot. He sighed, shook a Winston out of his soft pack, and snapped it to his lips.

"All right, boy. What you got?"

"Sheriff, I'm not making this up. I swear I ain't. I—"

"Get to it, will you? Catfish are calling me."

"What?"

"You found a body?"

"Yes, sir. Me and Billy were walkin' along the river, and all we had was this little flashlight and we didn't see her till we were right on her and—"

"Who?" Charlie said, and as soon as the word was out of his mouth, he felt like a fool. Jumbo had baited him again, and like a hungry catfish, he'd taken hook, line, and sinker.

"I don't know. It was dark and all we had was the little flashlight and her face was down in the grass, and, and—"

"Where are you, Jumbo?"

"The pay phone down by the Hess Station. We started to turn her over, but—"

"I hope you didn't touch her."

"No. No, sir. We started to turn her over, but—"

"All right. Good. Crime scene would not appreciate that. Now, where is the body? Exactly."

As Jumbo talked, Charlie's face got hot. If this was another of the boy's pranks, he'd kill him. On the other hand, if it was not a prank . . .

He thought of his boat, all packed and ready, behind his truck in his driveway.

He sighed. "Listen, you and Bozo go straight home, right now. You got that? I'll check this out, and if it's another one of your—"

"It's not, Sheriff. I swear it ain't."

"If it is, it's the last one you'll ever pull in my town. You understand me? Go home. Now!"

Charlie slammed down the receiver. He realized the cigarette, still unlit, was dangling from the corner of his mouth. He took a book of matches from his desk drawer, lit it, and dropped the match in an ashtray.

If it isn't a prank . . . He cut the thought off mid-sentence. Considering where it might lead, he found himself hoping it was just another one of Jumbo's stupid jokes.

Charlie stood up, turned off the light, and slammed his office door behind him. His long strides began to sound in the hallway as he headed toward the exit door.

Chapter 2

Officer Mike Evers drove past Uncle Buck's Blue Duck Café for the third time in fifteen minutes. He wanted to stop, but not as long as Wanda's Pinto was parked there. Wanda was the last person he wanted to see this morning.

Mike believed he was justified for indulging in despondency today, of reflecting a little upon his miserable past.

He was having a bad morning. He'd had a bad night too. His whole week had sucked. Hell, his whole damn life sucked.

His father, whom he'd never known, had been a drunk, so his mother said, and so said everyone who'd known him. Mike had no reason to doubt it. And that meant Mike probably had an alcoholic gene or two floating around in his system. He had no reason to doubt that either. That sucked too.

Mike's mother had divorced his father when Mike was two. Not long after the divorce, and with a week of heavy drinking, his father ran his car off a bridge over the Peace River and drowned. It had never been determined whether it was an accident or suicide, but Mike refused to consider it had been anything other than an accident.

When Mike was four, his mother married his stepfather, Al Evers. Mike and Al clashed like sin and church from the get-go. Al was no-nonsense, distant, and cold, with never a word to say about anyone unless it was judgmental, crude, or contemptuous. But he didn't drink, and he was a good provider. Mike's mother stood by him through his rants, rages, pouts, and depressions. Mike believed that if his mother had been a woman of less character and more imagination, she would have poisoned the son of a bitch. If she'd asked, he would have helped her.

In his mother's time, in the tiny, rural, central Florida town of Flowing Wells, where she was born and raised, divorce was almost unheard of. She had been forgiven for leaving his father because he was a drunk, but for her to have divorced Al Evers simply because he was a son of a bitch would have branded her for life. Mike believed the main reason she stuck with Al was because he provided well for her and himself, better than she thought she could do alone.

Mike shook himself. He was aware of his tendency toward melancholy, especially when he was hung over, which was more often than he liked to admit to himself.

But anyone in his situation would have gotten drunk last night. It had been a hell of a week. He'd been through the wringer.

His girlfriend had dumped him for another guy. He'd been dumped before, but the difference was that this time, he'd been truly in love. He'd thought he'd been in love those other times, but when he met Wanda Dunn, he realized all his other relationships with women had been puppy love, infatuation, or maybe just lust. Wanda was a woman where the other girls had been . . . well, girls. At twenty-five, she was two years older than Mike, and she had showed him things he'd only heard whispered in locker rooms.

Mike first met Wanda ten years ago when she came down from Tampa one summer to work for her Uncle Buck in The Blue Duck Café. She was fifteen then, Mike was thirteen, and he thought she was the prettiest girl he'd ever seen.

Two months ago, she came back to Flowing Wells and went to work at The Duck full time. Mike stopped in for a cup of coffee her first day on the job.

It was midmorning, and there were only a few other customers in the restaurant. Mike took a seat in a booth by a window. The moment he sat down, Wanda came over to him, smiling and holding her order pad. Mike looked at her and couldn't speak.

Her smile widened.

"Coffee?"

Mike nodded. He knew he'd seen her before, but to say so seemed too much like a line, a come-on. He was trying to remember where he'd seen her when she set his coffee before him.

"I remember you," she said.

Mike looked at her. He felt the thump of his heart on his breastbone. "You do?"

"Sure. You used to come in with your mama that summer I worked here when I was in high school."

A light went on in Mike's head, and again he was seeing fifteen-year-old Wanda through thirteen-year-old eyes. His mouth went dry.

"You're a cop," Wanda stated.

Mike nodded.

"I have a lot of respect for police officers. Y'all do such dangerous work." She looked toward the cash register and then moved her eyes back to Mike. "You look handsome in that uniform, if you don't mind me saying so. How's your mama?"

"Uh, she passed away. Two years ago."

"Oh. I'm sorry, Mike. And your dad, the man who used to come in with y'all, how's he doing?"

"Step dad. He moved to Orlando. He landed a job at Disney World." Mike drank some coffee and swallowed it hard. "So what brings you back to Flowing Wells, Wanda?"

"I got divorced."

Her voice was lyrical, Mike noticed; and although it was the mature voice of a woman, it contained the high-pitched lilt of a little girl's, like the country singer Kitty Wells. Mike wondered if Wanda could sing.

"Tampa isn't big enough for me and that bastard both."

Mike laughed.

"Tampa's a big place."

"Yeah, but he's a bigger bastard."

Mike laughed again, and they talked until some customers came in. He finished his coffee and headed for the door, and as he started down the steps, he felt a tap on his shoulder. He turned to see Wanda smiling, the morning sun soft on her face. She reached out and stuffed a napkin down into his shirt pocket beside his pen. For a few timeless seconds, they looked at each other; then Wanda turned and went back inside. Mike walked to his car.

*   *   *

As he sat with the motor running, he took the napkin out of his pocket and unfolded it. Wanda's phone number was on it.

Mike laid his head back against the headrest and let the grin spread across his face.

"Oh boy," he said. "Oh boy oh boy oh boy."

*   *   *

Now Mike wished he had torn that phone number into pieces and dropped it out the window. He drove by The Duck for the fourth time, and Wanda's Pinto was still there. He thought, *the hell with it,* and pulled into the parking space by the front door. He had to have something in his stomach; maybe he'd get a piece of toast and a bowl of cheese grits.

As he reached for the door handle, his radio beeped; he snapped to attention as if he'd been caught napping on the job. He grabbed it.

"Evers."

"Where are you, Mike?"

Mike sat up straighter when he recognized Charlie's voice.

"Just pulled into The Duck. I'm goin' in for coffee."

"Get it to go. Get me one too—large, four sugars, two creams—you know how I like it. Stir it good. I'll be right there."

"Yes, sir. What's up? Thought you and Tom were going fishing today."

"We are. Hurry up and get the coffee."

Mike climbed out of his car. His head throbbed, and there was a foul taste in his mouth. Inside he didn't see Wanda; he was glad she wasn't there. But if her car was there, where was she? *Shacked up,* he thought, sinking deeper into despair. *Shacked up with that rich college boy bastard, Gilbert Vancini, whose folks owned the Vancini Pepper Plant, the biggest industry in Pinewood County.*

He ordered two large coffees to go and fixed his just like Charlie's. He also ordered two pieces of toast, knowing he didn't have time for grits. He ate the toast quickly, washing down small bites with sips of water.

Just as Mike stepped out the door, Charlie wheeled his patrol car off the highway and put down his window.

"Get in, Mike."

Mike handed him his large Styrofoam cup. "Want me to move my—"

"Get in."

As Mike got in, Charlie ripped the tab off the lid of his cup, tested the temperature. He drank a long swallow. He tucked the cup between his legs and backed out onto the highway.

*   *   *

Charlie glanced at Mike who was slouched in the seat beside him. Tall, lanky, dark-haired, and thin-shouldered, he looked to Charlie more like a high school English teacher, or maybe a med student, than a deputy. But he'd been on the force for a year and a half, and he was proving to be a fine officer.

At forty-six, Charlie didn't think of himself as old enough to be Mike's father, but he felt fatherly toward him. He'd warned him not to get involved with Wanda. He looked at the kid again. This time his gaze lingered.

"You look rough, Mike."

"I reckon I feel worse than I look."

"You must feel pretty bad then."

"I do."

Charlie sniffed.

"Booze won't help."

"I thought you and Tom were going fishing."

"I had this stupid dream . . ." Charlie told him about his nightmare, how the mountain of paperwork on his desk had inspired the dream to manipulate him to go to his office, and the phone call from Jumbo Jones.

"Wait a minute, Charlie. I may not be the sharpest arrow in the quiver this morning, so let me get this straight. Jumbo Jones called you, before daylight, on a Saturday morning, and said he found a body on Peace River?"

"Yep."

"And you fell for it?"

"What could I do, Mike? Ignore it? I have to check it out."

"Yeah, I know. Just seems like a waste of time though."

Mike sipped his coffee.

"Why'd you call me instead of Tom?"

"I sent Tom to Tallahassee yesterday afternoon to pick up a prisoner. Talk about a waste of time. Before Tom got there, the guy escaped. Don't have the details yet. Anyway, Tom made that long drive for nothing, and he was late gettin' back, so I thought I'd let him sleep some before we get on the river."

"If you get on it—what with this dead body and all."

Charlie gave him a nasty look.

"We'll get on it, all right. Don't worry about that. And don't make any more smart remarks about dead bodies."

"Sorry."

"A dead body isn't anything to joke about."

"You're right. It's not. I said I was sorry."

The sky was still overcast, and Charlie drove slowly with his bright lights on so as not to miss the turnoff between the rows of orange trees. Hoping Jumbo had given him the right directions, he made the turn and drove through the grove and headed across a stretch of pasture toward an oak hammock.

Mike thought his head would come off each time the cruiser bounced over a rough spot. Near the hammock, a herd of wild hogs quit their rooting and trotted off into the trees, squealing and stomping each other as they tried to get away from the car. Buzzards circled overhead, and one perched in the top of a dead pine.

Charlie parked in the edge of the hammock. He looked at Mike.

"How're you doing?"

"I don't like it. Buzzards."

"Snakes and coons die all the time. Buzzards will circle for a dead mouse."

"Yeah."

Mike got out of the car.

They walked through wet grass. A covey of quail thundered out from beneath a palmetto thicket, startling both men. Charlie grabbed for his gun. He let out a humorless laugh. "I'll see you babies again come hunting season."

Mike's chuckle precipitated a wave of nausea that almost dropped him to his knees. He staggered to a nearby oak on to which he leaned as he vomited vehemently into a pile of moss and rotten leaves. Tears streaked his face. Wincing at the bitter taste, he straightened up, trembling and cursing himself for a fool. Charlie was right. Booze did not help. All it did was make misery more miserable. He wiped his face with his hands and spat into the grass.

Turning back toward Charlie, he caught sight of a shade of blue that stood out from the browns and greens of the surrounding woods.

"Charlie!"

When the retching started, Charlie had walked away; now he hurried back toward Mike, watching his step.

"Look." Mike pointed into the hammock at what he now could see was an automobile.

They walked fast, side by side. Mike's foot tangled in a wad of vines, and he fell hard, but he got up and caught up with Charlie who stood beside a baby blue Mustang parked between palmettos and crape myrtle shrubs.

"That's Sandy Carlton's car. What's going on here, Charlie?"

Charlie stepped forward and laid his open palm on the hood.

"Cold. Been here a while."

He opened the front door and looked inside. The key was in the ignition. A purse lay on the seat. Charlie closed the door and called Sandy's name. He called again, louder. The only reply was the cry of a blue jay.

"What's going on, Charlie?"

"Come on."

Mike followed him through the hammock; they ran across a clearing toward the river.

"Sandy! Sandy Carlton!"

They walked along the grass at the river's edge. Just before they came to a bend, Charlie froze. He reached for his weapon.

"Good god!"

On the ground in front of them lay a body. The lower legs lolled in the water, the upper body sprawled face down in the grass. One arm was tucked beneath the body to the elbow, the other stretched straight out to the side. In the back of the head was a dark smudge Charlie knew was blood.

Mike thought he was going to be sick again.

"Sandy? Charlie, what the hell?"

Chapter 3

"Go radio the station, Mike. Get an ambulance out here. Call FDLE—number's in my book on the seat. Tell them we need a crime scene crew here fast."

"Looks like Jumbo and Bozo did a war dance around here, the way this grass is smashed. We've walked on it too."

"Go."

When Mike returned, Charlie was standing away from the body, not wanting to contaminate the crime scene any more than it already had been. Mike glanced at him, but then he looked away. The expression on Charlie's face was one he hoped he'd never have to see again.

"Sandy Carlton, of all people." Charlie said it as if he were speaking to himself. "I can't believe it."

"Why would anybody kill Sandy? What was she doing out here? Who—"

"If it were anybody else, I'd say drug deal gone bad."

"Not Sandy."

"No."

Mike followed Charlie up the riverbank and back across the clearing to the hammock.

"Don't touch the car, Mike. Don't even go near it till crime scene gets here."

Charlie walked to his car, turned, and looked at Mike.

"I don't know when the last murder was committed in Flowing Wells, but it was a long time ago. I was a deputy when Tom killed Eddie Huggins, but that was an accident. The shit's going to hit the fan when this gets out."

"Sandy Carlton? Murdered? I've seen the body, but I still can't believe it. I'm glad Jumbo didn't see who it was or the news would be all over town already."

"Listen, I've got to get back to town. You stay here."

"What?"

"Don't let Oscar near the body till crime scene gets here."

"Well—"

Charlie looked across the pasture toward the orange grove.

"Mike, you know what this is going to do to Connie and David?"

"Yes."

Charlie got in his car and looked out the window.

"When crime scene's done, drive Sandy's car back to the office."

Mike nodded.

Charlie started his engine and put the car in reverse.

"Mike?"

Mike looked at him.

"Don't come to work in this condition again."

Mike looked down at his feet.

"No, sir."

"The demon's in your blood, Mike. You know what it did to your daddy. He was a good man, but no match for the demon, and you're not either. I don't want to see happen to you what happened to him."

Mike's throat tightened as his eyes moved back up to Charlie's.

"Yes, sir."

As Charlie started across the pasture, he saw the ambulance come out of the orange grove and head toward him. He stopped and let his motor idle until the vehicle stopped beside him. Oscar Thomas stuck his head out the window and spat a stream of tobacco juice into the grass; a few drops dribbled down the outside of his door.

"That's gross," Charlie said.

"Yeah. So I've been told. I'm gonna quit tomorrow."

"Tomorrow, huh?"

"Yeah. What you got here, Sheriff? I don't believe I've been out to this place since I used to bring Shirley Ann parking when we were in high school."

"I ought to tell her daddy."

Oscar grinned, revealing a gap between tobacco-stained front teeth the size of Chiclets. A lock of bushy red hair tumbled down over one eye.

"He knows it. When we got married, we told him all about it. Well, maybe not *all* about it. Haha. Whatcha got?"

"Mike's over there." Charlie pointed. "He'll tell you. Don't do anything until crime scene gets here."

"Crime scene? What the hell is it?"

"Mike'll tell you."

Charlie drove on across the pasture and through the grove. He turned back toward town and drove slow.

How long had he known David and Connie Carlton? A long time. No finer people anywhere. Worshipped that girl whose body . . . How was he going to tell them? Maybe he could get Tom to—no, it was his hand. He would deal it.

Charlie passed The Blue Duck Café and turned west at Flowing Wells' only traffic light; three minutes later, he pulled into the driveway at 329 North Elm Street, his home. There sat his boat, fully loaded, waiting. It would keep on waiting too.

He got out of his car, lifted the Igloo out of the boat, and put it in the garage. He set it on the floor and started to unpack it.

"What the hell?" he said out loud, flinching at the sound of his own voice.

He hurried to the house, kicked off his wet shoes on the front porch. In the bathroom, he took off his pants, which were wet to the knees, and tossed them in the laundry hamper. How was he going to break this thing to Connie and Dave?

Smelling coffee, he walked to the kitchen. Sally had left the coffee maker full. He poured a mug. *No time for this*, he thought as he sipped.

Charlie was glad Sally and Peg, their nine-year-old daughter, had gotten in the habit of going to The Duck for breakfast on Saturdays. They didn't need to hear this now. He didn't need to tell them.

He walked into the living room and set his mug on the coffee table in front of the couch. He started to sit down, but remembering his socks were soaking wet, he pulled them off and took them to the bathroom and put them in the hamper with his pants.

Back in the living room, he sat on the sofa and sipped his coffee. He remembered he hadn't added sugar and cream. Well, hell, he ought to be drinking black coffee, anyway. Every cop he'd ever seen in the movies or read about in books drank their coffee black. You had to be tough to drink black coffee. And cops were tough; they were real men. Real tough men who drank their coffee black.

"Screw it," he said to all the idiots responsible for creating the myth that all cops were real men who were tough and drank black coffee.

He got up and went back to the kitchen and spooned two heaping teaspoonfuls of sugar into his mug and poured in a double shot of half-and-half. He tested the temperature again and gulped half the mug. Good. Just the way all six-foot-three-inch 230-pound real men like him liked their coffee: sweet and creamy, just like they liked their women.

He refilled his mug, unplugged the pot, and went back into the living room and stood by the window. He shivered with contempt and disgust for himself. There was work to be done, and here he stood in his drawers, drinking sweet, creamy coffee.

Procrastinating.

That was the word for it. It's what he'd been doing since he'd seen Sandy's lifeless body sprawled by the river in the wet grass. But he wasn't being paid the big bucks to procrastinate.

He set his mug on the TV and ran to the bedroom. He quickly showered again and put on clean, dry clothes. He was shaken, and he knew it. He'd known Sandy since she was a baby. He loved her. Shouldn't he be shaken?

No. He was the sheriff. He was big, and he was bad, and he was a real man and a tough cop even if he did like his coffee sweet and creamy.

Charlie sighed as he sat down on the side of the bed and reached for the phone on the bedside table to call Tom.

Chapter 4

Kitty frowned and hung up the phone. Tom and Charlie had planned this fishing trip a month ago. Tom talked about it all the time. He could hardly wait. The boat was packed and ready to go. And now, at the last minute, Charlie called to cancel.

"What's going on, Charlie?" Kitty had asked.

But he'd been evasive. Just said something had come up; he said he had a call to make and would be by for Tom in a few minutes.

"What's so important you'd cancel this fishing trip?"

"Police business."

That's all he'd say.

"That was a dirty trick, sending Tom off to Tallahassee. He didn't get home till three this morning—*without* a prisoner."

Charlie had hesitated. Charlie was not one to hesitate.

"Sorry, Kitty. Those things happen."

"Tom's looking forward to—"

"Listen, Kitty, I'll be there in—"

Kitty hung up.

*　　*　　*

After hanging up on Charlie, Kitty walked into the kitchen for a glass of water. As she began to open the refrigerator door, a pain hit her. She knew it was way too soon, but she was scared. She wanted Tom there.

Leaning against the refrigerator, pressing the palm of each hand against her bulging belly and feeling the squirming life inside her, she sighed. She loved that life, as she loved the man who helped create it; it scared her that sometimes it just seemed too good to last.

Every time Tom strapped on his gun, she cringed. He told her more roofers were hurt on the job than police officers, but she didn't buy it, and it didn't make her worry any less. When she told Tom how she worried, he neither laughed nor ridiculed; he listened. He let her talk, and then he held her, and that made her love him even more.

Sometimes she almost wished Tom hadn't gotten the pardon. She blushed at the realization of her capacity for selfishness. Still, if the governor hadn't granted Tom the pardon, he couldn't have pinned on the badge. No badge, no gun.

Kitty didn't care what kind of work Tom did, as long as it didn't require that he wear a gun. He could work at Vancini's Pepper Plant, pump gas, hoe orange trees, dig ditches—anything that didn't require a gun.

Kitty had been married once before, while Tom was in prison. Dewayne Cutter had seemed the perfect mate, until they got married. That's when she discovered the Hyde side of the Jekyll she'd dated all through high school.

The handsome face Dewayne presented to the public could become, in the privacy of their home, the face of a monster. The marriage had lasted less than a year and cost Kitty a broken heart that ached more than her bruised body. The body healed; she didn't think her heart ever would—until she met Tom.

*   *   *

Kitty removed her hands from her belly and stepped away from the refrigerator. She walked into the living room, eased herself down into Tom's recliner, and wished this pregnancy was over and the baby was snug in her arms.

She wanted Tom now, beside her. He'd walked down the block to the Circle K for a newspaper and a quart of half-and-half; Charlie got him started on that. Tom would be sick about the fishing trip being off.

Why wouldn't Charlie tell her what had happened? There could be only one reason. He didn't want to worry her.

As big as Charlie was, an inch under Tom's six-foot-four and twenty pounds heavier, he was basically a teddy bear. In spite of her fear of him—or rather, what he stood for: badges, guns, and enforcing the law—she loved him like a brother. She'd known him since she was a kid and like a big brother, he'd taken up for her when bullies or bad boys bothered her. He'd called her his little princess.

A car crunching on the gravel driveway interrupted her thoughts. Leaning forward and looking out the window, she saw Tom climb out of the passenger's seat of Charlie's patrol car. His face confirmed her suspicion. Whatever had prompted Charlie to call off the fishing trip was not anything any good.

*　　*　　*

Charlie followed Tom into the house and closed the door behind him. He looked around the room. Tom had done a fine job remodeling. The house had been run-down before Tom and Kitty bought it. It looked cute now, what with Tom's carpentry skills and Kitty's good taste in secondhand furnishings.

"What do you think?" Kitty asked.

"Looks good."

"Lots of hard work," said Tom.

Tom went into the kitchen and came back with two mugs. He handed one to Charlie.

Charlie sipped and nodded approval.

"You fix a fine cup, Tom."

"Learned from the master."

"Cut the crap, boys. What's going on? I don't think Charlie would have called this fishing trip off for anything less than an axe murder."

Charlie cut his eyes to Tom as Tom studied the floor at his feet. Charlie stepped to the window and looked out at the neatly mowed front lawn. An oak with waist-high azaleas around its trunk stood between the house and the road. The azaleas were blooming, and in spite of the sick feeling inside him, Charlie couldn't keep from admiring the shades of pink that blended together to form a glorious front for the home.

"Sit down, Kitty."

"I *am* sitting down. What is going on?"

Charlie turned from the window to Kitty. He looked at her for several moments before he spoke.

"This morning I went to the office to catch up on some paperwork. But as soon as I walked in the door, the phone rang. Jumbo Jones—"

"Jumbo?"

"He and Bozo were fishing down on the river. They found a body, Kitty."

"A body?"

"I didn't believe him at first, but—"

"Whose body, Charlie?"

Charlie started to speak but turned back to the window and looked out at the marigolds lining either side of the sidewalk that ran from the front porch to the road. A smattering of blackbirds pecked in the grass on the lawn as a pair of redbirds flitted about in the azaleas around the oak.

Still staring out the window, Charlie said, "I never would've thought you'd get this place looking so good, Tom. I love this neighborhood. Plenty of elbow room."

"That's why I bought it. It's quiet."

"Give it a few years. My place was quiet too when I bought it."

"Whose body?"

Tom walked behind his wife and put his hands on her shoulders.

"Sandy Carlton's been murdered, honey."

"*What?*"

Kitty's hand flew up to cover her mouth, then slid down to her stomach and lingered there.

"Somebody killed Sandy? No. Who? Why?"

Charlie told her all that had happened from the time he received Jumbo's phone call.

"And now I have to do the hardest thing I've ever had to do in my life. I've got to tell Connie and David."

"I've known Sandy since she was this big." Kitty held out her hands to indicate about a foot. "When I was in high school, Connie and David lived right across the street from us. I went over and saw Sandy the first day she was home from the hospital. I used to baby sit her."

Kitty swallowed as her eyes filled with tears.

"A couple weeks ago, before I went on maternity leave, Sandy came into the bank with Connie. While Connie was tending to business, Sandy came over to my desk. She looked so happy. Radiant, I guess you could say. She said she'd gotten the scholarship to FSU. She also told me she had a new boyfriend, but she wouldn't say who. She said she was really and truly in love for the first time in her life. And she—she . . ."

Kitty struggled to her feet and collapsed into Tom's arms.

Charlie wondered if crime scene had gotten there yet. If it had to come from Tampa, probably not. Maybe, if it came from Lakeland.

This was the first time Charlie had needed a crime scene crew, so he was speculating. He'd had all the training, of course, and he knew procedure, knew the drill backward and forward. But this was no drill. The body he'd seen on the river was real, flesh, blood, and bone—no plastic dummy. And it belonged to one of the town's own. A girl everyone loved.

Kitty moved away from Tom and looked at Charlie.

"We're wasting time."

Before Charlie could reply, she left the room. She returned looking fresher, wearing a different dress.

"You came by to get Tom for moral support, didn't you, Charlie? You're getting two for the price of one. I'm coming with you."

"Kitty, I don't think—"

"Sandy was my friend, Charlie. I loved her. I love her mama and daddy. I think it'll be good if I'm there. I'm going with you."

"Honey, in your condition—"

"I'm fine, Tom."

"Well—"

"Charlie, don't you think we've wasted enough time?"

Charlie nodded.

"Too much."

Kitty took Tom's hand, and they followed Charlie outside to his car. Tom opened the back door and helped Kitty in. As he opened the front door, he saw Charlie looking at him over the roof of the car.

"What?"

Charlie bit his lower lip so hard a speck of blood appeared.

"Sometimes I hate this job."

He and Tom looked at each other for several moments before getting into the car.

Chapter 5

Backing out of the driveway, Charlie looked up at the sky. It was still overcast, but the blanket of clouds was thinning, and Charlie thought the sun might peek through. He hoped so. This day would be dreary enough even if the sky were blue.

Charlie punched his radio.

"Evers."

The radio squawked.

"Evers here, copy?"

"Loud and clear. What's happening, Mike? Crime scene there?"

"Yes, sir. They got here faster than I'd have believed. They've printed the car, inside and out, and looked under every rock and behind every bush. By god, they're thorough. They're dragging the river now."

"Have they found anything?"

"If they have, they haven't told me."

"What are *you* doing, Mike?"

After a silence so long Charlie was beginning to wonder if he'd lost him, Mike said, "They told me I could help the most by staying out of the way."

Charlie chuckled. "You do that then. What about the body?"

"The medical examiner—we had our own man, Dr. Collier—released it a few minutes ago. Oscar just drove off. Body's on its way to town."

"Okay, Mike. You stay there until they're done. Then come on in. Drive Sandy's car."

"Right."

Another pause.

"Uh . . . Charlie?"

"Yeah?"

"There's this guy here, Raul Garcia—"

"Detective Garcia? From Tampa?"

"That's him. He said he was in Fort Meade when he heard the call come in."

"Doing what?"

"Says he has a girlfriend there."

"Oh."

Charlie listened to the hum on the line and waited for Mike to go on.

"Well, what about it, Mike? Garcia is there, so what?"

"Well . . . ah, nothing, I guess. Only, well, I just met the guy, and I hate his guts."

Kitty laughed. Charlie hushed her.

"Well, Mike, just stay out of his way. And whatever you do, don't shoot him."

Charlie punched off his radio.

"You know Garcia?" Tom asked.

"I've met him."

"What did you think of him?" asked Kitty.

"Well, to tell you the truth, I hated his guts too."

The three of them broke into peals of laughter. Relief from the morning's tension swept over each of them, and they howled till tears blurred their vision. Then, as suddenly as if someone had flipped a switch, they remembered their mission, and the laughter stopped. No one spoke during the remainder of the drive.

*   *   *

The Carlton house, a sprawling two-story structure built in 1902 by David Carlton's grandfather, Daniel, stood on a hill halfway between Flowing Wells and Wasahatchee, a town with six stoplights.

Acres and acres of orange grove stretched out behind the house; pastureland spread as far as you could see on either side. The half-acre front lawn was shaded by oak and pecan trees, queen palms, pines, magnolias, and a Jerusalem thorn.

Decorating the lawn were attractive plantings of azaleas, caladiums, crotons, gardenias, hibiscus, oleander, and crape myrtles. Although David and Connie employed a part-time gardener, they spent many hours working on the lawn themselves, and often Sandy helped.

As Charlie pulled onto the red brick driveway and parked in front of the house, he remembered the story of Daniel Carlton who, in 1894, had drifted into Flowing Wells on a horse, his only worldly possession except for his saddle and the clothes he was wearing. He got a job with the railroad and managed to buy pieces of pasture land and orange grove, which in those days were dirt cheap. In 1898, he built a sawmill that made him his first real money, money with which he bought more land in Arcadia and Fort Meade. Daniel Carlton married in 1901, the year he began construction on the house upon which Charlie now gazed.

By the time the depression rolled around, Daniel had passed on, and David's father, Durston, was running the show. Durston was not as shrewd, or as ruthless, as his father, and he made some bad investments. Much of the Carlton estate was lost, but enough remained that David, blessed with the same business acumen as his grandfather, was able to salvage what was left and begin to rebuild the Carlton fortune.

David and Connie, high school sweethearts who had married one year after graduation, were not vastly wealthy, but very well off. Both held real estate licenses, and David owned several auto dealerships and a concrete company.

For years they tried to conceive a baby. When men of medicine were of no help, they turned to prayer.

Their prayers and patience brought them Sandy, a healthy, good-natured infant who grew into a beautiful child. By age three, she could sing the national anthem on key, and she could read almost the entire library of Little Golden Books by the time she was four. At twelve, the woman began to evolve, and by fifteen, her beauty was so striking adults often stared while classmates loved and envied her.

*　　*　　*

Reaching for the door handle, Charlie looked across the seat at Tom. "Well, this is why we get paid the big bucks, pal."

"Right."

Tom took Kitty's hand and helped her out of the car. Charlie walked around the car and took her other hand.

"Sure you're up to this?"

"No. Are you?"

"No."

They went up the stone steps to the front door. Charlie rang the bell. Connie, wearing jeans and a pink blouse, opened the door.

"I thought I heard a car," she said. "What brings y'all out here? I mean, I'm glad to see you, of course, but . . ."

She looked from one face to another, closed her mouth, and stepped back. "Please, come in."

She led Kitty to the sofa.

"My goodness, it can't be long now."

"Not long."

"I remember when I was that big with Sandy. One day I was in the kitchen cooking, and three hours later, I was a mother! According to the doctor, she wasn't due for another two weeks. Babies don't always follow the schedule the doctors put them on."

Sunlight had pierced the cloud cover, and a ray shone into the big room through a window that overlooked the lawn. Beneath the window, a window seat was strewn with books.

The wallpaper in the room was a cheerful yellow with green and white flowers. The hardwood floor was light pinewood so brightly polished you could see the sunshine reflected from it. Connie's face looked pale.

Pieces of an old song buzzed through Charlie's head; something about turning cartwheels, calling out for another drink, feeling seasick, the ceiling flying away, Vestal virgins, the miller telling his tale, and the face of the lady turning a whiter shade of pale.

When Connie turned from Kitty to face Charlie, something she saw in his eyes seemed to deliver a blow to her solar plexus; her heart jumped, and her knees went rubbery. She tried to speak, but the tightness of her throat choked off any sound.

"I'll get David," she finally managed.

Tom eased himself down on the sofa by Kitty as Charlie stepped over to the window and looked out at a pair of robins pecking on the lawn. A redbird splashed in a birdbath. A few buzzards circled lazily above the grove across the road. The air, even inside the house, was perfumed with the scent of orange blossoms.

David Carlton stepped through the hallway into the living room, Connie close behind him. David was as tall as Charlie, but thirty pounds lighter. He had narrow shoulders, a long neck, and thick dark hair graying at the temples. He shook hands with his visitors and said to Charlie, "Sorry to keep you waiting. I've been trying—for two weeks!—to fix a leak under that sink in the bathroom. Guess I'm gonna have to break down and call a plumber."

David and Connie sat down on a love seat facing Tom and Kitty on the sofa. He motioned Charlie to a chair, but Charlie stayed on his feet, near the window.

"How're you, Tom?" David said. "Kitty, you look . . . pregnant."

Kitty laughed.

"I am."

"You'll have your figure back in no time," said Connie.

David was watching Charlie. Charlie looked at him, but he looked away fast.

"Charlie, I'd like to think this is a social call, but I don't believe it is. What's up?"

"It's about Sandy."

"Sandy? What about her? She went over to Kara's this morning, as she does most every Saturday morning. She had some errands to run after that. She'll be back soon. What do you want to see her about?"

Charlie saw Connie's hands go to her mouth. He heard a soft gasp and saw fear flash in her eyes. He knew her intuition was telling her something bad was coming. He didn't want to look at her.

"David, I . . ." Charlie fidgeted, and then he straightened himself to his full six-foot-three. He made himself look into David's eyes.

"I'd rather be horsewhipped than to have to tell you this, but—"

Connie stifled a scream.

"No!"

Kitty got up and went to her.

The color drained from David's face.

"What are you trying to say, Charlie? What are you telling us?"

For one more moment, Charlie put off what he'd dreaded doing from the moment he'd seen Sandy's body on the riverbank. He shook his head from side to side, slowly, looked at his feet, and finally lifted his eyes.

"Sandy's dead."

Connie slumped, but David sat rigidly, as if strapped to a body brace. As his face turned whiter, his jaws slackened so his face seemed to melt. His lips made little shapes as a fish's mouth might, but no sound emerged. Tears slid down his cheeks.

"I'm sorry," said Charlie.

The room was quiet but for Connie's sobs. David stood up, moved behind her, and touched her hair; he walked to the window, looked out on to the lawn. "What happened, Charlie? Car accident? Sandy was a good driver."

"It wasn't an accident."

David stood as still as a statue of himself. Charlie began to wonder if David had heard him. Then, in a voice barely audible, David whispered, "Not an accident?"

"Sandy was murdered."

Outside in the pasture, a cow bellowed. A bobwhite quail whistled. In the living room of the Carlton house, silence hung so thick Charlie thought he would choke on it.

"She was shot," Charlie heard himself say.

Connie cried out.

"Somebody shot Sandy? Somebody shot my baby? Good lord, man, why?"

"We don't know yet, David."

David's eyes were wide as he stared through Charlie and spoke. He seemed to speak more to the wall behind Charlie than to anyone in the room. His voice was flat, a monotone.

"I was forty-one years old when our Sandy was born. Connie was thirty-nine. We'd almost given up hope of ever having a child of our own . . . We were about ready to adopt. I knew Sandy was special the moment I laid eyes on her. She was such a good baby—hardly ever cried. Smiled and laughed a lot. And smart? I've never heard of anyone learning as fast as Sandy. She had so much talent. Such a kind heart. Why would anyone want to hurt her?"

Charlie let David go on until he stopped talking and began to breathe heavily. Then, using his sheriff's voice, "David, can you think of anybody, anybody at all, who might have had some kind of grudge against Sandy? Anything will help no matter how small or insignificant it might seem."

"No."

Charlie let several moments pass.

"She didn't have any problems with anyone? That seems unlikely, even for Sandy. She was becoming a precocious young lady . . . and a striking beauty. Surely some girls were jealous of her."

"What, jealous? Oh, of course. But girls don't murder other girls because they're jealous. There'd be murders every day."

"I know it. I'm just—"

"I know damn well what you're doing, Charlie. But do we have to do it now?"

"No. You want us to come back later?"

David walked across the room to the fireplace, leaned against the mantle.

"It won't be any easier then—or ever."

"Sandy's been to Tallahassee a few times checking out FSU. Has she said anything about anybody she might have met there?"

"She hasn't mentioned anyone."

"Can you think of anyone she could have had any kind of conflict with? How about teachers? Did she get along with all her teachers? What about boyfriends?"

David moved away from the fireplace and flopped down in a chair. He held his head in his hands. When he looked up, his face was streaked with tears.

"Well, she broke up with Jim Ed Pace a couple months ago."

"There you go. That's something."

"You don't think *he* did it? I never liked him much, but—"

"No no, we're not accusing anybody. We're grabbing for straws. Give us something else."

"Well, there was this new teacher Sandy didn't like much, Mr. Pratt. This is his first year here. He came from California, I think. I met him on 'Back-to-School Night.' He seemed all right, I guess. He's young—too damn good looking for a high school teacher, if you ask me. Too many impressionable young girls, you know. Sandy didn't like him. I heard her tell Kara he was a creep."

"Do you know *why* she called him a creep?"

"No."

"So what do you think of Mr. Pratt, David, aside from him being too young and good looking?"

"Well, to tell you the truth, he seemed weird. I don't know quite how to explain that though. Just something not right about the guy, but nothing I can put my finger on."

"He's single too, isn't he?"

"Yes, that too. A single man that young and handsome ought not to be around all those young girls. You know what I mean?"

"Come on, David."

"Hey, you wait till Peg's a few years older. You'll know what I'm talking about."

Connie groaned. David got up and went to her. He took her hands as he sat down beside her.

"I'm going to wake up in a minute and go, 'Good gosh, what a dream.' This can't be happening, Charlie."

"What time did Sandy go to Kara's?" Tom asked.

"Early, like she does most every Saturday morning. She left before Connie and I got up. Sandy's an early bird. Always has been."

"You say Sandy went over there every Saturday morning?"

"Most every Saturday."

Connie sat up and started to speak but collapsed into spasms of sobs.

"Why'd she go over there?"

"They had coffee together, and talked. Kara hasn't been well for some time. You know that. She's all right as long as she takes her meds, but when she doesn't . . . Well, she and Sandy have been best friends since kindergarten when they were in that play together, and Kara's an early bird too; I don't know why, it's just a habit they got into."

"Was she going anywhere else? After she left Kara's, I mean."

"Not that I know of."

"You said she had some errands?"

"Oh yes. She did say she was meeting someone after she left Kara's, but she didn't say who."

"You didn't ask?"

"No. What about it?"

"Nothing. I know you trusted her."

"I had damn good reason to trust her. She never lied to us once, about anything."

"I know it. Believe me, I'm not implying anything."

Kitty shifted her weight, trying to get comfortable. "Kara just did another stint in the hospital."

Connie wiped her eyes with a handful of Kleenex and managed to speak.

"Yes. I—I talked to Lois yesterday." She looked at Charlie. "Charlie, where was the . . . ?"

Charlie told her.

"What on earth was Sandy doing way out there?" David asked.

"That's part of the puzzle, David. We don't know yet. Is there anything you need? Anything we can do for you?"

"Just find the son of a bitch that killed my baby."

"I promise you that."

"Charlie?"

"Yeah?"

"Could it have been an accident?"

"No."

"Why not?" Connie asked.

Charlie had wanted to spare them any gruesome details, but now he had to tell them about the bullet wound in the back of Sandy's head.

"God," Connie whispered.

"I can't tell you how sorry I am," Charlie said. "There are just no words to—"

"No," said David. "There aren't. There are no words. Words can't even come close."

Kitty asked Connie, "Would you like me to stay?"

Connie's tears had spotted the front of her blouse. She shook her head. "I want to be alone, Kitty. I—I think I'm in shock. I can't believe this is real."

"Call me if there's anything I can do. Will you?"

Connie nodded.

She and David walked them to the door. As Charlie opened his car door, David called to him from the top of the steps.

"You go get that son of a bitch that killed my baby, Charlie."

Charlie looked back at them, a pair of broken dolls wrapped in each other's arms.

"We'll get him."

David's head bobbed up and down, like the head on a mechanical doll. His lips pressed together, making a firm, thin line.

"You do that, Charlie. You find the dirty bastard that killed my Sandy."

"You can count on it."

Charlie steered his vehicle back down the red brick driveway toward the road. No one spoke as they headed back toward town.

Chapter 6

Gasping, the man rolled off the girl and onto his back. He lay still, staring up at the thin, jagged crack in the ceiling. *Damn that crack*, he thought. *Damn this crummy apartment. And damn this shitty little town.*

How in hell had he wound up in this hick one-traffic-light town anyway?

He knew how, of course. When he resigned from his position in California, before the administrative idiots fired him, he'd decided to move to the Sunshine State. He liked sunshine and beaches and bikinis.

One evening, fueled with a six-pack of beer and several fat lines of cocaine, he spread out his Florida map on his kitchen table, raised an ice pick over his head, and drove it down into the wooden tabletop. He squinted at the name of the town where the pick had stuck: Flowing Wells.

Now isn't that a sweet name, he thought; it sounded like the most hick place on the planet. Right smack dab in the middle of Florida. The nearest place to it he'd ever even heard of was Tampa, and that looked to be about eighty miles away. Flowing Wells? It was probably crawling with spiders and snakes, and alive with alligators.

It took several yanks to pull the ice pick out of the tabletop. He raised it again, but in the middle of his downward thrust, he changed his mind.

He leaned over the map and looked at the name of the town again; just to be sure he'd read it right. Yep, Flowing Wells. He liked the name. It kind of, well, flowed, as flowing wells do. It might be just the kind of place he needed, one that was off the beaten path, one no one had heard of.

What the hell? It might be fun. It would be an adventure. Nature should be abundant—not that he gave a shit about nature. There'd probably be plenty of wildlife; maybe some wild pussy.

He'd got that right. He sat up on the side of the bed and lit a cigarette. Exhaling, he reached for the bottle of beer on the bedside table. As he guzzled it, the girl sat up and pulled up the sheet to cover her breasts.

"Let's do another line," she said.

The adoring eyes reminded him there were compensations for living in this backward shit-hole where you had to drive thirty miles to get to a decent movie theater, fifty to the nearest mall.

He looked at the girl. She was a beauty, all right, with a perfect body and a face as gorgeous as any movie star. Her father was one of the wealthiest men in Pinewood County, maybe in the state. She was quite a catch, almost as prized as that bitch Sandy Carlton would have been. Well, her majesty Miss Sandy wouldn't have another opportunity to turn Jim Pratt down. Jim Pratt didn't take kindly to being turned down by anyone, especially a naïve country hick who thought coke was something you drink.

But for all Pratt's bravado, he suffered stabs of fear like the one jabbing him now as he sucked down the rest of the beer.

Diana was a beauty with a body as good as any centerfold; but she was only seventeen. Although his own classically sculpted face could pass for twenty-one, or two, the truth was he was pushing thirty.

The incident that drove him from California weighed heavily on him. After he'd gotten settled here in Hicksville, he'd called his pal Steve in Los Angles.

"You got out just in time," Steve told him. "Scarletti's boys have turned over every rock in California looking for your sorry ass. He wants your balls, man. And then your blood."

There was no doubt in Pratt's mind that Carlo Scarletti would kill him, and in a most unpleasant way. The man was ass deep in organized crime and had more money than God.

When sixteen-year-old Serena Scarletti had appeared in Pratt's classroom, she was manna from heaven. The girl was a ripe peach, begging to be plucked. Oozing youthful health and vitality, radiating sexual energy as a physical force, she succumbed to Pratt's charms and floated right into his arms.

Pratt's friends warned him. Told him he was playing with fire. He knew it was true, but he was smitten. Not that he was in love, but the lust this dark-haired, dark-eyed beauty aroused in him was the most intense he had ever experienced. There were times, right in the classroom, he would actually ejaculate into his underwear just looking at her; he had not done that since he was sixteen.

Word of Pratt's dalliance had gotten out, of course. The school administrators demanded that Pratt either resign or be fired. He'd chosen the former and had not even gone back to his room to clean out his desk. The only thing he really wanted, and could not allow anyone else to find, was a small white envelope he kept hidden in his bottom desk drawer.

He asked Steve, a first-year assistant principal, to retrieve it, and Pratt had his envelope that very afternoon. Good old Steve.

Having a small stash discovered in his desk at school was one thing; being butchered by Carlo Scarletti's thugs was something else.

Pratt had gotten the hell out fast, and, according to Steve, not a second too soon. He had known Scarletti would hunt to hell and back for him, so he'd given fake references with phone numbers of friends. The scam had worked. He was in like Flint. He'd rather be "in" in a more cosmopolitan place, one more suited to his own finer tastes. But looking at the young beauty in his bed, he knew things could be worse.

*   *   *

Pratt stood up and walked into the kitchen for another brew. The shades were drawn, and in the late afternoon, the light in the apartment was dim. When he came back into the bedroom, he sat down in the chair at his desk and set his beer down on a neatly folded paper towel.

From the bottom drawer, he took out a vial and spooned out two little piles of coarse white powder onto the compact mirror he carried in his jacket. From the same drawer, he withdrew a razor blade. He began a steady, rhythmical *chop-chop-chop*, and then laid out two lines about an inch and a half long.

Diana smiled, stretched, and ran her long, manicured nails through her boyishly short golden hair. She slid out of bed and walked to Pratt and knelt on the floor beside him. As he'd taught her, she took the straw and touched an open end to a nostril and closed her other nostril with her fingertip; holding her breath so as not to blow the precious powder into oblivion, she touched the other end of the straw to a line and sniffed. Pratt took the straw and sucked up the other line.

He stood up and took Diana's hands and pulled her to him. He knew she adored him, and why shouldn't she? He had changed her from a girl into a woman. He had made real her pleasures that before had only snuck into her wildest fantasies.

Reaching out with both hands, Pratt ruffled the short golden hair that one week ago had tumbled in silky piles down upon her shoulders. That she had cut it at his command to prove her love and loyalty made him swell with pride. His hands moved to her breasts, and with the backs of his fingers, he began to softly brush the nipples. The nipples became erect, and he led her back to the bed.

*   *   *

The revving of a monstrous engine blasted through the quiet of the apartment.

Pratt jumped out of bed and ran to the window. He shoved the shade aside and looked down on the parking lot. "Shit!" The redneck that lived in the unit below him was playing with his hot rod again. Pratt let go of the shade and turned to Diana, who also got up to look.

"Listen, Diana," he said, "I think you better go now, honey. It's getting late, and your folks might start to wonder where you are. I have to grade some papers, anyway."

Diana pirouetted in front of the full-length mirror mounted on the back of the closet door then glided across the carpeted floor to her lover's arms.

"Mama doesn't keep tabs on me anymore. And Daddy doesn't even know I'm alive. Little Di is all grown up. Or hasn't the big bad wolf noticed?"

She pursed her lips into a sexy pout, rotated her shapely hips.

Pratt grinned and moistened his lips with the tip of his tongue. "He's noticed, all right. If you didn't live at home with Mommy and Daddy, he just might hogtie you to that bed and keep you here all night."

She swayed before him, cupping her breasts in her hands.

"Oh, he would, would he?"

"Damn right. He might anyway if you don't get the hell out of here fast." He was hard again. She reached for him.

"Can't Little Red Riding Hood stay just a little bit longer? Let's do another line."

"No. Really, honey, you need to go. No use pushing our luck."

"All right, then. If that's the way you want it."

"It's not what I want, but it's what has to be."

When she was dressed, he gave her an envelope, and she slipped a couple of hundred dollar bills into his pocket.

As he kissed her good-bye, he was thinking that thanks to her and a few of her friends he soon would be able to blow this town. There was plenty of pussy here, but pussy was everywhere. The problem here was that there was no culture. Except for the girls—and no matter how good they looked, they were light years beneath him in sophistication—there was absolutely nothing for him to do.

Truth was Pratt had plenty of money. He could pull out today to anywhere in the country and live high for six months before having to work. He made very little teaching, but he had other interests, investments, and connections more lucrative than educating children. It wasn't money keeping him here; he stayed because he believed he was safe.

But townspeople had become suspicious of him. He could feel their eyes on him when he walked down the sidewalk, stepped into a building, or drove down the road in his Corvette. He was used to women looking at him, but it disturbed him that the looks he got from Flowing Wells women were not looks of admiration.

And the men were Neanderthals, light years behind the cultured gentlemen in California. The men here were tough, hard-assed, no-nonsense, church-going country bumpkins still living in the dark ages. They most certainly did not look at Jim Pratt with admiration or envy. They didn't like him, they didn't trust him, and they were waiting for him to slip. He was an outsider with a past. A past he did not want known.

*   *   *

"Did you park down the block where I told you?" Pratt asked as he cracked the door and peeked out into the hallway.

"I always do, sweetheart," she said, sniffling and touching her nose with a tissue. "Are you getting paranoid, Jim?"

"Hell, no, I'm not paranoid."

He crossed the room and looked out the window.

Diana let out a drug-induced laugh, the shrillness of which grated on Pratt's nerves.

"Keep it down. Make sure no one sees you sneaking out of here."

"Diana doesn't sneak, honey. See you tomorrow at the monkey house."

*   *   *

When she was gone, relief swept over Pratt like the rush of a good drug. *By god, I must be getting paranoid*, he thought.

He got another beer, then went back to the desk and laid out two more lines. This stuff was better than the occasional shit Steve sent him. He wanted to buy a bunch of it. But he could not get Leon to tell him the name of the local heavyweight.

Leon shared his own stash, but Leon was lightweight, and Pratt never really had all he wanted. If not for Steve, he'd have to press Leon harder. Pratt didn't like being kept in the dark, especially by a guy he was sleeping with.

As he was laying out the lines, the phone rang, more shrilly than Diana's silly laugh, and it startled him. He swore and grabbed the receiver.

"Listen, Jim," a male voice said. "Don't say anything, just listen."

As he listened, Pratt's hands began to tremble, and he felt blood rush to his face. He slid the phone into its cradle and began to scurry about looking for a place to hide his stash; a place where no one would ever think to look. It might never be looked for, but that was not a chance he was willing to take. Shit was going to hit the fan now, for sure.

For half an hour, he scrambled around his apartment, exploring every nook and cranny for the perfect hiding place. Succumbing to exhaustion and despair, he flopped down on the couch and rolled his eyes up toward the ceiling; as they moved back down, it hit him. It was perfect. Why hadn't he thought of it before?

A portrait of Christ hung on the wall directly in front of him, the famous one of Jesus looking up toward heaven with an otherworldly look about him, his hair long and soft looking, a halo around his head. The portrait had been there when Pratt moved in, and he hadn't gotten around to taking it down. Now he was glad he hadn't.

Pratt's mood lightened. He almost wished he hadn't been in such a hurry to send Diana home. He whistled as he removed the cardboard backing, taped a white envelope to the back of the canvas, replaced the backing, and re-hung the portrait.

Then the voice on the phone replayed itself in his head. Fear stabbed his gut like a knife and began to twist. He stood up and stumbled into the bathroom, vomited into the toilet.

He climbed into the shower, turned the cold water on, and stared wide-eyed up into the fine, painful spray.

Chapter 7

As Charlie drove back toward town with Tom in the front seat beside him, Kitty sat in back with her hands pressed firmly over the bulge of her belly.

She thought, with awe, about the life inside her. She marveled that eight and a half months ago, two microscopic cells had joined within her to become the living, breathing human being that was about to come into the world.

In high school, she had taken science classes, and she understood, sort of, the biology involved in making a baby. But to Kitty, the creation of life would always remain a mystery, a miracle.

And then she became aware of Tom's voice.

"I don't think I'll ever get the image of those two standing on the top of those steps like broken dolls out of my head. Charlie, do you ever get used to it?"

"I don't see how you could unless you were a heartless bastard to begin with."

"I'll never get over the looks on their faces," Kitty said. "I can't even begin to imagine that kind of pain."

No one spoke again until the police cruiser crunched onto Tom's driveway. Charlie switched off the engine. He watched a pair of redbirds flit about in the azalea bushes around the oak. A squirrel chased another squirrel down a limb that hung out over the road.

"Well, Charlie, it looks like we can forget our fishing trip."

"Yep."

"Let me take Kitty inside, and I'll go with you."

Charlie looked at him.

"Go with me where?"

"To Pratt's place. Isn't that where you're going?"

Charlie nodded.

"I'm going with you."

"Kitty needs you here."

"I'm all right, Charlie." Kitty opened her door and starting to climb out. "Besides, y'all would've been gone fishing all day anyway. What's the difference?"

Sandy is dead now, that's the difference, Charlie thought. But he did not speak.

Tom got out and helped her out of the car. She gasped, made a little grunting sound, stood straighter, and smoothed her blouse over her belly.

She looked at Charlie who had also gotten out of the car and was standing by his door.

"Charlie, you don't really think Mr. Pratt had anything to do with this, do you? I mean, he's a weird guy, all right, but—murder? What possible reason could he have to kill Sandy?"

"I'm not saying he killed her. I just want to talk to him. We'll be talking to lots of people."

"Maybe Mr. Pratt was trying to broaden Sandy's horizons," Tom said, "and things got complicated."

"Oh, come on, honey. Guys don't kill girls because they won't jump in the sack with them, if that's what you're saying."

"Yeah, but what if the guy is an ounce or two short of a quart? Maybe he told her something he shouldn't have and felt the only way he could be 100 percent certain she wouldn't blab was to shut her up for good."

"We have plenty of 'what-ifs' and 'maybes,'" Charlie said.

"I'd like to go with you."

"Why don't you call Sally, Kitty? She and Peg ought to be home by now. She'll be wondering why the boat's still in the driveway. Tell her what's going on. Maybe she can come over and stay with you for a while."

"You want *me* to tell Sally about Sandy?"

"I just mean with you here alone, and Sally and Peg over there alone, maybe y'all could . . . I mean—"

"I know what you mean. Y'all go on. I'm going inside to lie down. I might call Sally when I get up."

As Tom walked Kitty to the door, Charlie leaned against the car and lit a cigarette.

"She okay?" he asked when Tom came back.

"She's being brave, but this is a hell of a shock. The baby isn't due for two weeks, but the doctor says it could come any time. This could hurry it up some, I guess."

"Stay here."

"Like she says, if it weren't for this, we'd be fishing."

*   *   *

Cabbage Palm Apartments, a two-story eight-unit apartment house, stands one block west of Highway 17, between Flowing Wells and Wasahatchee, behind a small strip mall with a Circle K, a beauty shop, a pawnshop, and a video store.

As Charlie turned off 17 on to Cabbage Palm Drive, he glanced at his watch and realized it was past noon. He pulled into a parking space in front of the Circle K and said to Tom, "Let's get a hot dog."

Tom pointed to an emerald green Jaguar parked on the east end of Ms. Betty's Beauty Emporium. "Diana Matthews is spending a lot of time in Ms. Betty's. This is the third time this week I've seen her car parked there."

"Maybe she's got a new boyfriend. Trying to make herself beautiful."

"Diana doesn't have to try to be beautiful. She just is. If I was a few years younger, and single—"

"You're not."

Tom grinned. "I know it. Wouldn't have it any other way either."

They went inside the Circle K, came back out with hot dogs and cokes, and leaned against the car, using the hood as a table. Charlie finished his first hot dog and opened the container holding the second.

"Fishing makes you hungry, doesn't it?"

Tom gave him a look but did not answer. They ate in silence.

Charlie wiped his mouth with a napkin. "Tom, what do we know about Jim Pratt?"

Tom thought about it. "Not much. This is his first year teaching here. Came from California, they say. He drives a Corvette—an expensive car for a teacher. Of course, maybe the guy's rich and just teaches for a hobby.

Who knows? Keeps pretty much to himself, maybe he's writing a book. I hear he's popular with the kids at school, especially the girls."

"The girls?"

"That's what I hear. He's a good-looking guy, if you like that pretty-boy type."

"Hmm. Good-looking guy in a little town like this. Doesn't date." Charlie glanced at Diana's Jaguar. "You reckon Pratt's got a girlfriend?"

Before Tom could reply, Ms. Betty Ledford stepped out of her beauty shop and stood on the sidewalk. She yawned, stretched, and lit a cigarette. Her bleached hair hung just over her ears. She inhaled a deep drag, saw the police officers, and walked toward them, her wide hips bouncing inside her loose slacks. She smiled, revealing small teeth that needed dental work.

"You ought to quit those smokes, Ms. Betty," Charlie said, lighting one up. "The surgeon general has determined cigarette smoke can be hazardous to your health."

"The surgeon general can kiss my fat ass," Ms. Betty said. "If he had a man like mine to put up with, he'd smoke too. And drink. Anything to help him forget. Me, I quit drinkin' the day I opened this shop—'cept on weekends."

"Oh, come on, Ms. Betty. You've got a good life. What are you tryin' to forget?"

"I can't remember!"

She squealed and shook with laughter.

"See, it works."

Charlie grinned.

"You're a caution, girl. But that's an old one."

"Yeah? It's still funny."

"I quit smoking two years ago," Tom said. "It's not that hard, once you make up your mind."

"That's the hard part," Charlie offered, "making up your mind."

"I make up my mind to quit every night I go to bed," Ms. Betty declared. "Next morning, I decide to start again.

"Say, what're you boys hangin' out in front of my shop for? You run out of something to do, or what?"

"Just hopin' to get a glimpse of you, Ms. Betty." Charlie winked. "You're looking mighty fine these days."

Ms. Betty threw back her head and laughed, then broke into a coughing spasm that went on for more than a minute. When she got her breath, she hacked up a glob of phlegm and spat it into an empty parking space beyond the sidewalk.

"Goddamn, Charlie, no wonder you got elected sheriff, anybody that can spin a line of shit like that. But let me tell you something, I might be old and ugly, but I can still get it wet."

Charlie reddened as Tom watched a pair of sand cranes sail lazily above the treetops. High above the cranes, floating in broad circles on air currents, buzzards appeared as dark specks in the sky that now was blue.

Charlie looked at the Jaguar.

"Is Diana getting a haircut?"

Ms. Betty sucked smoke deep into her lungs.

"You must not have seen Diana lately, hon. She won't be needin' another haircut for a long time, the way she made me cut it. I hated to do it, long beautiful hair like that, but she was payin' for it, so I just did what she told me to."

"You cut off her hair?"

"Short as yours."

"That's her car," Tom said.

"Yep."

"I've seen it parked here a lot lately."

"So?"

"What's it doing here?"

"Sitting there mindin' its own business."

Her eyes moved slowly from Tom to Charlie, then back to Tom.

"Listen, I get paid to mind my own business."

She lit another cigarette and looked off across the highway.

"But to tell you the truth, something has been bothering me, and since you're askin' about it, I'll tell you. It's not only Diana that parks here a lot. It's other girls too. They park in one of those spaces there"—she indicated the row of parking spaces with her eyes—"and disappear sometimes two, three hours."

"Where do they go?"

"Cabbage Palm Apartments back yonder is the only place there is to go. Unless they just leave their cars here and go off with friends, which is possible. But what I think is they're goin' to see that teacher from California, that Pratt feller."

She added with a leer, "Maybe he's helping 'em with their homework."

Charlie waited for her to go on.

"Listen, it's just a hunch, but I'm a pretty good judge of character. Workin' with people every day like I do, you develop instincts, and I guarantee you that son of a bitch is lower than whale shit. He comes in here every two, three weeks for a haircut, and it makes my skin crawl to touch him. He's too goddamn pretty for a man, and he thinks his shit don't stink. I could tell that right off."

"Let me ask you something, Ms. Betty. Did Sandy Carlton ever leave her car parked here?"

"I think she did—a time or two. But I don't believe Sandy was having a fling with that asshole. If she went to see him, it was about something else."

"How do you know?"

"Like I said, I'm a good judge of character. Sandy wouldn't have touched that piece of shit with a ten-foot pole.

"Listen, to tell you the truth, I've almost called y'all a couple of times about Mr. Pratt, but I don't have proof of anything. It's just a feeling I have. But you ask my old man—if you can find him home and sober—and he'll tell you about 90 percent of the time, my hunches are right on the money."

A car pulled into the parking space on to which Ms. Betty had spat.

"Well, there's my next appointment. Y'all check that Pratt bastard out. I'm tellin' you, he's no good."

As Ms. Betty went back inside her shop, a beautiful young girl with very short golden hair came around the corner of the building. As she opened the door of the Jag, she glanced around the parking lot and scanned the sidewalk.

When she spotted Tom and Charlie, she froze. Then her head bobbed a quick hello as she got into her car; she did not look back as she pulled out onto the highway.

"Good god, Charlie. I see what Ms. Betty means about her hair."

"Did you notice her eyes?"

"The dark bags under them?"

"The haunted look."

"What the hell is goin' on, Charlie?"

"Whatever it is, it's happening right under our noses."

"How'd we miss it?"

"Because we couldn't imagine it. Are you ready to go see the teacher of the year?"

"Damn right."

*   *   *

As Jim Pratt stepped out of the shower and reached for a towel, he thought he heard a car door slam. He ran to the window and peeked out.

Tom Wilson and Charlie Morris were standing beside his Corvette, looking up toward his apartment. He swore. Although he hated having no time to rehearse, he performed well under pressure. And the curtain was about to rise.

He rushed to his desk, grabbed a spiral notebook, and ripped out a sheet of paper. With a black marker he scribbled, "Gone for weekend—be back late Sunday."

As he had not been outside of his apartment all day, and no one except Diana had been inside, this ruse seemed safe. Congratulating himself on his quick thinking and fast action, he scratched his signature, taped the note to the outside of his door and dropped to the floor. He lay on his belly and scarcely dared to breathe.

His senses were heightened, and he could hear the police officers' footsteps coming up the short flight of stairs. When they stopped outside his door, he could picture them reading the note, only inches from where he lay.

He heard Charlie say, "Darn it, we missed him."

"One thing about it," Tom said, "we were wrong about Diana. She couldn't have been up here with Pratt—not with him gone."

Goddamn that bitch! She let herself be seen!

"What'd he do, walk? His car's right out there."

"Someone must've picked him up."

Pratt pictured the two men looking at each other.

The sheriff said, "What if he didn't go anywhere, Tom? What if he saw us and stuck that note on the door and he's inside right now, maybe hiding and listening to us?"

Oh shit oh shit oh shit oh shit!

Pratt took deep breaths. They'd seen Diana. Well, so what? They couldn't prove she'd been in his apartment. But even if they could, he believed he could convince them there was a legitimate reason for her being there. These weren't brain surgeons, these two. He could say she stopped by to pick up an exam he had graded. Or that she was stuck on a particular problem and came by to get help.

Hell, if he had to, he could think of all kinds of good reasons for her having come to his apartment. But he didn't really think it would come to that. Still, he was glad he'd hidden his stash.

"Think we ought to go get a warrant, come back, and turn this place inside out?"

Oh shit oh shit oh shit oh shit!

"Nah. All we have, really, is hearsay and speculation. We'll see him tomorrow or Monday."

As footsteps receded from his door and started down the stairway, Pratt heaved a sigh of relief. He peeped out the window, and when he saw the police car drive away, he ran to the phone and punched in a number.

"Walker residence."

"Listen, Leon," Pratt whispered. "Diana Matthews just left here, and not ten minutes later, Charlie Morris and Tom Wilson were standing at my door!"

The silence on the line lasted so long Pratt was beginning to think they'd been disconnected.

Then Walker said, "Oh, Jim. How many times have I told you not to bring kids up there to your room? It's too risky. It's foolish. What did you say to the sheriff?"

"What did I say to the sheriff? I told him to go fuck himself! Hell, Leon, what kind of fool do you think I am? I didn't say anything to him. I hid like a goddamn rat. They left, but I heard Morris tell Tom they'd see me tomorrow or Monday. You don't think they'll come to the school, do you?"

"You never know. They do things differently here. Don't let that drawl fool you. Morris is smart, and so is Wilson. I'd about as soon have Carlo Scarletti after me as those two."

"No, you wouldn't."

"You're right, I wouldn't. But don't underestimate them. That's what I'm saying."

"Leon, I'm scared. What am I going to do?"

"Listen, Jim, I love you, but you're taking too many risks. I've gotten along as well as I have in this town because I'm careful, very careful. I told you, things are different here."

"Don't you think I know that?"

"Yes, I'm sure you do, but you aren't acting like you do. What were you thinking, Jim, bringing those kids up to your apartment in a little town like this? Don't you know people know each other here? They see things and they talk. You're being way too reckless, Jim. You're stirring up trouble. Now there's this Sandy Carlton thing."

Pratt gulped.

"Look, Jim, I don't think you realize how bad this thing's going to get. It's imperative you keep your nose clean. Do you understand?"

"Yes yes, I do, Leon. I'm sorry. I've been a damned fool."

"Well, you certainly haven't behaved very wisely, Jim. That's for sure. But from now on, you will, you have to. Do you understand?"

"Yes."

"Answer me one more question. And please, Jim, tell me the truth. Do you know anything about Sandy's murder?"

"No. You don't think I had anything to do with that?"

"I'm just asking if you know anything about it."

"No."

"In the days ahead, the cops will be asking everyone questions like that. Keep cool. If you go blowing your stack, you'll just make things worse."

Pratt groaned.

"Why me, Leon? Why does trouble follow me around like my shadow? I couldn't help being born beautiful. I can't help it if chicks dig me. I'm not a bad guy. Leon, I've got to get out of this town."

"Jim, that's precisely what you *don't* want to do. To take off now, right after the murder, in the middle of the school term, would be as good as a confession. Use your head for something besides holding your ears apart and looking beautiful."

Pratt groaned again.

"What am I going to do?"

"Just be cool. Take it easy. Keep your nose squeaky clean. And for God's sake, leave your students alone!"

"I miss you, Leon. When can I see you?"

"Monday, at school."

"I don't mean see you that way."

"I don't know. I'll see what I can do. But we have to be very, very careful, both of us. There's too much at stake."

"All right, Leon."

Pratt hung up the phone.

He stood up and walked to the window and peeked out again. No one was spying on him, unless they were well hidden.

Things were getting too complicated, just as they had in California. Pratt had had his share of bad luck. Trouble, like a nasty little dog, growled and nipped his heels wherever he went.

So far he'd managed to keep the mutt away from his throat. But the heat was on. Leon was right about the folly of him leaving town now, right after the murder. Still, if things got too hot, he'd have to do something.

After a while, he moved away from the window, trudged into the kitchen for a beer. Then, still naked, he walked back into the living room and stood for a long time, staring longingly at the picture of Christ hanging on his living room wall.

Chapter 8

At three o'clock in the afternoon, business was slow at Uncle Buck's Blue Duck Café, but dinnertime was coming, and employees were busy preparing for the evening rush, which started in spurts at around four thirty or five.

The head cook, a young Mexican called Taco, whose given name was Manuel, had worked for Uncle Buck for four years. Taco was born in Pinewood County General Hospital twenty-three years ago to illegal immigrants. Both parents were now legal citizens, and they worked full-time—"For peanuts," they joked—at Vancini's Pepper Plant.

Taco's food was mostly American, but sometimes he would sneak in some secret ingredient, giving it a hint of Mexican flavor, which usually went unnoticed. But occasionally a customer would say something like "Hey, Uncle Buck, this beef stew is fine today. There's something a little different about it. What's that seasoning?"

Uncle Buck would laugh.

"Hey, man, Taco won't even tell *me* what his secret spices are."

This Saturday afternoon, while Uncle Buck and Taco worked in the kitchen, Wanda Dunn and Gloria Simms, a high school senior who worked on weekends, were working the front of the restaurant, filling napkin holders, salt and pepper shakers, sugar bowls, and rolling silverware into paper napkins.

A solitary customer sat at the counter drinking coffee, smoking cigarettes, and eyeing Wanda Dunn as a hawk might watch a field mouse. Wanda was flattered by the attention, but the constant stare made her so nervous she dropped a sugar bowl.

She said, "Gilbert, I don't get off until nine. You don't have to hang around here all day."

Gilbert took a long pull on his cigarette, sucked the smoke deep into his lungs, and let it out slowly, sniffing the used smoke up into his nostrils.

"Got nothin' better to do."

Wanda was down on her knees cleaning up the mess. She glanced up at him. She tried to smile, but drops of sweat that rolled from her forehead into her eyes made the smile appear as a scowl as she closed her eyes to squeeze out the burn.

"Whatever, sweetheart. I'm just sayin' you don't need to hang around here all afternoon unless you want to. I'm not gonna run off with anybody else, if that's what you're worried about."

"I'm not worried about it."

Wanda swept the shards of glass and the sugar onto a dustpan. With a wet rag, she swabbed the floor to clean up the remaining sugar.

"Well, that's good," she said, "because it's not even an issue. I lost interest in every other man the minute I laid eyes on you."

Gilbert grinned with a complacent cockiness that Wanda wasn't sure she liked. She liked men to be confident and self-assured, but arrogant and snotty was something else. She wasn't quite sure which side of the fine line Gilbert was on.

It was true the serious money Gilbert had been born into would make his cockiness easier to stomach. And he was awfully easy on the eyes. In fact, she could honestly say he was among the top 10 best looking guys she'd ever seen. The only better looking guy in Pinewood County was that teacher that came in occasionally, Jim Pratt. But he was so creepy. Maybe, if she would admit it, Gilbert was creepy too.

"Wanda."

And although she hated to admit it, she missed Mike Evers.

"Wanda!"

Uncle Buck was yelling from the kitchen.

She stood up and, touching Gilbert's hand, whispered, "Uh-oh, sounds like I'm in trouble." She pushed through the swinging doors into the kitchen.

"What is it, Uncle Buck?"

Buck Jernigan was a bear. He stood five-nine and weighed two hundred and ten pounds. His back, shoulders, chest, and stomach were matted with thick swirls of black hair, which also covered his arms and grew down the backs of his hands and onto his fingers. Those who had seen Buck barefoot claimed his feet and toes were as hairy as his hands.

But Buck's head was as bald as an onion. To compensate for that loss, he grew a beard that began just below his eyes, grew down his face and neck, and hung to his navel. Health inspectors said there was no use wasting a hair net on a head as bald as Buck's but insisted he wear a net on his beard.

At first Buck had balked, but after several fines and threats of being closed down, he finally complied. Every moment of the fifteen-hour days he spent at his restaurant, he wore the net on his beard; he tied it with pieces of yarn behind his ears to keep it from falling off.

When Uncle Buck first began to wear the net, the teasing was merciless. But one day, after he picked up a couple of drunks by the seat of their pants and heaved them out into the parking lot, the kidding stopped.

But Wanda had known her uncle all her life, and she knew that inside the grizzly exterior lived a very gentle soul.

"What is it, Uncle Buck?"

He wriggled his finger for her to come closer.

When she stood right next to him, he said, "I told you an hour ago to get that boy out of here. What's he still doin' here, hunched over my counter, sipping on the same cup of coffee he's had in front of him for an hour? It's bad for business, him sitting there all afternoon making goo-goo eyes at you."

"Uncle Buck, he's not bothering anybody."

"He's damn well bothering *me*. I can't stand the creepy little bastard, anyway, if you want to know the truth—and I sure don't like you going out with him. I've known him his whole life, and he's never been anything but a spoiled, rotten brat. He's a surly son of a bitch too. Why you dumped Mike Evers for something like that is more than I'll ever understand. I guess it's gotta be the money he comes from, and that car he drives."

"Uncle Buck, that's not true. He's handsome too."

"Handsome? So was Ted Bundy. Now you go back out there and get rid of him before customers start comin' in."

"I've already told him I don't get off until nine and he doesn't need to hang around."

"Go tell him again. And if he can't take a hint, I'll come out there and show him the door like I did those drunks."

"I'll tell him," Wanda said pushing through the swinging doors.

*   *   *

Wanda's daddy, Merle Jernigan, Buck's brother, had been killed when Wanda was fourteen. An "accidental shooting," was the official ruling, but Buck knew the truth; Merle's little redheaded fireball of a wife, Marsha, Wanda's mother, had murdered him.

One month before the shooting, Merle had called Buck and told him he'd found out that on all those Saturday nights Marsha said she was going out with the girls, she was in fact hooking on Tampa's hottest strip, Dale Mabry Boulevard. Merle said he was going to an attorney to find out, when he filed for divorce, what the odds would be under the circumstances of him getting custody of Wanda, with Marsha having to pay him child support.

Buck reckoned Marsha somehow found out about Merle's plan because a week after the phone call, Merle was shot in the chest with a .38 Colt revolver. Marsha's story to the police was that Merle had bought the weapon for her for protection, and he was teaching her to shoot it when it went off, accidentally, killing him instantly. Marsha had gotten a big life insurance claim that put her on Easy Street, giving her the financial freedom to go to Dale Mabry Boulevard and give herself away, thus avoiding any embarrassing prostitution charge.

Buck adored his niece. Every year on Wanda's birthday, he sent her cards with money in them, and every Christmas, she found plenty of presents under the tree from her Uncle Buck.

A few times, Wanda had spent her entire summer vacation with Uncle Buck, who never married and was glad for the company. One year, when he was short handed, he let her work in The Blue Duck.

When Wanda had called after her divorce and said she just had to get out of Tampa and asked for a job, Buck remembered how well she'd worked the summer she was still in high school and said, *Sure, come on.*

She'd stayed with him the first few days, and then moved into a duplex he owned in Wasahatchee. She didn't know he charged her a hundred and fifty dollars a month less than he charged any of his other renters.

*   *   *

Wanda went back into the kitchen.

"He won't leave, Uncle Buck."

Uncle Buck looked up from his salad making.

"What?"

"He says he won't leave, that this is a public place and he can stay here as long as he wants to, and you can't do anything about it."

Uncle Buck's face turned as red as the tomato he was slicing. He set the tomato down on the table and wiped his hands on his apron. "Well, we'll see—"

"Wanda, Mr. Buck!" Gloria called from the front. "Y'all come here quick, take a look at this."

Wanda went through the swinging doors into the restaurant with Uncle Buck right behind her.

"Gloria," Buck said, "what're you hollering about?"

"Look!"

Through the big window that looked out over the parking lot toward the highway and pastureland beyond, Buck saw a black Lincoln Continental almost as long as a limo parked on the shoulder of the road.

"What's a car like that doin' here?" Wanda wondered out loud. "Must be movie stars or something. You think they're comin' in, Uncle Buck?"

"If they do, I hope they've got their appetites and their wallets with 'em."

Gilbert, lighting a cigarette, sneered.

"Anybody who'd drive a car like that wouldn't eat in a dump like this."

Wanda froze, and then whirled around to face him.

"Gilbert, that is so *rude*. You apologize to my uncle right now!"

Gilbert sneered again.

"You're kidding."

"No, I'm not."

"Look!" Gloria exclaimed. "They're getting out!"

The driver's door and the passenger door opened at the same time, and two men got out and looked around, stretched, and then started walking across the street. Each was immaculately dressed in a dark suit, and they reminded Buck of a movie he'd seen in which very serious men made people offers they couldn't refuse. He shooed his employees back to work.

The door opened, and the taller of the two men walked in first. They sat at the counter, a couple stools down from Gilbert. The tall man reached inside his suit coat, pulled out a gold cigarette case, snapped it open, and took out a long, unfiltered cigarette. Holding one end with his thumb and forefinger, he slid the cigarette underneath his nostrils, savoring the scent of the tobacco. His eyes then moved toward Gilbert. He saw the boy looking at him.

The tall man smiled.

"Got a light, sonny?"

Gilbert grinned and slid his Zippo down the counter. The man picked it up, looked at it, and nodded approval.

"Beats the hell out of those disposable pieces of crap," he said.

He lit his cigarette, looked at the lighter again. Then, with a flick of his wrist, spun it through the air at Gilbert; if Gilbert hadn't snatched it out of the air, it would've struck him square in the forehead.

Wanda watched from behind the counter, her heart beating fast. She was afraid Gilbert was going to say something smart, and these did not look like the kind of men you wanted to get smart with. She'd seen such men in Tampa, in clubs in Ybor City, who exuded the same aura. Even when they were smiling, their eyes told you they could kill you and think no more of it than stepping on a bug.

Wanda could feel the tension growing in the room.

"Can I get you gentlemen something?"

The tall man pulled his eyes away from Gilbert and looked at Wanda. He smiled. His teeth were small, like a child's, and yellowed by nicotine.

"Yes." His voice was gentle. "I'll have a coffee, please. Black."

"The same," said the other man.

As Wanda poured coffee, the tall man said, "I'm Eddie. This is Bruce. We're headed down to the Keys."

Wanda set their coffee cups on the counter and smiled.

"You're a little bit off the beaten path, gentlemen. How'd you wind up in Flowing Wells?"

Eddie tasted his coffee.

"Good." He set his cup down. "Actually, it isn't an accident that we're here. We heard an old buddy of ours is staying here, and we thought, being this close, we ought to stop by and say hello."

Gilbert was listening. He hadn't taken his eyes off the man named Eddie since he tossed his lighter at him.

Eddie knew Gilbert was watching but pretended not to notice.

"Why'd you throw my lighter at me like that, man?"

Eddie cupped his ear in his hand, and leaned slightly toward the boy. "Eh? Excuse me?"

"You heard me. Why'd you throw my lighter like that?"

Wanda cut in, "Who is your friend, Mr. Eddie? Maybe I know him."

Gilbert got loud.

"Wanda! Don't interrupt me. Mister, I said, why did you throw my lighter at me?"

Eddie winked at Wanda and turned his head, slow, to look at the boy.

Their eyes locked, but only for an instant. Gilbert was struck with the insane notion he was eyeballing the devil. He even fancied he saw scales, horns, and cloven hooves.

Gilbert shivered as an icy fist clutched his heart. His stomach churned, and he sprang from the stool and ran for the bathroom, but not fast enough. Halfway there, he felt something wet and warm running down the backs of his legs.

Wanda sniffed the air and went pale.

"Gilbert!"

"Must be something he ate."

"Something he ate," Bruce said. "That's a good one, Eddie. Must've been something he ate."

"What'd you do to him?" Wanda's voice was tinged with awe and fear.

Eddie frowned and shrugged his shoulders.

"What'd I do to him? Nothing, honey. You were standing right there. You know I didn't do anything to him. You saw what happened."

"I'm not quite sure what I saw."

Uncle Buck came out of the kitchen, drying his hands on a towel. When the visitors saw the beard and the hairnet, they began to howl. Buck ignored them, hoping they'd drop some money.

"How're you fellas doing?" he asked. "Get you anything to eat?"

Eddie's face took on a very concerned look. "I don't think so, sir, not after what happened to that young man. We just stopped for coffee anyway.

"As I was just telling this lovely young lady, we're headed down to the Keys and thought we'd swing through here to say hello to an old buddy of ours, Jim Pratt. He's a school teacher—or used to be. Do you happen to know him?"

"Sure, I know him," Buck said. "He comes in here once in a while. Doesn't say much though. Kinda keeps to himself."

"You know where he lives?"

"I hear he's stayin' over at the Cabbage Palm Apartments."

"Where's that, sir?"

Uncle Buck scratched his bald head. Looked out the window.

"Say you're friends of his? You must not be school teachers, driving a car like that."

"Actually, we're just renting that car. We're not teachers though. We're businessmen."

"I thought so."
"Can you tell us where the Cabbage Palm Apartments are located?"
"Sure," Buck said. "Boy, he'll be surprised to see y'all, won't he?"
The tall man chuckled.
"You got no idea, pal."

Chapter 9

In the mid 1980s, when phosphate mining in central Florida was at its peak, Dick Mendel was managing a restaurant in Miami. Dick hated the aggravation and the long hours; when he heard from a friend that mines all over Polk County were hiring and paying well, he moved wife Lois and one-year-old daughter Kara to Bartow, a medium-sized town smack in the center of Polk County. Dick found work in less than a week. He was a good, conscientious worker, and in only six months, his foreman gave him a raise and assured him he had a future with Brightway Mining Corporation.

But Dick was dismayed at the devastation his livelihood wrought on the land. When Kara was starting kindergarten, and son, Sean, was a baby, Dick moved his family again, forty miles south to Pinewood County, to make a home on less tortured ground. The commute was tiresome but better than living on the land he was helping to rape. Now that the phosphate miners had almost sucked Polk County dry, they were eyeing areas farther south.

Dick despaired at the probability that the howling, rattling old phosphate trains and the monster mining draglines that gobbled up the earth in enormous mouthfuls would soon be soiling his own backyard, and there was nowhere else to run.

Dick, Lois, Sean, and Kara settled into a three-bedroom two-bath house in a subdivision near Wasahatchee called Peace River Pines. The Peace River was nowhere near, nor were there any pines.

*   *   *

It was late in the afternoon when Charlie pulled his patrol car onto the Mendel's driveway. He sat in silence for several moments, reached for the door handle, and climbed out of the car. "Something feels weird, Tom."

"Creepy."

They walked toward the house.

"It's so quiet, Charlie."

"That's why it's creepy."

*   *   *

A short, bald man in the yard across the street stood with a hose in his hand, watering marigolds that lined both sides of his sidewalk while watching Charlie and Tom. Charlie threw up his hand in an exaggerated wave.

"Hey, Tiny! Nice day!"

Embarrassed at having been caught staring, Tiny coughed into his hand, waved, turned his back to the police officers, and continued to water his plants.

*   *   *

Tom followed Charlie up the steps to the front porch. Charlie knocked on the door. They could hear movement inside. Lois Mendel opened the door.

"Hi, Lois."

"Hey, Charlie. Tom."

Her eyes were red and puffy, as if she'd been crying. She motioned them inside.

"I can't get over this thing about Sandy," she said, stifling a sob. "I can't believe it. I absolutely cannot believe it. Why in the name of the Lord Almighty would anyone want to kill Sandy?"

"Well, that's the sixty-four-thousand-dollar-question. Why? When we figure that out, we won't be too far from knowing who."

Lois looked at the sofa.

"Will you sit down?"

Charlie shook his head.

"We're in kind of a hurry, Lois. We need to talk to Kara. We know Sandy came by here early this morning, and we want to know if she said anything to Kara that might be helpful to us."

"Sandy came by here every Saturday morning, between six and six thirty. They'd just sit out on the porch and talk, sometimes for an hour or two. Kara looked forward to those visits all week.

"She's awfully upset, Charlie. I gave her a sedative a while ago, but I don't think it's doing any good. She's only been out of the hospital a couple of weeks. I hope you won't upset her any more than she already is."

"I'll try not to, Lois. We just need to ask her a few questions."

"How are Connie and David taking it?"

"Hard."

"My god, how can they stand it? How do you live with something like that?"

"You just keep breathing, I guess. Put one foot in front of the other."

"It's just too awful. Too goddamned awful—oh, I'm sorry! I don't even swear, and listen to me. I'm just so . . . What do you think Kara can tell you?"

"We won't know until we talk to her. It's possible she knows something but doesn't know it's important. That's why we need to talk to her, to find out what she knows and to see if it's anything we can use. We'll be talking to all of Sandy's friends."

"Come on, then. I just hope you don't upset her."

$*$ $*$ $*$

Lois led Charlie and Tom through the living room and down a short hallway to a closed door. She knocked lightly, opened the door, and went inside; she closed it softly behind her. In a few moments, she opened it again and motioned them in.

Charlie and Tom stepped into Kara's bedroom.

"Y'all want some coffee?" Lois asked.

"Sure. Cream and sugar."

"Same here," said Tom.

"It'll just take a few minutes." Lois Mendel hurried off toward the kitchen.

Charlie glanced around the room at four bare walls. No banners or posters or anything except one 5 x 7 above Kara's bed of Kara and Sandy made up as bluebirds. Charlie remembered the play. The girls had been in kindergarten. Their whistling in mock birdsong had brought cheers and applause from the audience and sealed the girls' friendship.

In the eighth grade, when Kara's mental illness began to manifest itself in unpredictable and bizarre ways, many of her friends shied away, but Sandy stuck.

The room was unnaturally neat. Not a magazine, shoe, blouse, belt, or anything was out of place. Everything was immaculate, and except for the wrinkled bed, the room looked unlived in.

A comforter with a great stalking tiger covered the bed, and at least a dozen pillows made of animal skin prints were piled against the headboard. Kara, dressed in blue jeans and a white T-shirt, sat on the bed, leaning back against the pillows. Her eyes, like her mother's, were puffy and red.

Kara stared at the police officers but did not speak. Her lower lip quivered. She touched a big cotton handkerchief, which Charlie guessed belonged to her father, to her eyes.

A brown leather chair stood against one wall. Its matching love seat was adjacent to it, with a jungle throw spread neatly across it. Charlie eased himself onto the edge of the bed. He reached out and patted Kara's hand.

"Kara, I know you're upset, but we need to ask you a few questions. Think you're up to it?"

Kara closed her eyes, squeezing out tears.

"How could anybody kill Sandy? She was the most wonderful person in the whole world. She was my best friend. Why would anybody do it?"

Kara covered her face with her hands and sobbed. Charlie looked at the desk against a wall near a window. On it were books, papers, pencils, and a computer. Each item occupied its own particular space. Everything was in perfect order.

"You keep a mighty nice room, Kara," Charlie said. "Looks like you take pride in it. Neat as a pin. Clean as a whistle."

Kara opened her eyes. "What? Oh, thanks. I like neat. Sandy was neat too. We had a lot in common."

Kara's mother came back into the bedroom with a plastic tray holding two steaming mugs.

"Take one, guys," she said. "They're both the same. I thought cops drank coffee black."

"A myth I'm working hard to shatter," said Charlie. He took a mug off the tray and sipped. "*Mmm*, just right, Lois. Thanks."

Lois looked at her daughter. "Please, try to help the sheriff, honey. It's the only thing you can do for Sandy now. Let me know if you need anything, Charlie."

She went out the door, closed it, but lingered protectively in the hallway.

Charlie said, "Look, Kara, we really want to get the person who did this. The faster we move, the better our chances of catching him. But if this is too much for you to handle right now, we can come back another time."

"I'm all right. I mean, I can talk. It's just that I can't believe Sandy's dead. It's like I'm in a nightmare, and I want to wake up, only I can't. Like those dreams where you know you're dreaming—it's like you're awake in your dream, sort of—but you want to wake up for real, but you can't, so you just have to go on in the dream, hoping every moment you'll wake up. Do you ever dream like that, Sheriff? Like you're trapped in your dream and can't get out?"

"I've had dreams like that."

"So have I," said Tom.

"You're not dreaming now, Kara," Charlie said. "I wish you were. I wish we all were dreaming, and we'd wake up and Sandy would be alive, but that's not going to happen because this is real and Sandy is dead, and that's the sad truth of it."

Kara sniffled.

"What do you want to know?"

"What time did Sandy leave here this morning?"

"Real early, before seven. More like six thirty, I think. She didn't stay long."

"How did Sandy seem this morning, Kara? I mean, was she angry, upset, depressed, happy, what?"

"She was nervous."

"Nervous?"

"She said she'd found something out, and she wanted to tell you about it. But she was afraid. She said if she told, people would get hurt, even some of her friends."

"Did she say which friends?"

"No."

"Could you have been one of them?"

"I asked her that, and she said I had nothing to worry about. I wasn't involved. Actually, she didn't tell me that this morning. She told me last week, I think it was. I-I get confused on just when she told me what."

"That's all right, as long as you remember. Involved in what?"

"I don't know."

"She wouldn't say?"

"No."

"And she wouldn't tell you who could get hurt?"

"No."

Tom said, "Kara, how did she mean people would be hurt? Do you think she meant hurt physically, emotionally, or what?"

Kara picked at a loose thread on a pillowcase and was quiet for a moment. "I think she might have meant all of those ways. But I don't know."

Tom leaned forward. "Kara, you and Sandy have been friends a long time. Do you have any idea what it was she knew that could get people hurt?"

"Well, I've thought about it and thought about it, and I have an idea, I guess, but that's all it is, a guess."

"Well," Charlie said, "that's more than we've got. Tell us anything you can think of."

"Well, I've heard our new math teacher, Mr. Pratt, is maybe going out with some of his students. I don't pay much attention to stories like that because they start up every time a cute new teacher comes to town. Remember Mr. Belcher, the art teacher, and all the stupid stories that were going 'round about him? And all of it was a bunch of lies!

"It's probably the same thing with Mr. Pratt," Kara said, "only . . ."

"Only what?"

"Well, for one thing, Mr. Pratt is just such an absolutely gorgeous man. I can see almost any girl going out with him, if she got the chance. I'm not saying any girls *are* going out with him, I'm just saying I can see how it could happen. But it isn't just his looks. Mr. Pratt is so friendly—"

"Especially to the girls, huh?"

"Oh no. Boys too. He's friendly to everybody. He's a real friendly person."

Charlie said, "So what you're saying is, Mr. Pratt might have been dating Sandy, and she broke it off and threatened to tell on him, and he killed her to keep her quiet?"

"Oh no! *No!* That's not what I'm saying at all! Why Ji—Mr. Pratt would never ever hurt anyone. Besides, Sandy didn't date him. That's one thing of which I am 100 percent certain! He might have asked her, but Sandy would never have gone out with him. That's the truth. Sandy didn't like him."

"Why not?"

"I don't know. I asked her, but all she would say was she didn't trust him."

"What are you saying then?"

Kara put her thumb between her teeth and began to bite the nail. When she looked at Charlie, she saw him watching her and took her thumb out of her mouth.

"Well, I probably shouldn't say this, because I know it isn't true, but they say Mr. Pratt is dating Diana Matthews."

"Really?"

"Yes, sir. Diana does cocaine. What I think happened is that Diana got high and got jealous of Sandy—she was *always* jealous of her, you know—because she thought Sandy was trying to take Ji—Mr. Pratt—away from her, so Diana killed her."

"You think Diana Matthews killed Sandy?"

"Well, why not? Sandy was more beautiful than Diana, and she was smarter too. Diana can't stand not to be the best at everything."

"But you said Sandy wouldn't have anything to do with Mr. Pratt."

"Yes, but Diana didn't know that. You don't know how jealous Diana can get."

"Who told you Diana was dating Mr. Pratt?"

"Martin told me. He was dating Diana, you know, until they broke up a little while ago."

"Did Martin tell you Diana was doing cocaine?"

"Yes. But I think he's doing it too. Lots of kids are."

"We hear Sandy had a new boyfriend," Tom said.

Kara bit off a speck of thumbnail.

"Well, she was seeing somebody, I think. But I don't know who. She was making it out to be a big secret."

Charlie said, "We hear Jim Ed was pretty burned up when Sandy broke up with him. Do you think he might have found out who she was seeing?"

"He could have, I guess."

"Is there anything else you can tell us, Kara?"

"No, not really. Sandy told me she was going to meet someone, but she wouldn't tell me who. She said she'd tell me about it tomorrow."

"Do you think it could have been her new boyfriend?"

"No, I don't think so. I don't know."

Kara took a tissue from the box on the bed beside her and wiped her eyes.

"I don't know anything else to tell you. And I don't know if anything I've said is worth anything because I don't know if any of it's true. Only I know Mr. Pratt didn't do it. I think Diana did it."

"I thought the three of you were friends, Kara," Tom said. "I thought you and Diana and Sandy used to run around together all the time."

"That was before I found out what Diana is really like. Just because her daddy is rich she thinks . . . Oh, never mind. That's nothing. But I hope something I've said helps you. I loved Sandy. I think Diana killed her, but if she didn't, I want you to find out who did." Kara sat straight up in bed.

"You've been a big help," Charlie said. "Thanks for talking to us, Kara. I know it wasn't easy."

"It wasn't that bad."

"Take care now," Tom said, standing up. "We'll see you later. Okay?"

"Sure. I'm not going anywhere."

As the men started for the door, Kara said, "Listen, I shouldn't have said that about Diana. I don't know that she killed Sandy. I really don't think she did. I'm sorry I said that."

"I asked you to tell me everything, even your guesses, and you did."

Kara smiled weakly, slumped back against her pillows, and closed her eyes. Tom and Charlie left the room.

*　　*　　*

In the living room, Lois was sitting on the sofa, waiting. When she saw Charlie and Tom, she stood up.

"How is she, Charlie? Is she all right? You didn't upset her, did you?"

"I don't think so. I think she's all right."

Lois spoke so softly Charlie had to lean closer to hear.

"As long as Kara takes her medicine like she's supposed to, she's okay. She's as normal as you and I. Thing is, she starts feeling too normal, too good, and she thinks she's well, and quits taking her pills. She says they bring her down, make her feel tired. Then her 'illness' comes back. Sometimes she has trouble knowing what's real and what isn't. And she gets time sequences mixed up. Maybe someone tells her something last week, or last month, and she gets it in her head they told her yesterday, or today. She has mood swings. One day she'll be sweet as pie, the next day mean as the devil. And she imagines things. When we put her back in the hospital this last time, she was blabbing about wanting to kill somebody for stealing her boyfriend."

"Who'd she want to kill?"

"I don't know."

"Who was her boyfriend?"

Mrs. Mendel shook her head and looked down at her feet.

"Charlie, Kara doesn't have a boyfriend."

"Oh."

"You caught her at a good time. She's okay now. She's okay as long as we can keep her on her prescriptions."

Charlie nodded.

"Well, we appreciate it, Lois. Thanks for letting us talk to her."

"Charlie?"

"Yes, ma'am?"

"I've got to be honest with you. I say Kara is fine now, but the truth is, I don't know." She dabbed her eyes with a tissue. Charlie waited for her to go on. "In the hospital, they *make* her take her pills. They put them in her mouth and make her swallow them and then look into her mouth to make sure she hasn't hidden them under her tongue or anything. Well, of course, I don't do that, and, since she's been home, well, I'm just not sure she's taking it as she should."

"Why do you say that?"

"I can't explain it. I just know my daughter. It's a look she gets, how she snaps at one of us for no reason. I called her doctor, and he said her dose wasn't real powerful, and a little more wouldn't hurt her, so I've been putting a little bit into the glass of orange juice she drinks every morning. I can't put much because she'd taste it. Next week we're taking her in to have a blood test done. Then we'll know for sure."

"Thank you for your confidence, Lois."

"I hope you find that killer."

"We will. Will you let me know what Kara's blood test shows?"

"You bet I will."

*   *   *

As Charlie backed out of the driveway, Tom said, "If it's true about Pratt and Diana, I wouldn't give two cents for what'll be left of him if word gets out."

"It's our job to make sure nothing happens to him, except what he gets in a court of law."

Tom looked at the last rosy thread of light hanging above the horizon.

"You know, Charlie, there *is* a lot of cocaine trade here. Seems like every week, we bust some kid. If Diana Matthews is into it, and if she's seeing Pratt, then maybe Pratt's our pusher. These kids are getting it somewhere, and it seems like there's more of it now than ever. Even the good kids are into it."

"Well, drugs aren't just in the cities anymore. I wish they were, but they're not. Besides, this coke business was going on before Pratt got here. There's a top dog who's bringing it in, all right, but it isn't Pratt. That's not saying Pratt isn't involved in it."

"Charlie, did you notice a couple of times Kara slipped and almost called Mr. Pratt Jim."

"Yeah. It also struck me she seemed purely positive Pratt did not kill Sandy."

"I think she knows more than she's telling."

"You can bet on it."

"Are we going back to Pratt's place now?"

"No. I'm taking you home to Kitty, before she calls the cops on us."

"I imagine Peg and Sally are glad to see you once in a while too."

"Listen, Tom, tomorrow, you and Kitty take it easy. Sometimes I think I worry about her more than you do. Nobody's going anywhere, and if they do, we'll get wind of it fast, so you and Kitty relax tomorrow. I'll nose around a little bit. Meet me at the high school at seven thirty Monday morning. It might not set right with some people, us hauling kids down to the station, so we'll go to school."

Tom frowned. "Maybe I'll do better my second shot at it. I wasn't exactly a prize pupil my first go-round."

"Don't worry about it. I didn't set any academic or good conduct records myself. Listen, I'm sending Mike to see John Matthews. If there's anything to this business about Pratt and Diana, maybe John's got wind of it."

"I doubt it. Kitty says Diana and her daddy haven't gotten along in a long time. Seems John doesn't have any time for her anymore, and she resents it. Kitty's worked for Matthews for years now, you know, and she doesn't think much of him."

"Oh?"

"She says he's changed. Says he used to be okay, but he's gotten cold, and now he only cares about himself and business. You know how money changes some people. The more they make, the more they want. They get greedy. Kitty says Matthews has gotten greedy, and mean."

"I've never had much use for him either, to tell you the truth. He rubs me the wrong way, always has. But he's a man you don't want to cross, unless you just have to."

"Kitty says the shame is Diana used to worship him, and still does, says it kills her that he never has time for anything but business."

"Hmm, maybe I'd better see Matthews myself."

The porch light was on when Charlie pulled onto Tom's driveway. The front door opened, and Kitty stood in the lighted doorway.

"See you, Sheriff."

As Charlie was backing out of the driveway, he saw Kitty take Tom's hand and lead him into the house; the door closed behind them, and Charlie smiled.

Chapter 10

Tom closed the door, reached for his wife, and pulled her as close to him as her condition would allow. He held her gently in his arms and kissed her.

"I love you," he said.

They kissed again.

"I love you too."

Suddenly aware of the delicious smells coming from the kitchen, Tom remembered how little he'd eaten all day and realized he was starving.

"Whatever that is, I hope you made a washtub full of it."

"Pot roast, with lots of onions, potatoes, mushrooms, and gravy. After my nap, I felt better and decided to cook the man of the house some supper."

"Baby, you're the greatest."

"Now where have I heard that?"

"Never mind, let's eat."

"You look beat. How about a drink first?"

"Are you trying to soften me up, lady?"

"Get that gun off before I change my mind and let you get your own drink."

Tom gave an exaggerated salute.

"Yes, ma'am. Right away, ma'am."

*   *   *

As Kitty went to the kitchen, Tom stepped into the bedroom, unbuckled his gun belt, wrapped the belt snuggly around the holster and gun handle, and placed it in its designated spot high up in the right rear corner of the top shelf in the small walk-in closet.

He slipped out of his uniform and hung the pants and shirt on a hook on the closet door. He pulled off his socks and underwear and tossed them into a clothes hamper against the rear wall in the closet.

After he showered, he put on a pair of boxers, faded Levi jeans, and a clean white T-shirt. As he shaved, he watched in the bathroom mirror the rippling muscles in his arms and chest bulge beneath his T-shirt. *One thing about prison*, he thought, *it gives you plenty of time to work out*. Before he began his workout regimen, he was a lanky six-foot-four, a perfect bull's-eye for bullies. But after a year of intense training, even the baddest of the bad left him alone.

Tom winced at the memories and nicked his face. Dabbing the blood with a tissue, he shoved the memories of those awful days into the back of his mind where they joined all the other buried memories of the horrors of prison.

He toweled off his face, dabbed on some of the aftershave Kitty had bought him, combed his hair, brushed his teeth, and smiled at himself in the mirror.

"You've come a long way, baby," he said to himself.

He turned from the mirror, then looked back at his reflection once more. His nose was crooked from being broken twice; hazel eyes with small scars around each; long chin and high cheekbones, giving his face an oval shape; scar on his forehead the size of a guinea egg, dragging a tail that thickened then narrowed into his hairline; hair that was still thick and dark but for small patches of gray around the temples.

He turned away from the mirror again and, this time, did not look back. His was not the face of a man he'd want his daughter to bring home for dinner, but it was one he had learned to live with.

He went back into the living room and sat down on the sofa, lifted his feet up off the floor, and stretched his long legs out on the coffee table.

"Need some help?"

"Nope, I've got it under control. I've had all afternoon to do this. I want you to enjoy it."

Tom breathed in the aroma of the pot roast.

"*Mmm*," he said. "I'm delirious with joy, just sitting here smelling it."

He heard her laugh, a sweet sound.

A corner lamp made patterns on the wall as cars passed by on the road in front of the house. A breeze blew in through the open window, moving the beige curtains Kitty had hung up back when she was still able to climb onto a chair.

Tom breathed in deep, sucking the air as far down into his lungs as he could, savoring the scent of the pot roast, fancying a whiff of his wife's hair and a hint of the clean freshness of her warm body.

*   *   *

Kitty walked across the living room to Tom and handed him a glass. He took a sip and set the glass on the table at the end of the sofa. He stood up, looked into her eyes, reached for her hands, and helped her down onto the couch beside him.

She nuzzled against him. "My handsome husband sure does smell good. Makes me want to . . ."

Tom stroked her hair, fragrant from a recent shampoo.

"What did I ever do to deserve you?"

"You came back home."

"If I'd had any say-so, I never would have gone away."

"I know."

They were quiet for a while.

"How'd it go today, Tom? Did you see Kara? How is she?"

"I'm not sure. I'm not sure how much of what she says we can believe."

"You think she's lying?"

"According to her, Flowing Wells is becoming sin city. Mostly she was repeating rumors—or so she said—about that new teacher, Jim Pratt. She says he's playing around with students and turning 'em on to cocaine."

"Do you believe it?"

"Well, it's hard to figure. Kara told us all this stuff about Pratt, but I think she's got a crush on him. A couple of times she started to call him Jim. But it's more than that. I don't know. Just a feeling I got listening to her talk about him. The sound of her voice, a hunch, I guess."

Kitty was quiet, waiting for him to go on.

"Kitty, you've worked for John Matthews a long time. You've known Diana since she was a baby. Kara says Diana is seeing Pratt. Is that possible?"

Kitty thought about it. "Well, a couple of years ago, I'd have said, 'No way, not ever.' But now, well, she's changed, Tom. I've seen it happen. John has buried himself more and more in his business and neglected his family, and Diana has gotten more and more angry and rebellious. Is it possible? Yeah, it's possible, I guess. Anything's possible."

Tom stared at the wall across the room. Kitty took his hand. "Come on. Finish your drink. Let's eat."

He raised his glass.

"That," he said, "sounds like a great idea."

*   *   *

The long black Lincoln Continental looked out of place among the old, gas-guzzling cars and pickups with gun racks spanning the rear windows that were parked around the Cabbage Palm Apartments.

The men inside the Lincoln had taken off their jackets and loosened their ties. The man named Bruce flipped his half-smoked cigarette out the window and lit another one.

"How much longer are we going to sit here and wait, Eddie?"

Eddie drew deeply on his cigarette and watched the smoke that he blew forcefully into the windshield.

"Take it easy, Bruce. Relax. We could be here a while."

"We've already been here a while."

"The boss said to wait here till he calls back. That's what we've got to do. No matter how long it is."

"We stick out like a sore thumb, sitting here in this car. What if somebody calls the cops?"

"Listen, we're getting big bucks to find this guy. Now we've found him. Where else are we going to make this kind of dough sitting on our asses?"

"But the note says Pratt won't be back till tomorrow. Why can't we go get a room and come back in the morning? I need some sleep."

"What if he gets back sooner than he expected? It took us a month to find this bird. I don't want to take a chance on losing him."

Just then, a pickup pulled in and parked a few spaces down from the Lincoln. Country music blasted from out of the open windows until the driver killed the engine. He got out of the truck and lit a cigarette. His high-heeled cowboy boots clicked on the concrete as he walked along the sidewalk in front of the apartment building and went up the stairs.

Eddie turned toward Bruce.

"How in hell did Jim Pratt wind up here?"

"Must've been stoned out of his mind."

"How many little cowgirls do you think he's popped?"

The cell phone on the seat between the two rang. Eddie snatched it up. "Yeah?"

He listened, and then snapped the phone shut and started the engine.

"What, Eddie? What the hell?"

"We go get a room, get some rest, and head home tomorrow."

"What? We spend a month looking for this son of a bitch, sit here half the goddamn night waiting, and now we just drive away? I can't fucking believe it!"

Eddie smiled as he took out a cigarette. "We're done, Bruce. The boss says what he's got planned for Jim Pratt is too nasty for clean-cut guys like us. I'd bet good dough that right about now in Tampa the Zebra is getting a phone call that'll have him licking his chops and spanking the monkey all night, when he's done honing his blades. I don't mind shooting some fucker, but what the boss wants done to this boy is way past anything I'd ever hire out for."

"Well, shit. Step on it, then. Let's get the hell out of here."

$$* \quad * \quad *$$

Upstairs, in apartment number 7, Jim Pratt slept fitfully. As the big Lincoln rolled out of the parking lot, he turned over in his sleep and cried out as though demons were chasing him in his dreams.

Chapter 11

Pinewood County Senior High School lay off Chancy Road on the southwestern edge of Wasahatchee, set back amid acres of piney woods, orange groves, and pasture land. Palmettos grew along the road leading to the school, as well as guava trees, crape myrtle shrubs, Australian pines, cabbage palms, kumquat, dog fennel, and wildflowers.

The school was only six years old, but already the buildings showed the strain of housing hundreds of hormone-driven teenagers who, for the most part, did not want to be there. Vandalism happened on a daily basis, and graffiti grew like fungus. Despite ongoing efforts to beautify the campus, the students' destructiveness was taking its toll.

It was difficult for Pinewood County natives to grasp the fact that in 1960, only 6 percent of its population had been Hispanic, and now it had grown to 47 percent. Puerto Ricans, Haitians, Cubans, and Middle Easterners had migrated there also.

Pinewood Senior High School reflected the diversity of the population of the county, and in spite of multicultural and sensitivity training for the students and staff, fistfights erupted daily. Those who had created the sensitivity training defended it, claiming that without it, there would be even more fights.

*   *   *

At seven thirty Monday morning, when Tom Wilson pulled into the student parking lot, the morning air was fragrant with the scent of orange blossoms. Tom climbed out of his car and looked around. It was plenty different from the cramped red two-story brick building he'd attended.

Tom leaned against his car and breathed. He was glad he'd quit smoking, but he wanted one bad. People told him the craving would go away. He hoped it was true.

As he waited for Charlie, Tom watched the students drive into the parking lot. Radios blasted hip-hop, rock, rap, country, and Spanish music; there was also something Tom assumed was Middle-Eastern music, although he had no idea what Middle-Eastern music sounded like.

A few rows ahead of him, Diana Mathews parked her Jaguar and walked toward the cafeteria. East of the main entrance a school bus unloaded students under a canopy in front of the gym.

Charlie drove through the parking lot and parked in a "visitor" space next to Tom. He ground his cigarette out in the ashtray and climbed out of the car.

"Morning, Tom."

"You're late," Tom said.

The sheriff rubbed his eyes with his fists.

"Didn't sleep much last night. Kept thinking about Diana and Pratt."

"You believe they're doing it?"

"No. But if it's true, and if Sandy got wind of it and threatened to let the cat out of the bag—well, that could've been the end of Pratt's career. Motive for murder?"

"It's a possibility." Tom pointed to Diana's Jag. "She pulled in just ahead of you."

"Come on," said Charlie.

*   *   *

They walked across the parking lot to the office. As they entered, every head turned. Behind the counter, a secretary scribbled a note with one hand as she held a phone to her ear with the other. She was a short heavyset woman with white hair and thick glasses. She hung up the phone.

"Hello, Charlie. The school is in shock. Parents are calling in right and left to say their kids won't be here today."

"Is Mr. Pratt here?"

"Why, yes, he is. Why do you—"

"We need to talk to him."

"Well—"

"Just routine, Mrs. Johnson. We'll need to talk to all of Sandy's teachers; some of her friends too."

"Oh yes, of course."

Mrs. Johnson forced a smile.

"I'm just stunned, Charlie. Sandy Carlton—of all people! Why in God's name would anybody kill Sandy?"

"Well, that's what we aim to find out, Mrs. Johnson," Tom said. "Is Mr. Walker in?"

"You want to see him?"

"Yes, ma'am."

As Mrs. Johnson knocked on the principal's door, she looked back at Charlie. "I'll tell you one thing, this is a dark day at Pinewood County High School."

"Come in," said a voice behind the door.

Mrs. Johnson turned the knob, stepped inside, and came right back out. "Come in."

She pulled back the waist-high swinging door at the end of the counter. Charlie stepped through and went into the principal's office.

Tom lingered at the counter and said to Mrs. Johnson, "I noticed you waited until Mr. Walker answered your knock before you entered his office. Most secretaries just go right in."

Mrs. Johnson glanced toward the office and smiled.

"You don't do that with Mr. Walker—not but once, anyway. He told me to knock before I came in, but I forgot one day and walked in, and when he got through with me, well, I haven't done it again. Mr. Walker is a nice man, but he's peculiar."

"Huh."

"Excuse me," Mrs. Johnson said, turning to a parent.

Tom walked into the office to find Walker on his feet facing Charlie. Walker shut the door and went back behind his desk and sat down.

"I know the whole town, not just the school, is in shock over this thing. No one can quite believe it. Sandy Carlton, murdered!"

Tom looked at the dark circles under Walker's eyes.

"It's hard to believe, all right."

"Have a seat, Tom. You too, Charlie."

He indicated two black leather chairs facing his desk.

"Coffee?"

"Sure."

"Black?"

"Cream and sugar."

"I thought all cops drank their coffee black."

"It's a myth."

"Cream and sugar for me too," Tom said.

"Huh."

Walker turned in his chair to the table behind him and poured coffee into Styrofoam cups, stirred in sugar.

"All I have is Coffee-Mate. The powdered stuff."

"Have to do then."

"Better than nothing, I guess," said Tom.

Walker finished fixing the coffee, leaned over his desk, and handed it to them. As he turned back to refill his own mug, Charlie glanced around the room at the paintings covering the walls.

"That's fine artwork, Mr. Walker. The detail in that portrait of you looks almost like a photograph. Who did it?"

"A student. I try to let all the students know I appreciate their work. Kids in wood shop made this desk last year." He moved his hand slowly over the smooth, shiny surface of his desk.

"I'm surprised to see that picture of Christ," Charlie said. "I mean, I'm all for Jesus, but I didn't think he was allowed in school anymore."

Walker shrugged.

"If it offends anyone, I'll take it down. So far, no one has complained. Are you offended, Charlie?"

"Like I said, I'm all for Jesus."

Tom changed the subject.

"Mr. Walker, excuse me for saying so, but you don't look well. Are you sick?"

"N-no—well, yes. I've had a cold. I'm pretty much over it now. I didn't sleep much last night, with this murder on my mind."

Walker took a handkerchief out of his pocket and blew his nose.

"Do you have any idea who could have done this horrible thing?"

Tom said, "Mr. Walker, did Sandy have any enemies that you know of?"

"Enemies? Sandy? I've never known a girl as well liked as Sandy. Everybody loved her."

"How about her teachers?" Charlie asked. "Did she get along all right with all of her teachers?"

"She was a straight-A student, active in half a dozen clubs, president of the senior class, president of the honor society . . . If any teacher had a problem with her, I haven't heard anything about it."

Tom glanced at Charlie, then looked back at Walker.

"How'd she get along with Mr. Pratt?"

Walker lifted his chin and loosened his tie.

"Mr. Pratt? Fine, as far as I know. I've never heard otherwise. Why?"

"We heard Sandy didn't like him much," Charlie said.

Walker's jaw dropped. It seemed to require physical effort for him to close his mouth.

"Who told you that?"

"Mr. Walker, if it's all right with you, we'd like to use your office for a little while. We need to talk to some kids, and rather than haul them down to my office, we'll just do it here, if you don't mind."

Walker cleared his throat and swallowed.

"Well, it's unusual, but under the circumstances, I guess so. Sure. Just tell Mrs. Johnson who you want to see. How much time do you think you'll need?"

"Oh, an hour, maybe two."

Walker stood up and began going through a stack of papers.

"Give me just a few minutes to get organized. I'll take some of this paperwork with me and do it somewhere else."

"We appreciate your cooperation. Go ahead and get your stuff. We'll wait outside."

"I won't be long."

"Take your time. Come on, Tom."

When Charlie and Tom left the room, Walker sighed, locked the door, and turned to the portrait of Christ.

Chapter 12

Charlie and Tom walked back through the outer office, nodded to Mrs. Johnson, went out a side door, and into a hallway that led to an exit.

They walked across the schoolyard to the parking lot and stood between their cars. Charlie took his cigarette pack from his shirt pocket and snapped one out. He looked at it for several moments, sniffed it, and slid it back into the pack.

"No use getting caught smoking and sent to the principal," he said, dropping the pack back into his pocket.

"Charlie, how long has Mr. Walker been principal here?"

"Five or six years, I think. I dunno. When he first came to Pinewood County, he was principal at Flowing Wells Elementary. Then when Mr. Peterson retired, they brought him over here to the high school. Never been married, that I know of.

"He knows John Matthews. They served together in Vietnam. It was Matthews who persuaded the school board to bring Walker here for an interview. Walker had kept in touch with Matthews and told him he was tired of LA and ready for a slower pace."

"LA, huh? Pratt's old stomping ground. You think they knew each other there?"

"LA is a big place, Tom."

"Still, it's a coincidence. I don't trust coincidences. You taught me that."

"I did?"

"Something about Walker bothers me, Charlie. I can't put my finger on it, but something isn't right. Whoever heard of a secretary being expected to knock first and get permission to enter the principal's office? I never saw anything like that before. Every school I was ever in—not that I've been in that many—the principal's door was open unless he was talking to a student or in a meeting with a parent or something."

"Yeah, I noticed that too, and I'll tell you something else. I've had a bad feeling about Leon Walker since the first time I laid eyes on him. But I've about convinced myself that it's just part of my nature that comes with the job, an occupational hazard, I guess you'd say, being too suspicious. Seems like I catch myself looking for the bad in people rather than the good, especially people I hardly know.

"The only problem I've had with Walker—if you can call it a problem—was one night, I got a call saying there was a lot of loud noise coming from his house. I drove by, and it was as quiet as a hospital. I decided it was just Jumbo and Bozo pulling a prank. It was Halloween."

Tom watched a gray squirrel chase another one along a telephone line. "Charlie?"

His tone turned the sheriff's head.

"Yeah?"

"Do you think Walker knows I've done time?"

"What if he does?"

"Sometimes I feel weird wearing this badge, when most everybody knows I've been in the joint. Sometimes I feel like people are whispering about me behind my back."

Charlie sighed.

"Tom, you've got to get past that and move on. It's history. You've got to put it out of your head and quit letting it sneak back in.

"Listen, you go to the same church I do, and you know that's just the devil trying to convince you you're no good. That's what the old rascal does, and he's a master at it.

"But, Tom, everybody in Pinewood County that knows anything at all about the case knows Huggins framed you, that his boy's death was an accident, not murder. He even admitted it, finally—that's how I got the governor to get the thing turned around and get you pardoned. Your slate's as clean as anybody's, Tom. You weren't guilty then, and you're not guilty now. Remember that, will you?"

"Yeah, but those years in the slammer are hard to forget. I have these dreams that I'm still in, and when I wake up, I feel dirty."

Charlie stepped closer and put his hand on Tom's shoulder.

"You had a bad break, you got a raw deal. But it's over, and you've got to forget it. The pardon's been signed by the governor. You hold your head high, son, and walk tall. You're a brave man and a good man. If I wasn't 100 percent certain of that, I wouldn't have hired you."

Tom looked a little embarrassed, but reached for Charlie's hand and shook it.

"Thanks for the pep talk. Seems like I need one every now and then. I guess being here at school got to me, being around educated people, and me with just my little GED I earned in prison."

"A GED is a thing to be proud of, like that badge you're wearing. Now ease up on yourself, give yourself a break, like you'd give anybody else."

Tom looked off toward an empty field; a buzzard perched near the top of a dead pine tree.

Charlie glanced at his watch.

"The man's had his few minutes, and more. Let's get back to work."

*   *   *

Walker was coming out of his office with an armload of papers. Charlie thought he looked better. He stood straighter, and his eyes were clearer. Maybe he'd taken some DayQuil, or popped a pill.

"I'm going to the cafeteria," the principal said. "It's quiet in there this time of day. If I can be of any assistance, just tell Mrs. Johnson, and she'll page me. You guys make yourselves at home, and good luck. Hanging will be too good for whoever did this thing."

"Thanks."

*   *   *

Charlie and Tom went into the office, and Charlie walked around behind the desk and sat down in Walker's big thick leather chair. Tom pulled one of the smaller chairs around and sat beside him.

"First time I've ever been on this side of a principal's desk," Tom said.

"Me too."

Mrs. Johnson looked in the open door.

"Anything I can do?"

"Yes, ma'am," Charlie replied. "We need to see Jim Ed Pace."

Mrs. Johnson nodded and closed the door.

As they waited, they studied the paintings.

"I don't know much about art," Charlie said, "but that looks like mighty good work, for high school kids."

"Yeah, but a student didn't paint that one of Jesus. That's a famous picture you see all over the place. There's one in our church. You know, back there on the wall behind the choir. You can buy them at Wally World, I think."

"Does Walker strike you as a religious man?"

"Not particularly."

There was a tap on the door.

"Come in."

Mrs. Johnson opened the door.

"Here's Jim Ed."

"Come in, son."

As Mrs. Johnson closed the door, Jim Ed Pace, eyes downcast, stepped into the room. Tom shook his hand and motioned to the other chair facing the desk.

For a little while, Charlie and Tom just sat back and looked at the boy. He kept his eyes down, picking at a fingernail. His face looked pale, drawn. A corner of his mouth twitched. When he looked up, his eyes darted between Charlie and Tom.

"How're you doing, Jim Ed?" Charlie asked politely.

Jim Ed cleared his throat.

"I'm all right, I guess."

"Heck of a thing, about Sandy."

"Unbelievable."

"Everybody feels that way. I know you want to help us. Are you up to answering a few questions?"

"I guess so."

"You probably knew Sandy about as well as anybody. Y'all dated, what, a year or so?"

"A year and two months."

"That's a long time. She broke up with you. What was that all about?"

The boy shrugged.

"She said she didn't want to go steady anymore, said she was too young to be tied down, wanted to be free to date when she went off to college."

"Must've pissed you off"

Jim Ed looked at his fingernail and began to pick at it again.

"It didn't bother me that much. There's other fish in the ocean."

"Did Sandy have another boyfriend?"

"I heard she did, but I don't know it for a fact."

"Who'd you hear it from?"

"I don't remember. Lots of people were saying she was seeing somebody."

"Who'd they say it was?"

"That's what was so weird. No one knew. And Sandy wouldn't talk about it. Like it was a big secret or something."

"Maybe she didn't want you to find out," Tom said. He saw the boy's jaws working, grinding his teeth. "Maybe she was afraid you'd hurt him."

"I would have. I'd have beat the . . ."

"The what? You'd have beaten the shit out of him?"

Jim Ed's face was red. His jaw worked.

"Damn right."

"But you didn't know who he was," Charlie said, "so maybe you decided to take it out on her."

"No, I . . . Hey, wait a minute. Are you suggesting—?"

"I'm not suggesting anything. When people get upset, they say things they don't mean—I know that—especially when they're in shock, like you are. You are in shock, aren't you, Jim Ed?"

"Shock? Yes, sir. I'm in so much shock I couldn't sleep a wink all night."

"You loved Sandy, didn't you?"

Jim Ed looked at his hands again. But this time he left the nail alone.

"I loved her more than anything."

"We know you wouldn't hurt her," Tom said sympathetically.

"No."

"Do you have any idea who would?"

"I can't think of anyone who could've had any reason to kill Sandy. It's crazy."

"Was there anybody she didn't get along with?"

"Sandy got along with everybody."

"Well, was there anybody she didn't especially like?"

Jim Ed thought a moment.

"There were probably people she didn't care that much about, but she didn't talk about it."

"What about the new teacher, Mr. Pratt?" Charlie asked.

He watched the boy's face, saw the twitch at the corner of his mouth, and saw him open his mouth to speak only to close it fast.

"Mr. Pratt? What about him?"

"Well, we've heard Sandy didn't like him much. She ever say anything to you about him?"

"No."

"I wonder why she didn't like him?"

"That's news to me. She never said anything to me about it. But, well, maybe she heard rumors or something."

"Rumors? About Mr. Pratt? What kind of rumors?"

"Uh, I didn't mean there *are* any rumors about him. I haven't heard any. I just meant that, well, any time a new teacher comes in who's young and single, somebody always starts rumors."

"What kind of rumors?"

"Rumors he's dating his students . . . You know."

Charlie's expression of horror struck Tom so funny that he had to look away so he wouldn't laugh.

"You mean there are rumors that Mr. Pratt is going out with *students?*" Charlie asked.

"No. I just told you I haven't heard any rumors about him."

Tom managed to get himself back together enough to say, "You don't think he is dating any of his students then?"

"No, I don't. Mr. Pratt's a great guy. He wouldn't do that."

"Whew," Charlie sighed, letting out a long breath. "Thank God for that."

Charlie leaned back in his chair and appeared to relax, as if a great weight had been lifted from him. No one spoke for a full minute. Then Charlie said in a voice so loud it was almost a shout, "You're captain of the baseball team this year."

Jim Ed jumped. Then he smiled for the first time since he entered the office.

"That's right. I am. Did you hear about that no-hitter I pitched last week?"

"I did. Congratulations, son. That's a heck of an achievement. I pitched a couple of years in high school, but I never threw a no-hitter."

Jim Ed beamed. The frightened kid was gone, replaced by the baseball hero.

Charlie's next question brought back the frightened kid.

"Jim Ed, I know you want to help us. Tell us the truth. Do you have any idea who Sandy's new boyfriend was? We really need to know."

"I told you I don't know. Do you think he killed her?"

"We just need to talk to him."

"I don't even know for sure if Sandy had another boyfriend. When she broke up with me, I just figured there had to be somebody else. But she never admitted it. She told me I was . . ."

"What?"

Jim Ed shifted his weight in the chair. His eyes darted around the room, as if looking for an exit. "I don't remember exactly. It doesn't matter. Uh, listen, I really ought to get back to class. I've got chemistry this period, and I'm havin' a tough time in there. I don't want to get any farther behind than I already am."

"Well, that's a good attitude, son. I bet your teachers wish all their students were that conscientious. Before you go, is there anything you can tell us that might help us? I know you want us to get the person that did this."

"No, sir, there's not. I wish there was, but there just isn't. I can't think of a thing."

"Well, if you do, will you call us?"

"Yes, sir."

Charlie stood up, so did Tom.

"Thanks for your cooperation, Jim Ed," Charlie said. "I know this has gotta be hard for you. Listen, on your way out, ask Mrs. Johnson to send for Martin Stanley."

A look of surprise or fear—Charlie wasn't sure which—passed over Jim Ed's face like a shadow. He turned to the door. With his hand on the doorknob, he looked back and shrugged.

"You'll be wasting your time. Martin doesn't know any more than I do."

Charlie looked at Jim Ed several moments before he spoke.

"Son, that sounds a little suspicious. Is there some reason you don't want us to talk to Martin?"

"No no. Talk to him all you want. I'm just saying he's not going to tell you anything because he doesn't know anything. You'll be wastin' your time."

Charlie smiled.

"Yeah, you're probably right, Jim Ed. We have to go through the routine though. You know?"

*　　*　　*

When Jim Ed was gone, Charlie looked at Tom.

"Well?"

"He's scared."

"Nervous, maybe?"

"He's nervous, all right. And scared. He's hiding something. Dresses nice, doesn't he?"

"His daddy's a dentist. He can afford nice clothes. Quick to stick up for Pratt, wasn't he?"

"Yeah, just like Kara."

Charlie put his fist to his mouth and cleared his throat.

"Tom, does Jim Ed seem just a little . . . ?" He held out his open hand, fingers spread, and turned it from side to side.

Tom shrugged and thought for a moment.

"I don't know. There's something about him. If it was that, it looks like we'd have heard of it before now. He reminds me of Pratt, almost too pretty for a guy. But that doesn't mean—"

There was a knock on the door, and Mrs. Johnson ushered in Martin Stanley. Whereas Jim Ed Pace had worn pressed Haggar slacks, a starched long-sleeved Arrow shirt, and Oxford loafers, Martin wore Wrangler jeans, an old pair of sneakers and a checkered short-sleeved shirt with the top three buttons open showing off a gold chain. Limp brown hair fell down on his forehead almost to his eyes and hung over his ears. He leveled his ice blue eyes at the sheriff.

"What y'all want with me?"

"How's your mama, son?" Charlie asked.

The boy visibly softened. He sat down.

"She's some better. She hasn't been right since Daddy left though. You know it."

Charlie oozed sympathy and shook his head.

"I'm sure am sorry, Martin. That was a heck of a thing, your daddy taking off like that."

Martin pulled his gaze from Charlie and glanced around the room at the paintings on the walls.

Tom said, "Nice necklace you got there, Martin. You and your mama must not be doing too bad, you sporting a gold chain."

"Mama works two jobs, and I'm working part time at the dry cleaners. We get by. What's it to you?"

"What's with the attitude?"

Before Martin could answer, Charlie said, "We hear you're taking a lot of powder up your nose, son, and maybe dealing it. Is that how you paid for that necklace?"

Martin jumped to his feet; his mouth twisted into a snarl as his fists balled at his sides. Although he was almost six-feet tall with wide shoulders and muscular arms, he was no match for Tom.

In one smooth, fluid movement, Tom sprang up, grabbed Martin's collar, and stuffed him back down into his chair. Tom moved back to his own chair and sat down, smiled, and shook his head as if Martin's action was incomprehensible to him.

Charlie leaned forward and looked into Martin's icy glare.

"I've heard you have a temper, son, but I didn't know you were stupid. Tom could hold a cup of coffee in one hand and beat you to a pulp with the other and not spill a drop. Tom's been places where they eat punks like you for breakfast.

"If we wanted to, we could arrest you for attempted battery on a police officer. Now are you gonna sit still, or would you rather we slap cuffs on you and finish this interview at my office?"

Martin squirmed. He muttered words Charlie didn't ask him to repeat. After a while, he said, "Go ahead and arrest me if you want to. You pissed me off, accusing me of dealing. Where'd you hear that shit? I think you're makin' it up."

"I'm not making it up, and it doesn't matter where we heard it. What matters is, is it true?"

"It's a goddamn lie. You tell me who told you that and I'll kill the son of a bitch."

Tom and Charlie stared at Martin without speaking.

"You'll do what?" Charlie asked.

"Wait a minute. I didn't mean like *kill* him. I just meant I'd beat his ass."

"You got a dirty mouth," Tom said. "Does your mama know you talk like that?"

"Don't worry about it."

"You're a smart ass, too."

"Have you ever killed anybody, Martin?" Charlie asked.

"What? I don't believe this shit!"

"There goes that gutter mouth again," Tom said.

"You killed Sandy." Charlie stated it as an obvious fact.

Martin tried again to come up out of his chair, but Tom grabbed him and stuffed him back down, harder than the first time.

"What're y'all tryin' to do, pin this thing on me? Well, you can't, goddamn it, because I didn't do it!"

"I bet you've got a neat little alibi, don't you?"

"You damn right I do. I was home asleep when she was killed."

"How do you know when she was killed?"

"It said in the newspapers and on TV that she was killed just before daylight Saturday morning."

"No, it said she was found at that time. It didn't say anything about what time she was murdered."

"Well, whenever it was, I didn't do it."

"Who did, then?"

"How the hell would I know?"

"Because you're a know-it-all," Charlie declared, "as well as a self-righteous, foul-mouthed, hot-tempered little creep."

As Martin sputtered and cursed under his breath, Charlie sighed, leaned back in his chair, took out a cigarette, slid it under his nose, sniffed it, laid it on the desk, and looked at it.

"Give me one of those," Martin said, grinding his teeth.

Charlie slowly lifted his eyes from the cigarette. He looked at Martin. "What did you say?"

"I said let me bum a cigarette."

"You're not old enough to smoke, Martin. And you're asking me, an officer of the law, for a cigarette?"

Several moments of silence passed as Martin fidgeted and fumed.

"How's Diana?" Charlie asked suddenly.

Martin sat up straight.

"What?"

"You heard me. How's Diana?"

"How would I know?"

"Aren't y'all still going together?" Tom asked.

"No, Tom," Charlie said. "Diana broke up with Martin right after Mr. Pratt moved to town, way back at the beginning of the school year. Isn't that right, Martin?"

Martin scowled. He started to speak but closed his mouth. It was clear to Charlie the boy was using all his willpower to hold his temper.

When he got himself under control, he growled, "Y'all know a lot, don't you?"

"Yes, we do," Charlie said. "You'd be surprised at all the things we know. And we've been hearing your name a lot lately."

"Look, I've already told you I don't know anything about it. But whoever it was, I hope you burn his ass. I liked Sandy."

"You haven't heard any rumors?"

"What rumors? What are you talking about now?"

"You know what I think, Martin? I think you're a liar. I think you know a lot you aren't telling us."

"How many times do I have to tell you, I don't know a goddamned thing!"

"Let me explain something so that even an idiot like you can understand it," Charlie said. "All the trouble you've ever been in so far in your life is kindergarten stuff compared to what you're headed for if you hold out on us. If we find out you know one little thing and didn't tell us, we'll charge you as an accessory to murder."

"What?"

"You heard me."

"You can't charge me with anything."

"You're stupid," Tom said.

"No wonder Diana broke up with him," said Charlie. "He's eaten up with the dumb ass."

Martin jumped up again, but this time he backed away from Tom and headed for the door. He was breathing hard, and sweat beaded on his forehead.

"Fuck y'all!"

"I've known you all your life, Martin," Charlie told him. "You've changed. You're not the same person you were even a year ago. If it isn't drugs that changed you, then it's something else. But I still believe that basically you're a good boy. Maybe you've gotten yourself into something you think you can't get out of. If you ever want to talk to me, you know where I am. If I were you, I wouldn't wait too long. Get out of here. Go on back to class."

Martin glared at Charlie for a long time. Twice he started to speak, but both times he closed his mouth and ground his teeth. He yanked open the door and stormed out.

"There goes one screwed up kid, Tom."

"You really think he knows something about the murder?"

"He might. It's for sure he's mixed up in something."

"Got a mean temper."

"Sure does."

Charlie stood up.

"Well, I've been saving the best for last."

"Let me guess. Mr. Pratt."

Charlie stepped out of the office to speak to Mrs. Johnson. He hurried back in.

"Let's go. Pratt signed out ten minutes ago."

"Let me call Kitty. Make sure she's okay."

"Make it fast."

As Tom reached for the phone, Charlie was already out the door.

*   *   *

"Mr. Morris!"

Charlie was reaching for the door handle of his car when he heard his name called. He turned to see Jim Ed Pace running across the parking lot toward him.

"Skipping class again?"

"No, sir." The boy was breathing hard. "I saw you out the window and wanted to see you before you got away. I got permission."

"Well, what is it?"

Jim Ed took some deep breaths and looked at the pavement.

"I wanted to, uh . . . Well, I didn't exactly lie, but—"

"That's good. This is murder investigation. You don't want to lie to a police officer during a murder investigation. You can get into more trouble than you know what to do with if you do."

"I didn't lie. I just didn't tell you all I know, or think I know."

"Don't split hairs with me, son. This is serious business."

"I know it is. I didn't say anything because I don't know if it's true."

"Get to the point."

"I think Sandy was seeing Elvis."

Charlie had known Roy Jenkins, nicknamed "Elvis" for his uncanny resemblance to the young Elvis Presley, all his life; he remembered when he was a happy child, before he'd become sullen and reclusive. He knew the boy's father, Sam, when he was a happily married man, before his wife died and booze took her place.

"What?"

"I said I think the guy Sandy was seeing is Elvis."

"Roy Jenkins?"

"Yes, sir."

"What makes you think so?"

"Well, one night before Sandy and I broke up, we were uptown talking in the parking lot behind the bank. Elvis drove by and saw us, then he turned around and came back."

"So?"

"He was drunk. He pulled up beside us and got out of his car and started talking dirty. I told him to shut up with that talk around Sandy and get the hell out of there before he got hurt."

"That doesn't sound like Elvis to me, Jim Ed. I've never heard of him drinking or bothering anybody."

"Maybe he's taking after his old man."

"Watch your mouth, son. And show a little respect. Sam Jenkins has suffered more pain and paid more dues than you can imagine, and I knew him before he picked up the bottle. As fine a man as I've ever known."

"I didn't mean—"

"Yeah, you did. Go on."

"Well, Elvis just got nastier. I told him to shut up again, and he took a swing at me. Can you believe it?"

"No."

"Well, he did. He swung at me, but missed—like I said, he was drunk—and I knocked him down. Sandy yelled at me and helped him up. She called me a bully for hitting someone smaller than I am."

"Sandy helped him up?"

"Not only that, she put him in his car, in the passenger's seat, and then she got in behind the wheel and drove off with him. Next day she said she was through with me for bullying a little guy like Elvis."

"Elvis isn't that little."

"Well, he's not as big as I am, and he doesn't work out and play sports like I do."

Charlie heard a car backfire and saw a student backing out a few rows over.

"You say Sandy left with him?"

"Yes."

"Elvis was drunk, and she helped him into his car and drove for him. That doesn't sound like Sandy to me."

"Well, it's what happened. And ever since that night, she wouldn't have anything to do with me."

"You ever see them together?"

Jim Ed paused a moment.

"No."

"Not even at school, talking in the hall, sitting together at lunch?"

"No."

"And yet you think Sandy was sneaking around with him, dating him?"

Jim Ed shrugged.

"What can I tell you? I don't know it for a fact. I wouldn't have mentioned it if you hadn't asked. Looks like I shouldn't have mentioned it at all."

"No no, you did the right thing, Jim Ed."

"You'll check it out?"

"Sure."

"I need to get back to class."

"Get going, then."

As Jim Ed hurried back across the parking lot toward the building, Charlie got into his car and started the engine.

"Damn," he said.

Then remembering the night he'd accepted the Lord Jesus as his personal Savior, he corrected himself.

"Darn."

Chapter 13

In her upstairs bedroom, Diana Matthews sat in a plush, purple velvet chair by a window, looking out onto the vast expanse of manicured lawn. She wiped tears that hung on her chin, ready to drop onto her blouse. Her convulsive sobs had subsided into whimpers; a flood of tears had become a slow, steady drip.

She had been awakened this morning by a crushing weight on her chest that pinned her to her bed and threatened to smother her. Terror had flooded her being as her mind pictured a mountainous pile of pure white powder piled on top of her, drowning her, smothering her, killing her. She tried to scream, but the tremendous pressure stifled any sound. She began to thrash wildly.

Just when she believed she would die, Sandy Carlton appeared in her vision. The image of Sandy frightened Diana even more than the crushing weight of the cocaine. Sandy, in a flowing aqua blue gown, seemed almost transparent as she held out her hands, smiled gently, and said, "Diana, you are dreaming. I'm not real, and this cocaine isn't real. Here, take my hand and get up."

Terrified to reach out, yet more afraid not to, Diana grasped her friend's hand; immediately Sandy was gone, and so was the crushing weight. Diana rolled out of bed and on to the floor, gasping.

When her mind cleared and she knew she could breathe, a throbbing sadness overwhelmed her. On the screen of her mind, she saw two pictures of herself, side by side: one, before Jim Pratt had come into her life; the other of herself as she was now, kneeling beside her bed, shivering in terror. The pictures faded as a huge fist punched her in the solar plexus. She dropped flat on the floor, drew up into a fetal position as sobs convulsed her.

After a while, she got up and sat in the chair. She realized she hated herself even more than she hated her father.

Truth be told, she didn't hate her father. She loved him and worshipped him, really. As he'd become more and more wrapped up in business and paid less and less attention to her, she'd convinced herself she hated him and had sworn to get even with him for hurting her so.

Her wild weeping had become quiet sobbing as Diana went on with facing truths about herself.

Jim Pratt had entered Pinewood High School, and her life, at the most opportune time. Pratt resembled old pictures she'd seen of her father, and she had imagined him to be exactly like her father as a younger man. When Pratt had come on to her, she had been not only willing, but eager. She had needed the love of an older man.

As she thought about it now, it seemed sick. If she had gone to bed with Jim, imagining him to be her younger father, then it was incest. How had she had been so blind? Maybe she was as crazy as her friend Kara.

No, Kara wasn't really crazy; she had some bad wiring, but when she took her medicine, she was all right, usually. Kara had an excuse for the way she acted sometimes. But what was her, Diana Matthews's, excuse? There was the cocaine, but not until after she'd slept with her teacher.

Diana stood up, paced her room, and sank back into her chair. She stared out the window. There was so much lawn. So much land. So much house. So many clothes in so many closets, so many jewels in so many jewelry boxes, so many . . . Well, there was so much of everything except—and even as she thought it, she realized how corny it sounded—love. There was so much stuff, and so little love. Once there had been lots of love, when they'd had a smaller house, fewer cars, and fewer clothes in fewer closets.

Diana knew her father had plenty on his mind. She knew a lot more than he thought she knew, not only about his businesses, but also about his other interests, like Shirley Spivey.

Matthews had no idea what he meant to his daughter, what she would do for him, what she had done for him. Diana knew too that the distance that had come between them had also come between him and her mother. They seldom looked at each other, and when they did, little was said.

Diana remembered when Shirley started working in her father's bank, only two years ago, as a teller; already she was a loan officer. Kitty Cole—Kitty Wilson now—on the other hand, had been at the bank much longer. But it had taken Kitty six years to become a loan officer. And Diana knew why.

Diana liked Kitty and had had long talks with her. Kitty admitted that John Matthews had made passes, and she'd turned him down, knowing it would prolong advancement. Diana respected Kitty. She liked Kitty's husband, Tom, too, even if he was a cop. What would Kitty and Tom think if they knew what Diana had done?

At that instant, Diana knew what she had to do. Although everything in her revolted at the idea, she had to tell Kitty; she had to come clean. Even if Kitty's husband, Tom, put her in jail, she had to do it, or she might never sleep again.

However, if she told Kitty and Kitty told Tom, that would only be the beginning. Her parents would have to know—not that her father would care; her friends and teachers would find out, and . . . she'd have to stop using! That frightened her more than anything else.

She could bear humiliation, even jail, if it came to that, but she honestly did not believe she could quit using cocaine. It was no longer a luxury; she had to have it. Without it, she would feel only half alive. In spite of the nightmare only minutes ago, when coke was killing her, she realized, with a shock, that what she wanted right now more than anything, even the love of her father, was a fix. And at that moment, she saw with startling and horrifying clarity what she'd become: a hopeless addict, lost and more alone than anyone she'd ever known.

When she thought her legs would hold her, she got up, shuffled to her phone, called school, and said she was sick, which was true.

Her parents would have to know because she would need help. Treatment probably would be necessary. She didn't know just what treatment was, but she'd heard about rehab centers, although she'd never seen one. There were none around Pinewood County. *Although there ought to be,* she thought.

She had to break free from this thing or die. But after all the bad things she'd done, did she deserve to be free? Should anything good come to the likes of her? Well, she'd only done what she had to do. Sure, she'd made mistakes, lots of them. But hadn't everyone made mistakes?

In her nightmare, it was Sandy who'd saved her. She missed Sandy so. She had been her best friend in the world. The person who'd killed Sandy deserved to die.

Feeling the start of a fresh flow of tears, Diana climbed into the shower, turned on the cold water, and held her face up to the spray. She slid down onto the cool tile floor, lay down on her back, and let water and tears mingle.

Chapter 14

Lois Mendel worked three days a week at Uncle Buck's Blue Duck Café. Today wasn't one of them, but Uncle Buck called her at 5:55 a.m. and told her one of his morning girls had called in sick and asked if she could help him out.

"Sure," Lois replied "Give me a few minutes to get the kids up and get things squared away here. Dick pulled a graveyard last night, won't be home till after eight. I'll leave him some breakfast in the oven, and coffee—"

"How soon can you be here?"

"By seven. Maybe sooner."

"Well, get here as fast as you can. People are starting to trickle in."

Lois hurried to her bedroom, hung up her robe, and put on the tan slacks and green blouse that she usually wore to work. She fried six slices of bacon, scrambled two eggs, and toasted two pieces of bread, all of which she put on a metal tray, covered with foil, and left in the oven. She set up the coffee maker and went to wake up Sean.

Sean didn't want to wake up. Sprawled across the bed, his head stuffed between two pillows, he groaned when his mother called his name. She put her hand on his shoulder and shook him gently, then harder.

He moaned.

"I can't go to school today, Mom. I'm sick."

"Get up," Lois demanded in her stern get-out-of-bed-now voice.

He moaned again.

She pulled the covers off him and promised if he was not out of bed in five minutes, she'd be back with a glass of cold water. The cold water never failed to bring him up fast, and usually just the threat of it was enough to get him moving.

When she went into Kara's room, she was surprised to see Kara already awake, sitting up and leaning back against the headboard. Kara leveled heavy-lidded eyes at her mother and stared without speaking.

"Are you all right, dear?" Lois asked.

"No," said Kara, her voice flat.

Lois went to her and touched her forehead with the back of her hand. "You have a temperature. How do you feel?"

"Lousy. I hardly slept all night."

"Listen, I'm working today, but I'll call you after a while and if you're not feeling any better I'll come home and take you to the doctor."

"I don't need to go to the doctor. I just need to stay home and rest."

"Well, we'll see. I'll call you after a while and see how you're feeling. Lie down and try to sleep."

Lois kissed Kara's forehead and went back out of the room and closed the door. She checked on Sean, who was pulling on his jeans, and then she headed toward the kitchen to fix his cereal. She glanced at her watch and realized she could make it to The Duck by 6:45, maybe even 6:40.

*   *   *

As soon as Lois closed the bedroom door, Kara got out of bed and put the heating pad back in the chest of drawers. Worked every time. If her mom did call later, wanting to take her to the doctor, her temperature would be gone.

Kara lay back down thinking it kind of funny that her mother didn't know her. Neither did her father. They thought they did, but they didn't. No one did, really. How could they? They had no idea what went on inside her head, in her secret places.

How could they possibly know what it was like to be free, as she could be without the horrible meds they'd had her on at one time or another, like Thorazine, Haldol, Lithium, and other shit they gave her. In the hospital, where they watched her through a microscope, she had to swallow the stuff or they'd tie her down and pop it into her with a needle.

But here at home, it was different. Here she often got away with faking it. She was beginning to feel good again. When she started feeling too good, they'd send her back to the hospital. But so what? That might be a week or two or three, or a month or six months. What did it matter? Kara felt good *now*, and *now* was what mattered. Jim had spoken in class one day about the wisdom of living in the eternal now, and the concept was immensely appealing.

People thought they knew her, knew what was best for her, how she ought to feel, how she ought to act, and what she ought to do. Even Sandy had been a little bit like that. She'd loved Sandy, but sometimes she got on her nerves. Like Saturday morning, when Sandy had picked on her for not taking her meds, just like her mother.

She remembered the first time she'd told Sandy she was in love with Jim and that she expected him to ask her out. Sandy had begged her not to go. When Sandy had kept on and on about it, Kara agreed to wait a few days and think it over. Big mistake. By then Jim was already messing around with Diana who was supposed to be her friend. It was Sandy's fault she'd missed her big chance with Jim.

Suddenly aware and ashamed of thinking ill of her best friend who was dead, Kara rolled over and looked at her clock. Only ten minutes had passed since her mother had closed her door. Seemed like an hour.

After what seemed like forever, she heard the front door open and close, and then she heard her mother's car start. She got up and put on her robe and went into the kitchen and poured a cup of coffee from the pot Lois had left for her father. She went into the living room and sat down in her father's chair.

Lois would be disappointed if she knew Kara had tricked her. Well, it wasn't the first time. She was tired of being told what to do. What irked her the most, but pleased her too because it gave her the upper hand, was that everybody underestimated her. Few knew there was more to her than big boobs and blonde hair.

Wouldn't folks be surprised to know some of the things she knew? She made it a point to know things. She looked and listened, and she'd gone to places and seen things she almost wished she hadn't.

It was hard to believe, even though she'd seen with her own eyes, that some of the people in this town, some of them big shots, could do some of the things she'd seen them do. She'd never known people did such things, except in books and movies. That people called *her* crazy made her laugh.

Of course, no one would believe her if she told what she knew. They'd say she was hallucinating and haul her back to the hospital.

Well, it didn't matter what people thought. She'd seen what she'd seen, and she knew what she knew, and no one would ever convince her otherwise. She could tell them things that would curl their hair.

What would people say if she told them about Jim's hideout on the Peace River, and some of the stuff she'd seen there? She knew somewhere there were pictures to prove it, but she had no idea where they were. What would people say if they knew that she had followed Sandy on Saturday when Sandy left her house? That would get their attention. Oh, there was a lot more to Kara Mendel than boobs and blonde hair. One day, this town would know it.

Kara finished her coffee and walked back into the kitchen. As she poured a glass of orange juice, she felt a gnawing certainty something was wrong. She tried to remember what she'd been thinking moments before, but her mind was blank. She was sure it was something urgent, but she could not remember. She slammed down her glass, sloshing orange juice onto the counter.

Where was her mother? Oh, of course, at work at the restaurant. Her dad had worked the graveyard shift and would be home soon. Her brother was in his room or had walked on to school. His cereal bowl was empty, so he was probably gone. But what was it she'd been trying to remember moments ago? Well, if it was important, it would come back. She hoped.

She sank back into her father's thick chair again and sighed. Had she taken her pills? She didn't think so. She didn't think she'd taken them in days. She ought to though. When she didn't, she got too many funny feelings. Most of them she enjoyed, like the energy and the clear thoughts and self-confidence; but others, like gloominess and forgetfulness, which she was experiencing more and more often, she could live without. Her bad feelings were beginning to catch up with her good ones. Was it worth it? Maybe she should . . .

She sprang to her feet. What kind of crazy thinking was that? Of course it was worth it. How could she even consider that it wasn't? She got those thoughts sometimes in the hospital when they made her take her meds regularly, but she had been off them now for . . . How long had it been?

She couldn't remember.

Chapter 15

As soon as Charlie turned off Highway 17, he saw Jim Pratt's Corvette parked outside his apartment building. At this time of day, when most people were working, there were few vehicles there.

"I can't get it out of my head," Tom said. "Sandy Carlton with Elvis. Roy Jenkins and Sandy Carlton. I can't believe it, but on the other hand, I sort of can."

"Yeah, me too," Charlie agreed. "But I don't see why Jim Ed would make it up. I mean, it's not like he had his lie all laid out. It was more like he just remembered it, like he hadn't altogether bought into it either."

Tom shook his head.

"I guess nothing should surprise me anymore, but it does. I mean, if it's true. But I still can't quite believe it."

Charlie snuffed out his cigarette in the ashtray.

"It's hard for me to believe Elvis was drunk."

"I can't imagine Elvis starting a fight, either. I think Jim Ed is lying."

"Well, if he isn't lying, he's twisting the facts in his favor, that's for sure. Even if Elvis was drunk, and I don't believe it, I can't see Jim Ed manhandling him the way he said he did."

"No way that happened."

"Elvis isn't a bad kid. After his mother died and Sam got drunk . . . Well, Elvis hasn't had it easy. I'm surprised he's done as well as he has."

"He hasn't quit," Tom said.

"Elvis is just so quiet and withdrawn, kind of gets into that outcast thing, I think. He's a darn good-looking boy. Looks just like Presley when he was a kid."

"Wonder if he can sing?"

Charlie shrugged.

"Sam was a fine man before Marge died. Then the booze got him. You knew Sam was Golden Gloves, didn't you? Sure was. Boxed pro for a while, and a lot of folks thought he could have gone big time. But then he met Marge and settled down, and gave it all up. You gotta respect him for that. He got on with the post office, and if the drink hadn't gotten him, he'd be postmaster today instead of a dishwasher at The Duck."

"Sam taught Elvis to box."

"Before Sam got sick, he worshipped that little boy and spent all the time he could with him. Taught him how to box, fish, build things, fix things. Sam was a great dad."

"I still can't see Sandy and Elvis together. I mean, hey, we're talking opposites here."

"Maybe and maybe not. Anyway, we're going to hear the other side of this story. I asked Mrs. Johnson to tell Elvis to come by the office after school."

Charlie parked beside Pratt's Corvette and sat with his arm out the window. "Remember Detective Garcia, the one Mike didn't like?"

"Yep."

"I forgot to tell you he called. Wanted to know how the case is going. Offered us some more manpower if we need it. Said if we need anything to give him a call."

"Well, that ought to redeem him some."

"He can come on a little strong, bossy and, well, just plain snotty. Gives you the impression he thinks he knows everything. But he's a man I wouldn't mind having in my corner if it came down to it."

"What'd you tell him?"

"Thanked him, said we'd call if we needed to, but that right now the investigation was going okay."

"Is it?"

"Yeah, I think so. Oh, one more thing. Garcia said there were hundreds of prints on Sandy's car, like every kid in Pinewood County had hand walked on it. Most of 'em smudged though. No help there. He said forensics is combing the inside, but not to expect much there either."

"Too bad."

Charlie opened his car door and got out and stood with his thumbs hooked in his belt, leaned back a little, and looked up toward Pratt's apartment.

"Ready?"

Tom was already out of the car and standing right by Charlie's side.

*   *   *

When Pratt had heard that Charlie and Tom were questioning people on campus, he flipped. To give himself a moment to gather his composure and to think, he rushed into the men's restroom across the hall from his classroom, went into a stall, locked the door, and plopped down on the hard porcelain seat.

Who'd ever heard of such a thing? Police interrogation on a high school campus? Unbelievable.

He'd known, of course, that he was different from country people, didn't understand their ways, but it was dawning on him just how different he was and how little he really understood them.

Pratt was a highly intelligent man. Intelligence tests he'd taken said so. On the long drive down from California, he'd had plenty of time to reflect on how to blend in with the people of Flowing Wells. He'd study them, follow their lead—monkey see, monkey do. If the majority of his colleagues attended a particular church on Sunday, he'd go there. He'd go to picnics, barbecues, dances—all the activities the locals attended. He'd soon be just another face in the crowd.

Wrong, he realized. These hicks weren't monkeys, nor were they stupid. There were no atomic physicists or brain surgeons among them, but what they lacked in academics, they compensated for in, as he'd heard several of them say, "good ol' common horse sense." There was wariness, a subtle suspiciousness about the homefolk that was unsettling. On everyone over twenty, his charm and good looks were wasted. No matter how thickly he laid it on, they'd just look at him as if they were trying to see into his brain and determine what made him tick. For a long time, he'd gone nowhere except work and The Blue Duck for an occasional meal. He'd let the world, or all of it he cared to see—young girls—come to him.

Pratt could not face a classroom of kids today, not now with the cops on the campus. When he came out of the bathroom, he hurried to the phone in the teachers' lounge, dialed Mrs. Johnson's extension, told her he'd come down with a stomach virus and had to go home. She told him to get better and said she'd call a sub.

*　　*　　*

Now he waited for the knock on the door, knowing it was only a matter of time. He looked around for telltale signs of anything illegal, changed into more casual clothes, mussed his hair, slipped on a robe, and tried to look more miserable than he actually felt, which he didn't think was possible. He sat down on the sofa in the living room with a copy of *The Pinewood Currier* and proceeded to wait.

The knock startled him even though he expected it. His hands trembled so much the newspaper fell to the floor. He stood up, took several long breaths, and wished he'd done a line. But if he had, he would be paranoid, and they'd see it in his eyes, so it was probably better he hadn't. Maybe if he guzzled a beer really fast that might take the edge off. No. They'd smell it. He picked up the newspaper and laid it on the table near the couch. Walking to the door, he almost panicked as he realized he would just have to be himself—whoever that was.

Pratt squeezed the doorknob hard until the trembling in his hand stopped. As he opened the door, he realized he couldn't remember any police officers anywhere, ever, who looked more threatening than these two. They were giants. Worse, he knew his charm would be about as effective on either of them as it would be on a grizzly bear.

"Sorry to bother you, Mr. Pratt, but we need to ask you a few questions."

Pratt managed a smile that he intended to look sickly, and had no doubt it did.

"Gosh, this is a surprise. I mean, how'd you know I was home? I'm usually at school. I went in this morning, but had to come home with a stomach virus. I hope you don't catch it."

"Mind if we come in?"

"Oh, sure. I mean, no, I don't mind. Come on in."

He led Charlie and Tom inside and motioned them to the sofa. He sat in a chair across the room, facing them.

Pratt leaned forward and pushed thick, dark hair back off his forehead. He looked vulnerable, Charlie thought, as if on the verge of tears.

"I knew I'd be seeing you guys sooner or later. I thought about coming to your office, but I knew how busy you'd be, and that you'd be around to see me when you had time. Like everyone else, I'm in shock over what happened to Sandy. It just doesn't seem quite real."

Charlie looked around the apartment. There were a few artificial plants, an aquarium, a TV, and a portrait of Christ identical to the one in Leon Walker's office.

"Can I get you guys something to drink? I can make coffee. I have soda."

"No, thanks," said Charlie. "We'd just like to ask you a few questions. You don't look well."

"I feel awful, but if there's anything I can do to help catch the maniac who killed Sandy, I'm at your service. Sandy was in my class. She was a beautiful young lady, from the inside out, a sweet, gentle spirit."

"Uh, yeah, she was. Mr. Pratt, the last time you saw her, how did she act? I mean, did she seem nervous, frightened, anything out of the ordinary?"

"No, she was her normal gregarious, scintillating self. Do you think she might have known she was in danger? I mean, do you think she saw it coming?"

Charlie glanced at Tom, moved his eyes back to Pratt.

"I used to know what 'scintillating' means."

A smile flashed across Pratt's handsome face. "It means, well, like sparkling."

"Right. Sparkling. That was Sandy, all right."

"Yes, it was."

"The way we figure it, Mr. Pratt, is that Sandy got into something she shouldn't have or, more likely, found out about something somebody didn't want her to know, and they killed her to keep her quiet. What do you think?"

"Well, it's an interesting theory, Sheriff, but I can't imagine what Sandy could have found out so serious someone would kill her over it."

"I can't either. Did she have problems with anyone?"

"Not that I know of. I'm sure she didn't. I don't think I've ever known anyone who got along with everyone like Sandy did. This might sound trite, corny even, but Sandy was full of love. It just bubbled up out of her and on to everyone around her."

"Mind if I smoke, Mr. Pratt?"

"Well, actually, Sheriff, I'd rather you didn't. Oh, it's all right. Let me look for an ashtray."

Pratt got up and went for an ashtray. He returned and gave it to Charlie and sat back down. Charlie lit up and set the ashtray on his knee.

"As you might know, Mr. Pratt, for the past few years, we've had an epidemic of cocaine here in Pinewood County—not meth, that any bimbo can make in the barn—but plain old-fashioned cocaine. We suspect there is one main man, a head honcho, importing the stuff. We've busted a few kids for possession, but we have no idea who the dealers are, or the big guy. If Sandy stumbled onto something like that, it might be reason enough for someone to want to shut her up permanently, don't you think?"

"It's possible, I guess. Do you think that's what happened? Do you think that's why she was murdered?"

"It's a theory." Charlie took a drag on his cigarette, exhaled slowly toward Pratt. "How do you like it here in Flowing Wells, Mr. Pratt?"

"I love it. I'd had about all I could take of the hustle and bustle of the city. I hardly had time for myself. Here, I've had time to think, to write. I'm writing a book, you know. I've begun to discover who James T. Pratt really is."

"And who is he?" Tom asked.

Pratt chuckled and smiled, showing even white teeth.

"Well, I haven't totally solved that mystery, but the picture's getting clearer. You know, all the world's great religions exhort us to know ourselves. However, in today's breakneck, dog-eat-dog society, I believe few have a clue who they are, especially people in cities. But it's so different here. It's like, well, stepping back a few years in time, to a time when life was simpler, when man had time to contemplate what was really important in his life."

Tom's eyes held the teacher's.

"And what's important in your life, Mr. Pratt?"

"Well, I'll admit that since I've come here, my values have changed. All I want now is to settle down and live a clean, moral life. We live in a sick society. If you don't believe it, just look at the movies our kids swarm to, the TV programs they watch, the music—if you can call it music—they listen to. Children are bombarded on a daily basis with sex, violence, and perversion. It's all around us, everywhere we look."

"Yeah, it's a sick society," Tom agreed. "Seems to be getting sicker too. Mr. Pratt, how is Diana Matthews doing these days? My wife, Kitty, has worked for her father for a long time. She's out on maternity leave now, Kitty is. She's known Diana since she was a baby. Kitty said the last few times she's seen Diana, she didn't seem to be herself."

Pratt cleared his throat.

"Diana is in my class, but I don't know her well enough to make a character assessment, and of course, I'm not qualified to do a psychological evaluation. Her grades have gone down some over the past couple of months. Otherwise, she seems to be doing all right, I guess."

"Pretty little thing, isn't she?"

Pratt swallowed.

"She is a very attractive young lady indeed, yes, sir."

Charlie held his eyes.

"You know what the rumor is, Mr. Pratt?"

"I try not to pay much attention to rumors, Sheriff. They've done too much harm to too many decent people."

Charlie nodded. "That's a fact. But occasionally, there's some truth behind one. Anyway, word is that Diana is strung out on cocaine."

Pratt looked shocked.

"No."

"That's what we're hearing. Any idea who might've turned her on?"

"No. This is a total surprise."

"So you haven't noticed any changes in her behavior?"

"A few days ago she cut her hair off. I think maybe she's lost some weight the past few weeks. But girls her age are always losing or gaining weight, trying this or that diet. I don't pay much attention."

Tom said, "There's another rumor going around that Diana is dating some man old enough to be her daddy."

Pratt took a breath.

"I haven't heard that one, either. But even if I had heard it, I would have dismissed it. Diana seems to be a very levelheaded young lady. I can't see her getting involved in something like that."

"How'd you happen to come to Pinewood County, Mr. Pratt?" Charlie asked. "It's a long way from LA."

"Well, when I decided to leave LA, I knew I wanted to come to Florida. I sent applications to several counties, and this was the first one to call me."

"I see. That portrait of Jesus looks just like the one in Leon Walker's office."

Pratt hoped he wouldn't vomit until they were gone.

"That's a pretty famous portrait. Copies of it are everywhere."

"You a religious man, Mr. Pratt?"

"You could say that, yes. I've studied all the major religions, and I try to live by spiritual principles. I believe Jesus was the greatest of all spiritual masters. And, yes, I do believe he was divine."

Charlie stood up so suddenly Pratt jumped.

"Mr. Pratt, we appreciate your time. You've been very helpful. If we think of anything else you can tell us, we'll come back."

"Y-yes, of course. Come by anytime. Or call."

Pratt stood up.

"I won't shake hands. Whatever I've got, I don't want to pass it on."

"Thanks."

Pratt stepped back and flopped down onto the couch where Charlie and Tom had sat. The color drained from his face.

"You all right?"

"No."

"You might ought to see a doctor," Tom told him.

"Yes, I might do that."

"You have a nice apartment."

"Thanks."

Pratt swallowed hard to push back bile that was rising in his throat. *Go! Go! Go! Get out of here, you bastards! Go!*

When the door closed behind them, Pratt's sweaty palms clamped over his mouth as he lunged for the bathroom.

*　*　*

"Where now?" Tom asked as Charlie pulled out onto the highway and turned south, back toward Flowing Wells.

Charlie glanced at his watch.

"I want to see Diana, but I'd rather wait until this evening, when John will be home. I reckon he will anyway. Mike is going to see him this afternoon, but I want to talk to him myself. What'd you think of Pratt?"

"I wish I'd worn boots. It was getting deep."

Charlie laughed.

"Sure was. The man's morally bankrupt, Tom, but slicker'n greased owl eggs. He should've been a lawyer or a politician. I wouldn't trust him any farther than I can fly."

"But could he commit murder?"

Charlie shrugged his broad shoulders.

"I guess most anybody could, under the right circumstances. Pratt had motive, if this cocaine business is true, and I believe it is. Whether he's dating Diana or not, if he turned her on and if Sandy found out about it and threatened to turn him in, there's motive aplenty."

At the police station, Charlie parked in his assigned parking space, glanced at his watch, and turned to Tom.

"It's getting on toward lunch time, Tom. You go on home to Kitty. Take a long lunch. Meet me here at the office at three. That's when Mike's supposed to report in. I'm gonna call the school and remind Mrs. Johnson to tell Elvis to come by. I want to talk to that boy."

"You're being awful generous with my time, Charlie. I remember days I couldn't even stop for a sandwich."

"Well, I had to break you in right. The thing is, I think I'm more worried about Kitty than you are."

Tom grinned.

"I doubt it. The baby's not due for two weeks."

"Yeah, but you never know about babies, Tom. Sometimes they don't pay any attention to the date the doctor gives them. They just come when they're ready."

Tom looked at Charlie and smiled.

"Thanks."

"Sure."

*   *   *

Charlie walked up the steps to the station and went inside. As he was opening his office door, Carol, his secretary, called him from across the hall.

"What?" he said.

"Kitty called a few minutes ago. She sounded pretty excited. Wants you or Tom to call her quick."

"Why didn't she call Tom?"

"Said she tried. Couldn't reach him on his cell."

"Is it the baby?"

"All she said was to call her as quick as possible."

Charlie hurried into his office, grabbed the phone and punched in Kitty's number. She picked up on the second ring.

"You okay, Kitty?"

"Where's Tom?"

"On his way home. What's wrong?"

"Listen, Charlie, you need to get over here. Hold on." Charlie could hear her speaking to someone, but he could not understand the words.

"Charlie? Yeah, I'm okay. Listen, there's someone here I think you'll want to talk to."

"Who?"

"Diana Matthews."

"I'm on my way."

Charlie took two steps toward the door before he remembered to hang up the phone.

Chapter 16

Tom put the front seat of his car all the way back and stretched out his legs as far as they would go. Usually lunch was a quick burger at the McDonald's that had recently come to Wasahatchee, a hot dog at the Circle K convenience store, or maybe the daily special at The Duck. Today he could eat a real meal, watch a little TV, and maybe even lie down and unwind.

His eyebrows went up as he pulled into his driveway and saw Diana Matthews's Jaguar parked in his yard. He parked his car and hurried inside. Kitty and Diana were sitting on the sofa.

"Hey, honey," Kitty said.

Diana nodded. Her cheeks were tearstained, eyes swollen.

"Hi, Diana."

Diana started to speak, but closed her mouth and looked at her nails.

"Excuse me." Tom walked into the bedroom and put away his weapon. In the bathroom, he washed his hands and face and dried them on the soft, clean towel Kitty kept hanging on the rack by the door.

He came back into the living room, grabbed the chair from the desk, set it facing the sofa, and sat down straddling it like a saddle. He put both hands on its back and looked at Diana.

"Diana's in trouble, Tom," Kitty said.

Tom nodded. He waited.

Diana said, "I knew I could talk to Kitty. I really unloaded on her. She says I have to talk to you too, and I knew I would—you or Mr. Morris, or both of you—but I don't know if I can."

Diana took some tissue from a box beside her.

"Well, Kitty tells me I'm a pretty good listener."

The sound of an automobile engine and the crunch of gravel drew Tom's eyes to the window. He saw Charlie's car stop behind his. Charlie climbed out of his car and walked to the front door. Tom opened the door before Charlie knocked.

Charlie took a chair close to Tom's. He sat down and looked at Diana.

"How're you doing?"

"I've been better."

"Do you mind me being here?"

"I told Kitty it was all right for you to come. I expected it."

"All right."

"Tell them what you told me," Kitty said. "Just go ahead and do it. You'll feel better, believe me."

Diana hung her head.

"I'm so ashamed."

"Everybody makes mistakes," Charlie said. "But most don't have the courage to admit their mistakes and come clean. I think you do."

Diana shook her head.

"I'm not brave. I'm a coward."

"If you were a coward, you wouldn't be here," Tom said.

"That's right, Diana. And you don't have to be afraid to tell me anything. No matter what you say, I guarantee you I've heard worse. And I don't judge people. That's not my job. I leave judging to the judges, and the good Lord. I've made too many mistakes myself to judge anyone else. I won't cast any stones at you."

Diana whispered, "Thank you for that."

"Go ahead, honey," Kitty prompted. "Tell them what you told me."

"Well, I-I don't hardly know where to start. I mean, this isn't just me. Lots of other people are going to get hurt too."

Charlie waited for her to go on. She sat for several moments, staring at her fingernails and biting her lower lip.

"People learn from their mistakes. If you do, maybe they will too. Maybe one day they'll thank you."

"I don't think so, Sheriff."

"You never know."

Diana began to speak, hesitantly at first, but gradually, with more assurance. She said her mother and father had grown apart and her father was seldom home, and when he was, he locked himself in his office. Her mother was drinking more and more to the point Diana worried that she was becoming an alcoholic. Most days, the three of them got up and went their separate ways without speaking and usually didn't see each other again until bedtime, if then.

Diana paused for breath.

"I probably shouldn't be talking about Mama and Daddy. It's me I came here to tell you about."

"If it's part of the picture, you can't leave it out. Go on."

"It's just that before Daddy got so rich, we used to go places together and do stuff, and now we never . . .

"I try not to show it, but it seems like I'm sad all the time. I miss my mama and daddy almost as much as if they were dead. I'm lonely, I guess.

"One day this guy got me to do some cocaine, and liked it. I mean really liked it a lot. Lots of kids are doing coke, you know?"

"Yeah."

"For a long time, I was scared to mess with it, but when I finally tried it, I loved it, and I think I was hooked the first time I used it. It made me feel so good. I wanted more the minute it wore off."

"Diana, I need to know where you got it."

Diana looked at Kitty.

"Heck, you can get it anywhere. It's all over the place."

"I know that. What I want to know is where you got yours. Who was the guy who got you to try it?"

She shook her head.

"I can't tell you that. I can't."

"Look, Diana, you came here to come clean. You can't go halfway. You can't hold back. You have to tell the whole story."

"Charlie's right," Kitty said. "You have to tell them everything."

Diana looked at the window across the room and didn't say anything. Her hands lay in her lap, and she flicked her thumbnails together, making clicking sounds.

"It was Mr. Pratt, wasn't it?"

Diana's head jerked up, and her eyes went wide as she stared at Charlie. "How did you . . . ?"

"We know more than you think we do. What we don't know is who's bringing it into our county. That we don't know. Do you?"

Diana's eyes darted around the room. Charlie thought she looked like a rabbit dropped into a cage.

"No," she said. "I don't. I don't know anything about that. How would I?"

"You might have heard talk."

"No, I haven't heard anything about that. I don't know anything about it."

"Did Sandy know Mr. Pratt is dealing drugs and turning on students?"

"Sandy?"

"Yes."

Diana didn't answer.

"She did, didn't she?"

"She might have heard about it. But not all that many people know. I didn't tell her."

"What did she say about it?"

"What did she *say* about it?"

"Yes, what did Sandy say about Mr. Pratt dealing drugs?"

"She didn't say anything, not to me."

"Did she say anything about turning Mr. Pratt in?"

"What? No, she didn't. I don't remember her saying anything about that, about turning him in. I don't think she knew about it. But I don't think she'd have turned him in even if she did."

"Why not?"

"Because it would ruin him."

"What about all the people he's ruining?"

Diana looked at the floor.

"Diana, how do Mr. Pratt and Mr. Walker get along?" Tom asked.

"What?"

"How do Mr. Pratt and Mr. Walker get along?"

"Fine, as far as I know. They're friendly enough. I've never heard they didn't get along. Why?"

"Mr. Pratt is a darn good-looking guy," Charlie said. "I bet lots of girls have crushes on him, huh?"

"Are you kidding me? Just about every girl in school is in love with him. Kara had it the worst before . . ."

"Kara?"

"Yes, Kara."

"Kara had it bad for Mr. Pratt?"

"Yes."

"Before what? You were saying Kara had it bad before . . ."

"Before Ji—Mr. Pratt started paying more attention to me than he did her. In class, I mean. She got so mad she wouldn't speak to me for a week. When she got back from the hospital, she acted like she was over it though."

Charlie looked straight at Diana, and his voice got louder. He made her look at him. "Diana, you've been honest with me, and I appreciate it, but we need to know one more thing. You and Jim Pratt have been more than friends, haven't you?"

Diana drew back into herself and seemed to freeze. She was quiet for so long Charlie wondered if he'd pushed too hard. But then, so slowly it barely showed, she began to nod her head.

"I'm such a damn fool. I wish it hadn't happened. But it did."

"Will you testify to that in court, if it comes to that?"

Charlie expected resistance and was surprised when Diana's answer came fast.

"Yes, I will."

"That's good, Diana. Do you use coke every day?"

"Yes."

"Do you want to quit?"

"I've tried to quit, to just 'say no.' But it isn't that easy. I want to quit, but I can't. I can't."

"Okay, listen. Here's what I want you to do. Go home and tell your parents everything you've told us. Call a powwow. Make them listen. They will. Tell them it's very, very important, which it is. Come clean with them, just like you've done with us."

"I don't think I can."

"I know you can. You've made a start here, and now you've got to go through with it. After it's done, you're going to feel brand new. Then you can decide what you think you need to do. You might want to check into a treatment center. That works for some people. One thing about it, your daddy can afford the best in the country."

Tom said, "Diana, we were going to drive out to see you tonight. You saved us a trip."

"What? You were coming to see me?"

"We still are," Charlie said. "I want to talk to your daddy."

"Daddy?"

"Yes."

"Why?"

"We just want to ask him a few questions. Routine stuff. We'll be talking to most everybody in town. Is there some reason you don't want us to talk to him?"

"No. But he doesn't know anything. Like I said, we don't talk much anymore. Hardly at all."

"That's too bad."

"Daddy is so busy, what with the bank and all his other business interests."

"Do you know much about your daddy's other interests?"

"No, not much. I just know he owns a couple of motels in Tampa and some restaurants and stuff."

Stroking the back of Diana's short, golden hair, Kitty said, "I know how close you and your daddy used to be. This must be so hard for you."

Diana didn't answer.

"You still love your daddy," Charlie said.

"Sure I do. I'd do anything for my daddy."

"I know you would. And I bet he'd do anything for you too. When it comes right down to it, I'm sure you come first in his life, just like my baby comes first in mine."

Diana started to cry again with her hands over her face.

"Not anymore," she said when she was able to speak.

Diana got up, shuffled to the door, her shoulders slumped. She resembled, Charlie thought, an old lady more than the vibrant young girl she'd been a few months ago. Her hand on the doorknob, she looked back. Her eyes moved from Kitty to Tom, then locked on to Charlie. Tears pooled in her eyes, and she went out the door.

* * *

"Poor kid," Kitty said.

"Think she'll do it?" Tom asked. "Call the powwow?"

"She'll do it," Charlie answered. "When I told that girl she has guts, I meant it."

"That Pratt bastard must be a real shit," Kitty said. "What the hell's he doing in a high school?"

"There's a teacher shortage," Tom said.

"He's in a class by himself, Kitty. What I'd like to do is take him out behind the barn and dispense a little country justice on his sorry butt. Of course, then I'd have to arrest myself."

"You ought to get a medal for it."

"Sometimes the system doesn't make a whole lot of sense," Tom offered.

"Sometimes it's as blind as a bat!" Kitty exclaimed.

"Our system's a far cry from perfect, but it's still the best one on the planet."

"You ought to run for governor, Charlie."

Charlie let that go.

"So now," Tom said, "do we get a warrant and pick up Pratt?"

"Yep."

Tom headed for the door.

"Hold on, Tom. Pratt's not going anywhere. I want to talk to Mike and Elvis before we pick him up."

"Elvis? What about Elvis?"

"Tell you later, Kitty."

"This just gets crazier."

Charlie smiled.

"Before this day is over, Mr. James T. Pratt is going to be behind bars."

"I hope you throw away the key."

Charlie stood up and stepped to the door. He looked back at Tom.

"I hate for you to miss that long lunch, but with these new developments . . ."

"Let me grab a few bites, and I'll meet you at the station at three."

Kitty looked at her watch.

"It's two ten already."

"See you at the station," Charlie said.

Tom and Kitty watched him go out the door. They watched through the window until he drove out of sight, and then looked at each other.

"I'm selfish, Tom."

"What?"

"I said I'm selfish. You heard what I said."

"What are you talking about?"

"Sandy is dead, Diana's in an ocean of trouble, Kara's messed up in her mind, and at this moment, I'm feeling sorry for myself because I'm fat!"

Tom had to laugh. He took her in his arms and kissed her on the lips. Then, assuming his best Ralph Kramden posture, he said, "Baby, you're the greatest!"

She shoved him away.

"All right, Mr. Comedian, I know you've got to eat and run, but you've got some explaining to do."

"I do?"

"Yes, you do."

"And what is it you want to know, ma'am?"

Kitty put her fists on her hips and looked into Tom's eyes.

"What's this about Elvis?"

Chapter 17

When Tom stepped into the office, Charlie was laid back in his chair with his feet up on his desk. He was smoking a cigarette and looking out the window.

Charlie took his feet off his desk, tapped his ash into an ashtray beside a Classic Coke can, looked at his watch and then at Tom.

"It's three ten."

"Yep."

"Mike just called. He's on his way."

"Is Elvis coming?"

"He'll be here."

Tom glanced at the ashtray and the Coke, then looked back at Charlie.

"You really ought to quit those things."

"The cigarettes or the Cokes?"

"Both. They're a deadly combination, but kick the cigarettes first."

Charlie grinned as he ground his cigarette out in the ashtray.

"I know it. Sally won't let me forget it. When they go up to four dollars a pack, I'm done."

"I've heard they're that much now in some places."

"I'm talking about here. Sit down. How's Kitty?"

"She's worried about Diana, of course, but she's okay. She's glad Diana knows she needs help and is willing to go for it."

"Diana will be all right."

Charlie's hand moved involuntarily toward the pack of cigarettes in his shirt pocket, stopped midway.

"Old habits are hard to break, Tom. I'm lucky I never got addicted to anything worse than these. They're bad enough."

"You have to make up your mind, Charlie."

"Yeah yeah, I know. That's the hard part, making up your mind. Once you get past that, it's easy. But what will I do with my hands? Seems like I do my best thinking when I'm holding a cigarette."

"Well, don't give up."

"Me?"

"Don't quit trying."

"Never."

Tom sat down in a chair facing Charlie.

"Tom, if you had one guess, who'd you say killed Sandy?"

"Pratt."

"Me too."

Charlie picked up a pencil and began to tap out a rhythm with the eraser end.

"Remember at first how we couldn't see how anybody in the world could have a reason to kill Sandy?"

"Yep."

"Then, after we poked around a while, it started to look like several people could have reason?"

"Yes."

"Well, what if there are other people, lots of them, maybe, who've got secrets, skeletons in their closets? What if Sandy found out about something we have no idea is even out there?"

"Yeah, but how many secrets are important enough for somebody to kill to keep them quiet?"

"I don't know. But what I'm saying is maybe we're going at this thing the wrong way. We've assumed Sandy's death is drug-related, that she knew something she shouldn't have. But what if the real motive had nothing to do with drugs?"

"That would let Pratt off the hook, wouldn't it?"

"Not necessarily. A pig that has wallowed in as much mud as that one has dirt all over it. I expect Sandy could have had just about anything on him. Maybe she threatened to tell Diana's parents."

"You think he'd kill to keep that quiet?"

"He might. Pratt wouldn't win the 'best judgment of the year' award. He might be smart, but that doesn't mean he isn't stupid."

Tom chuckled.

"True."

Both men were quiet for a while.

Tom said, "So we've gone from believing no one could have had a reason to kill Sandy to thinking half of Flowing Wells could have."

"I'm not saying that. I'm just saying that what goes on behind closed doors in our town would shock a lot of people if they knew about it. In little towns, everybody thinks they know everybody, but they don't, not really. We might be on to something bigger—or different, anyway—than we've imagined."

"So what do we do?"

"We keep on doing just what we've been doing. It's all we can do."

There was a tap on the door. Mike Evers came in looking much better, Charlie thought, than the last time he had seen him. Mike plopped down in the chair beside Tom, pulled off his glasses, and rubbed his eyes.

"Boy, I'm tired."

"You're sober though. Right?"

Evers reddened as he slid his glasses back onto his nose. He glanced at Tom and then looked back at Charlie.

"I'm on the wagon."

"That's good, Mike. Stay there."

"I intend to. How're you, Tom?"

"Sober."

"Now we've determined nobody's drunk," Charlie said, "tell us what you found out, Mike."

Mike lit a cigarette, leaned over the desk, and dropped his match into the ashtray beside the Classic Coke can. Charlie rolled his eyes and slid the ashtray toward Mike.

"Keep it. I just made up my mind to quit. You ought to too."

"Hell, Charlie, I just quit drinking. One thing at a time."

Mike drew on his cigarette, inhaled deeply.

"I don't know about this detective work, Charlie. I'm not that good at meddling in other people's business."

"Meddling in people's business *is* our business, Mike, especially when we're investigating a homicide."

"I'm better at busting up fights and dragging drunks out of bars. Of course, I've had more experience at that."

"Well, the meddling will get easier, just like breaking up fights did. If I remember right, the first few you busted up, I had to hold your hand and go in with you."

"There wasn't any hand-holding that I recall."

"Tell us about Matthews," Tom said.

"Well, I had to wait to see him, of course. He was with a client. While I was waiting, Shirley Spivey walked across the lobby and across the street to Riley's Rexall. I followed her over there and saw her sit down in a corner booth. I sat with her. She looked up with those big baby blues and goes, 'What's up, Mike?'

"I asked her how her mama and daddy are getting along, and for a while, we just shot the breeze. She said she was sorry about Wanda and me breakin' up, and that she thinks Wanda made a bad mistake dumping me for Gilbert Vancini. I told her Wanda spoke to me today in The Duck and—"

"She did?" Charlie cut in. "I didn't think y'all were speaking."

"Well, we talked a little bit today and—"

"You talked?" This interruption came from Tom. "She didn't just speak to you? Y'all talked?"

"That's what I said. Anyway, I—"

"Do I smell a get-back-together coming on?" Charlie asked.

Mike puffed hard on his cigarette.

"You wanta hear about Shirley or not?"

Smoke came out of his nose as he spoke.

"Sure. Go on."

"I asked her what happened to that guy from Bartow she was dating. Told her I heard they were getting married.

"And she goes, 'Oh, you mean Hank? I haven't seen Hank for a long time. He moved to Valdosta and got a job in a paper mill.'

"So we go on a little bit longer, just shootin' the shit, while I'm trying to think of a nice way to ask her if she's screwing her boss. I couldn't think of one, so I said I'd heard rumors that she's seeing him. I told her I didn't mean to be nosey or anything, but I was just wondering if it was true. I told her if it wasn't, I'd go to the guy I heard it from and tell him to keep his mouth shut. She didn't even try to deny it—said since I already knew, she might as well tell me the whole story."

Mike took in a breath and started to go on, but the amusement on Charlie's face stopped him.

"What?"

"For a guy who hates to meddle as much as you say you do, Mike, it sounds like you're getting the hang of it pretty fast."

"Thanks," Mike said, pleased. He pointed to the coffee maker on the counter behind Charlie. He ground out his cigarette as Charlie poured.

Charlie added sugar and cream and handed Mike the Styrofoam cup.

"Looks like yellow mud," Mike said.

"It is. It's free though. You can't complain about the price."

Mike took a sip and made a face as if he'd bitten into a lemon, and then drank some more.

"Perfect."

"Go on," Charlie coaxed. "What happened next?"

Mike drank more coffee and set the cup on the desk.

"Well, Shirley said John insists on keeping their affair a secret for now, but soon he's going to let the cat out of the bag and make a public announcement that he's going to divorce his wife and marry her, Shirley. When she told me that, she lit up like a Christmas tree."

Tom grunted. "Public announcement, huh?"

"John Matthews has no intention of marrying Shirley Spivey anymore than I do," Charlie said.

"Maybe not, but I believe he told her that. And she believes it. I can't see her getting all that excited about it if she was making it up."

"Oh, he told her, all right. I don't doubt that for a second. And I'm sure she believes him. John Matthews is a very convincing man, and he'll tell anybody anything to get what he wants. I just hate to see him hurt Shirley. I've known her since she was five, when her mama and daddy moved here from Okeechobee. She's a sweet kid. Got a heart of gold. I hate to see John Matthews break it."

"I'll tell you one thing," Mike said. "I don't know about her heart, but she sure has a body. I tell you that girl is built like a—"

"We know what she's built like, Mike." Charlie winked at Tom. "You ought not to be looking too hard though, what with you just going on the wagon and you and Wanda about to reconcile. You're vulnerable right now. You don't want to get caught up in a love triangle. I'd stay away from Shirley, if I were you."

"Charlie, I've got no interest in Shirley, and you know it. And I didn't say a damn word about Wanda and me reconciling."

"Take it easy, Mike," Tom said.

"Yeah, Mike, take it easy. Tom and I are just happy for your good fortune."

Mike snapped another cigarette out of his pack and lit up. He puffed hard and smoked the cigarette down until a long ash dropped in his lap. He brushed it off onto the floor and stared at the glowing tip of his cigarette without speaking.

"Go on with your story."

"Are you sure you want you hear it, or would you rather hear about my hot romance with Shirley and my rekindling with Wanda?"

"We want to hear all of it. But tell what happened in the drugstore with Shirley first."

"Well, she finished her coffee and said she had to get back to the bank. I waited a few minutes, and then I got up and followed her."

"Did you get in to see Matthews then?"

"As soon as I stepped back into the bank, he waved me into his office, like he'd been waiting for me. John Matthews is not an easy man to talk to, Charlie. He makes me nervous. The second I sat down, he said, 'If you have anything to ask me, Mike, ask it. I bet just about everybody in town will be questioned before this thing is finished.'

"I asked him if he meant he thinks it's gonna take us a long time to catch the killer, and he said, 'I don't know. You might get him today or tomorrow, or not at all. All I'm saying is, if I know Charlie Morris, and I do, he won't leave nary a stone unturned.' Then he asked me if I'd been talking to Shirley.

"I told him I had, and he said he didn't know what we'd talked about, but if I'd asked her about the rumor that they'd been seeing each other, it was true.

"That surprised me, and before I could think of anything to say, he goes, 'Linda and I were having problems, lots of them. Our marriage was on the rocks. It began to look like we were headed for a divorce. I was sore and lonesome and couldn't talk to anybody about it, and then one day, I opened my eyes and there stood Shirley, looking like an angel, sweet as sugar on honey. I took her to lunch a few times, we got to talking, got to be friends, and, well, one thing led to another, and the next thing you know, *pow!*'

"'Pow?' I asked him.

"'We became lovers,' he said.

"And I go, 'Are you still powing?'

"'No,' he said, 'my conscience got to bothering me, so I broke it off. The thing is, Shirley hasn't accepted that yet, and she talks as if we're still seeing each other.'

"'I see,' I say. 'Does Mrs. Matthews know about the powing?'

"Charlie, I expected him to tell me to mind my own damn business then, but he said, 'Yes. I confessed my sin, and since then, we've talked more than we have in years. It looks like Linda and I are going to make it after all.'"

"John Matthews wouldn't know what a conscience was if it bit his ear off," Charlie said.

"Yeah, well, I'm just telling you what he told me."

Mike looked at his cigarette that had burned down to the filter. He snuffed it out in the ashtray.

"Then I asked him about Diana, how she was getting along. That's when he got nasty. You'd have thought I pulled a gun on him. His face turned as red as a spring sunburn and, if looks could kill, I'd be a ghost. 'What the hell does Diana have to do with any of this?' he wanted to know.

"I said I was just wondering how she was handling Sandy's death, what with them being such good friends and all.

"That calmed him down some, and he gave me a little nod and said, 'She's taking it hard, Mike, real hard.'

"'She's lucky to have a father like you,' I told him. 'Everybody knows y'all are real close.'

"Matthews looked down at his desk for a minute and shuffled some papers and when he looked back up at me, I thought he might cry.

"He said, 'Frankly, I stay so damn busy these days we really don't spend that much time together anymore. But close? Hell, yes, we're close. I love my daughter more than anything in the world.'"

"That might be the only true thing he told you, Mike."

"I know it. Then I mentioned about Diana getting her hair cut off.

"'Who told you that?' he asked me.

"I told him I didn't remember.

"He started turning red again and goes, 'Look, let's leave Diana out of this. Okay? She's been through hell enough. You hear me?'"

Mike drank the last swallow of cold thick yellow coffee and tossed the cup in the trashcan.

"I don't know if Matthews has a conscience or not, but I believe he really does feel bad about not treating Diana right."

"Sure he does," said Charlie.

"I can't understand how he stays in such good standing around here," Tom said. "It looks to me like people could see him for what he really is, an asshole."

"M-o-n-e-y." Charlie spelled it out. "It's the magic word."

He looked back at Mike.

"Anything else?"

"That's about it. He told me he had another appointment and asked me to excuse him and showed me the door."

"Okay. Listen, Mike. Plumber called and would like to ride with you the rest of your shift. He goes on the clock tomorrow."

"I hate to see Crews leave," Tom said, "but Plumber was a good pick."

"He'll be a good part-time man. If the budget ever allows, I'll put him on full-time."

He looked at Mike.

"Is that it?"

"That's it."

"Well, you did some decent work, for an amateur who hates meddling in people's business."

Mike smiled and stood up and went to the door. He looked back at Charlie.

"Thanks. I think."

As he was walking out, Charlie stopped him.

"Mike?"

Mike looked back.

"Fasten your seat belt tight on that water wagon. I don't want you falling off it again."

Mike looked at Charlie without speaking and then walked on out into the hallway, not bothering to close the door.

Tom said, "Don't you think you were little rough on him, Charlie?"

Charlie didn't answer for several moments.

"Tom, you didn't know Mike's daddy like I did. He was as fine a man as I ever knew. But the booze beat him down. He couldn't handle it. And Mike's the same way. He can't drink one or two, like me and you. When he starts, he can't quit. Drinks till he's sloshed to the gills.

"Look at it like this. In every glass of alcohol, there's a demon. Mike can sit in a room full of glasses of demons, and as long as he doesn't take a drink and let that demon into his body, he's fine. But the second he does, that demon starts tickling his insides and nuzzling his brain, and it feels so good, he has to have another and another and another. One's too many, and a hundred isn't enough. It's a curse, a disease, they call it now, that Mike has to live with for the rest of his life. I don't want to see him go down like his daddy did. Mike's worth saving, and I'm gonna do my best to keep him on the straight and narrow. If it takes riding him now and then, I'll do it."

"Do you have to embarrass him?"

"Better he's embarrassed than passed out drunk somewhere, hung over bad, or dead. That's one reason I put Mike with Plumber. Plumber has been clean and sober in AA for six years. I want that to rub off on Mike. I want Mike to start going to some meetings."

"Plumber's in AA? Charlie, isn't that a gamble hiring a man into law enforcement you know is a drunk?"

"Forget I told you that, Tom. I, uh, slipped, so to speak. It's not called Alcoholics *Anonymous* for nothing. I knew Plumber before he got sober. That's the only reason I know about it."

"I guess you know what you're doing."

"Some of the best people I've ever known are recovering alcoholics. I could name some right here in Pinewood County that you'd be shocked to know they ever drank at all, much less got fallin' down drunk."

"I guess I missed a lot those years I was gone."

"You'll catch up. Listen, Tom, Shirley's folks are good, hard-working Christian people. And Shirley's a great gal. I hate to see Matthews use her that way."

"Her problem is she's just too darn pretty. Average guys fumble and stumble around her and make fools out of themselves. Then there's the guys like Matthews who think that because she isn't some kind of intellectual giant, like they think they are, the only thing she's good for is a roll in the hay."

"You think he's really broken it off with her, Tom?"

"No."

Charlie looked at his watch.

"Neither do I. Elvis should be here any minute. After we hear what he has to say, we'll go pick up Pratt."

That made Tom smile. Then he frowned.

"Charlie, I think we should have picked him as soon as Diana dropped the goods on him."

"Listen, Tom, when you've been in this business as long as I have, you learn that once you're sure you've got the right number, you don't have to be in such a hurry you break your finger dialing the phone. Besides, I like the idea of letting the jerk sweat for a while."

"But what if he runs?"

"Look, Pratt's a sociopath, a moral moron, and maybe a murderer, but he's not that stupid. He's got to know that to run now would be as good as a signed confession. He'll stick around a while. Oh, he'll run, all right, like a scared rabbit, but not right now."

"Charlie, I can't quit thinking about Kara. Something's bothering me, but I can't put my finger on it."

"You think she knows more than she's telling?"

"Oh, I'm sure of that. But why do you think she didn't just come out and tell us she had a crush on Pratt? I mean, it was so obvious she might as well have."

"Maybe she was embarrassed to come right out and admit it. But even if she wasn't embarrassed, if she's over the crush, why should she admit it? Why bring it up at all?"

"I don't think she's over it. She didn't sound to me like she was over it."

"Well, what if she isn't? So what? What's your point?"

Tom shook his head and looked out the window.

"That's the problem. I don't know my point. All I know is that something is bothering me."

"Well, maybe it'll come to you. Sometimes I stew over something for days. Then suddenly, it'll hit me when I'm not even thinking about it."

"Could be nothing."

"Don't knock your hunches, Tom. Hunches have solved a lot of cases. Cops develop an instinct."

"Yeah, but I—"

Footsteps in the hallway stopped Tom in mid-sentence. He looked at Charlie, who leaned back in his chair and moved his hand to his shirt pocket and took out the pack of cigarettes. He tapped one out and stuck it in the corner of his mouth.

"I thought you were quitting, Charlie."

"Elvis is in the building."

Chapter 18

When John Matthews closed the door behind Deputy Mike Evers, he dialed his secretary and told her to hold his next appointment for ten minutes. He needed some time to think.

Matthews walked to the window and lit a cigarette. Normally he didn't smoke in his office, but to hell with it.

He began to pace. How awful it was that Sandy Carlton had to be killed at such an inopportune time! Just when some of the biggest deals he'd ever made were going down. Now there would be questions, questions, and more questions. He knew Charlie Morris. The man was dogged. He'd been born with a dose of pit bull in his brain; when he latched on to something, he didn't turn loose.

Matthews remembered how Morris had stood staunchly by Tom Wilson when Homer Huggins was railroading Tom into prison. It was clear as air to anyone with eyes that Tom had not intended to kill Eddie, Homer's son. It was an accident, pure and simple, brought on by Eddie's drunken brawling. Yet Homer, with his immense wealth and power, had bought the judge, bribed jurors, and succeeded in turning nearly the whole county against Tom.

But not Charlie Morris. At the risk of losing his job—he was only a deputy then—Charlie had stuck by Tom and testified on his behalf at the trial.

Tom was convicted and sent to prison, but Charlie believed in Tom and never quit trying to prove his innocence. After ten years and endless interviews with every patron of the bar where the accident occurred, Charlie finally succeeded in proving Eddie's death was accidental and getting the governor to grant Tom a pardon. Now Tom was not only a free man with a clean slate, but a deputy sheriff.

Charlie Morris was no quitter. He was an old-fashioned man with old-fashioned values, but he was no quitter. When he got onto a scent, and believed he was right, there was no stopping him. Matthews wondered if Charlie was trailing a scent now, or was he was just sniffing around.

Except for a few enterprises that he hoped to be out of soon, Matthews was mostly legal now. And he was confident Charlie could not possibly know of any of his illegal activities. Charlie was fishing. He had to be. The trouble was, if he tossed his line into enough holes, eventually he was bound to get a nibble.

Charlie would have to dig deep to get to gold, but if he was anything, Charlie was a tenacious miner. It was that tenacity that had freed Tom Wilson from prison and pinned the badge on him. It was that same tenacity that could conceivably lead to Matthew's fall from grace.

Matthews sucked hard on his cigarette. That could not be allowed to happen. He had come too far, made too many sacrifices, taken too many risks, gone too far out on the proverbial limb. So that left only one thing.

But not yet. The thought of calling the Zebra made him cringe. He'd never met the man, never wanted to. He'd called him through contacts and mailed his money to a post office box in Tampa. He would wait to call the Zebra until it was clearly the last resort to save himself.

Sometimes when he was very tired and his guard was down, Matthews wondered if all the wealth was worth it. Although he had no intention of marrying Shirley, it was true Linda was almost ready to leave him. She was drinking too much and becoming more and more distant and withdrawn. He knew it was only a matter of time until one day he would go home to find her gone.

Worse was what had become of his relationship with his daughter, Diana. They never talked anymore, and days passed when they didn't even see each other. They were like strangers. Once they had been so close. She had worshipped him, and he'd adored her. What happened? What had changed things so? Matthews knew the answer, but he could not admit it to himself because if he did, it would break his heart.

Matthews snuffed out his cigarette and told his secretary he was ready for his next appointment. All this troubling, confusing stuff would have to wait. It was time to get back down to business.

*   *   *

When the dismissal bell rang at three thirty, Leon Walker was waiting in his car with the engine running so as not to get caught up in the rush of student traffic. Pulling out of the parking lot, he turned in the direction of the deserted hideout he'd first heard about from a student.

Walker turned off Highway 17, on to the dirt lane between rows of orange trees in an orange grove. He followed the lane for a ways and then bumped across a cow pasture dotted with clumps of palmettos, myrtle bushes, and scrub pines, then drove straight into the edge of a thick hammock bordering the Peace River. Plowing through dog fennels and weeds as high as his door handle, he drove farther into the hammock than he ever had before. He parked behind a head-high cluster of palmettos. He smiled when he saw the red Corvette nestled in myrtle bushes a short distance away.

Stepping carefully so as not to trip over fallen limbs and grapevines concealed under the grass and weeds, he made his way to the hideout. Even as close to it as ten feet, had he not known the old shack was there, he probably would not have noticed it. Spreading oak limbs and cabbage palms made a thick canopy above it; tall grasses and palmettos made a wall around it. The old shack itself was covered with wild grapevines and bougainvillea that the moonshine man, Cyrus Potter, had planted long ago when he'd built this tiny house.

Walker slipped through the overgrowth, pulled open the squeaky old door, and stepped inside. The floor was sand, leaves, moss, and stomped-down grass. Cracks in the walls and holes in the rusty tin roof let in strips of light to the dim interior. Both windows were broken and patched with plywood. Jim Pratt sat on a blanket in a corner, his arms wrapped around his knees, which were drawn up to his chest.

Walker sat down beside him and tenderly placed his hand on Pratt's knee. Both men stared straight ahead at a blank, brown wall.

Walker was first to speak.

"Well, Jim, the shit's hit the fan again."

Pratt nodded.

"Big time, Leon."

Pratt lit a cigarette, took a long draw, and turned his head to look at Walker. He held up his cigarette in front of his face.

"Look at me, Leon. I've been off these damn things for three years, and look at me now. This is my fault. Things were fine till I got here. I'm just damned bad luck, anywhere I go. Trouble follows me like my shadow."

"Don't be so hard on yourself, Jim. It isn't all your fault. And even if it is, it's been worth it, having you here. You don't know how much I've missed you. I've wished a thousand times I hadn't walked out."

"You were right to walk out, Leon. I was a real prick, bringing all those guys and girls in like I did. I don't blame you for leaving."

"Jim, did you ever think of me, wonder where I was? Did you miss me?"

"Only every day. I wanted to try to find you, to beg you to come back. But I knew you'd made up your mind, and I wasn't part of your plans. Besides, I had no idea where to look. Hell, you could have been anywhere."

"You'll never know how shocked I was the day you walked into my office to apply for a job. I nearly fainted. I thought I was dreaming. When I realized I wasn't, I couldn't get my breath."

"It took my breath away too," Pratt said.

Walker was quiet for a while. Then he began to chuckle. "I wish you could have seen your face when you walked in my office and saw me sitting there."

"You should've seen your own."

They laughed. Walker said, "It was fate, Jim. It had to be."

"I know it."

"After today, we can't see each other for a while, except at school, of course. Until this thing is finished, we have to be very, very careful."

Pratt sighed and lit another cigarette from the butt of the one in his hand.

"I'm afraid it's too late for me, Leon. I think that damned hick sheriff knows too much. But I promise you this, I will do everything within my power to keep you from getting dragged down with me."

Walker took Pratt's hand in both of his and held it tightly.

"I love you, Jim. I have from the day we met."

Pratt looked into his lover's eyes.

"If I have to do time, will you wait for me?"

"You know I will. And we'll go back to California where we won't have to hide our feelings and slip around like criminals, like we're doing now."

Walker scooted forward a few feet, scraped aside some grass and leaves, and opened a trap door. Reaching down into the hole, he pulled up a metal box and took out a pint-sized bag of white powder. He closed the metal box and the trap door and ruffled sand and leaves and grass over it again. He moved back beside Pratt.

"I'm going to ship this to a friend in Miami to hold for me until this is over. Chances of it being found here are slim, but any chance at all is too much."

Pratt nodded. "Good idea, Leon. But it's too late for me. My goose is cooked."

"You're not convicted of anything, Jim. You haven't even been charged."

"I tell you Charlie Morris knows too much. You weren't there when those two guys came to my apartment this morning. Even if he can't get me on the drug thing, there's my fling with Diana. She's jailbait. I don't know how they know about that, but they do. Morris said he heard she was seeing an older guy. Now who do you think he was talking about? Santa Claus?"

"Do you think Diana would testify against you, about the drugs? I doubt you'd do time just on the underage thing. I know for a fact her father wouldn't want her testifying to that in court."

"Who knows what a goddamn woman will do?"

A glint came into Walker's eye.

"Jim, there's one way to make sure Diana doesn't testify."

The coldness of Walker's voice startled Pratt. He'd never heard it before.

"What are you talking about, Leon?"

"What if the same thing happened to Diana that happened to Sandy?"

"What?"

"You heard me."

Pratt swallowed so hard it sounded like water gurgling in a pipe.

"Leon, if you think the shit's hitting the fan now, what do you think will happen if there's another high school homicide? Besides, I'd be the first one they'd look at."

"Maybe, but when they learn you were in the presence of a hundred witnesses at the time the crime was committed, they'd leave you alone. Do you think you might attend the FFA banquet next week? I like for my teachers to attend at least a few school functions."

"No. No. Leon, it's crazy. It would never work."

"How do you know?"

"Because I can't be in two places at once. I can't be at the banquet and be somewhere else killing Diana at the same time."

"What if someone else killed her?"

Walker's lips curled into a sneer that Pratt had never seen. He did not like it.

"Like who?"

Walker did not reply. He stared at a crack in the wall and continued to sneer.

"Who?"

"Me."

The small shack trembled like a frightened hand as a gust whipped through the low branches hanging on the roof.

Pratt gasped.

"What? Are you crazy? You couldn't kill anyone. I know you."

Walker looked into Pratt's eyes. His face softened as his sneer transformed into a smile.

"For you, dear Jim, I could. And if that's what it comes down to, I will."

Pratt thought about Diana cutting her hair to prove her love and loyalty, and he understood that had been nothing compared to this. He melted into Walker's arms and wept.

When his tears stopped, they lay back on the blanket and began to touch each other. A ray of light shone down through a hole in the roof onto the debris concealing the trap door. A blue jay lit on a limb outside a boarded-up window and screamed while a mockingbird, perched above the shack, sang its romantic warble.

Chapter 19

Although the door to Charlie's office was open, Elvis stopped in the hallway to knock. He saw Tom and Charlie inside.

"Come in."

Elvis stepped into the room and looked around. His gaze settled on Charlie.

"Nice office."

"Thanks. Sit down. You want a coke? Coffee?"

Sliding down into the chair next to Tom, Elvis nodded.

"Coke sounds good, I guess. If it's cold."

"You know Tom, don't you, Elvis?"

"Sure. Mr. Wilson."

"Call me Tom."

"Tom?"

"Sure."

Charlie opened the door of the small refrigerator at the end of his desk and took out a Classic Coke. He wrapped the can in both hands before giving it to Elvis.

"Feels cold to me."

He handed it over.

"Thanks."

Charlie watched the boy as he peeled back the tab and took a swallow of the drink. He needed a haircut and some new clothes, but he was a handsome kid, Charlie thought. He bore an amazing resemblance to pictures he had seen of the young Presley. It was easy to see how he got his nickname. With wide shoulders and narrow hips, he stood six feet, and he was still growing. He wasn't as small as Jim Ed Pace had said.

"Mrs. Johnson gave me your message, Mr. Morris. Said you wanted to see me. Here I am."

"Call me Charlie, Elvis. Mr. Morris was my daddy."

"Mind if I smoke, sir?"

"No, but it's not good for you, you know, you being a growing boy and all."

"I know it. But I reckon there are worse things I could be into."

"That's true."

"Elvis, if you ever plan to quit," Tom said, "the sooner you do it, the better. I smoked a long time and giving them up was hell. I keep telling Charlie that."

Elvis took a drag and inhaled. He blew the smoke out of the side of his mouth. Some came out of his nose.

"I keep telling myself I'm gonna quit, but I can't seem to make up my mind. You know what I mean?"

Charlie frowned. "Yes, I do."

"I'm glad you asked to see me, Mr. Mor—uh, Charlie. You want me to call you Charlie?"

"Why not?"

"All right, then, Charlie. Anyway, I've wanted to talk to you, but it's been like quitting smoking, I haven't gotten around to it."

"Well, I'm glad I asked to see you, then. What did you want to see me about?"

"Well, I think trouble is coming at me. I don't know where or when, and I don't know how bad it will be, but it's coming. When it does, I want you to know in advance what the deal is."

"What kind of trouble?" Tom asked.

"Well, I was cruising Main Street a while back when I saw Sandy's Mustang parked in the parking lot by the bank. Jim Ed's car was parked beside hers and they were both standing in the parking lot, talking. It looked to me like they were arguing.

"A little bit later, I drove by again, and just then Jim Ed slapped her. Now, Mr. Mor—Charlie, I mostly mind my own business, but when that jerk slapped Sandy—well, I made it my business. I whipped into the parking lot and jumped out of my car and asked him what the hell he thought he was doing, slapping a girl."

Charlie looked at Tom.

"I knew there had to be another side to this."

"What?"

"Go on, Elvis."

"Well, Jim Ed goes, 'Mind your own goddamn business and get the hell out of here before you get hurt.'

"I think you know, Charlie, my daddy taught me how to box almost before I could walk, and while Jim Ed might be a little bit bigger than me, I had a notion he couldn't fight his way out of a wet paper bag. So I say, 'You're a real tough guy, aren't you, slappin' a girl?'"

"Elvis, were you drinking that night?"

"I don't drink. Seeing what it has done to my daddy."

Charlie nodded.

"Go on."

"Jim Ed came at me. My notion that he couldn't fight was right. I side-stepped and jabbed him in the ribs, and he yelped. He rushed me again, and I slapped him a few times in the face—never did hit him with my fists—and he starts to cry. He hollers that he'll get me if it's the last thing he ever does and jumps in his car and burns rubber clear across the parking lot, all the way to the highway. Then he yells out his window to Sandy that he isn't through with her either."

Tom and Charlie looked at each other. Their eyes locked for a moment before they both looked back at Elvis.

Tom said, "I broke up a fight Jim Ed was in about a month ago. I got the impression he could fight pretty good. Messed a guy up bad. And he was no squirt."

"Jim Ed's a bluff. Oh, he's tough enough when Martin Stanley and some of those other clowns are with him, ready to back him up, but by himself, if anyone calls his bluff, he's a crybaby. He's a spoiled brat too, if you ask me."

Charlie's didn't attempt to hide his amusement. He started to speak, but closed his mouth when Elvis continued.

"Well, anyway, Sandy and I stood in the parking lot and talked for over an hour. That's the night I started believing in dreams. I mean, *Sandy Carlton* standing right there and talking to *me*, Roy Jenkins! And what made it so good was our talking was so easy and natural. Any other time, I would've been sputtering and stumbling all over myself. But that night, talking to Sandy was as easy as talking to my self in a mirror—easier."

"What'd you talk about?"

"I don't know. Ourselves, mostly, I guess. I told her about how my life had changed since Mama died and how tough it was having to work like I do and go to school too. You know I have to work to help pay the bills, with Daddy drinking like he does. Everybody knows he's a drunk, so I didn't try to hide it. I didn't hide anything. I didn't feel like I had to. I could tell she wasn't judging me. I was so comfortable just being myself, being honest with her. And I've never felt like that with anybody in my life."

"Sandy had that effect on people," Tom said. "She was special."

Elvis cut him a sharp glance.

"Yeah, well, maybe I'm crazy, but I believe there was something special between her and me. She said so too."

"I didn't mean to imply there wasn't, Elvis."

Charlie said, "This is interesting, Elvis, but what's it got to do—"

"Sandy was scared. She was scared that night, and she was scared every time I saw her after that."

"You mean scared of Jim Ed?"

"Not just him."

Elvis looked out the window and swallowed. He ran his fingers through his hair.

"Sandy and I kept on seeing each other every chance we got. But we never let anybody know it. She wanted us to go public. Go out to a movie or to dinner or something like that. But I didn't want to. I didn't figure being seen with me would do her reputation any good. I mean, I might look enough like that Presley fellow when he was young that people started calling me Elvis, teasing me, but I'm just Roy Jenkins, and a girl like Sandy has no business being seen with me. She was so beautiful and smart and popular. She could have had any boy in school. But for some reason I'll never understand, she picked me. I wasn't about to let that hurt her."

"You're too hard on yourself, son."

"Sandy said that too, Charlie."

"You should have listened to her. You say she wasn't *just* scared of Jim Ed. Who else was she scared of?"

Elvis shook his head.

"I don't know. Never found out. She wouldn't tell me. All she would say was she'd found out something she wished she hadn't. She said she just had to tell somebody about it and a lot of people were going to be hurt."

"She wouldn't say what she'd found out? Or who was going to be hurt?"

"No. But she wanted to tell me. I could feel it. The last time I saw her she almost did, but . . . Well, she never got another chance."

"When was the last time you saw her?"

"The night before she was killed. She told me she'd made up her mind, that she was coming to talk to you. She said she had to. She said there was someone she had to see the next morning, but right after that she was going to see you or Mr. Wi—Tom. She didn't make it that far."

"She didn't say who she was going to see?"

"No, sir."

"Kara Mendel, maybe?"

"She was going to see Kara, all right, like she did almost every Saturday morning, but there was someone else after that."

"Huh."

Moments of silence passed.

Elvis said, "You know what I think, Charlie?"

"What?"

"I've never ratted on anyone in my life, but, well, this is different."

"You bet it is. Sandy was murdered."

"Now I can't prove any of this, but I've heard Mr. Pratt is a cokehead and that he has turned some kids on to cocaine. I've heard he's given it to Jim Ed Pace and Martin Stanley, and I don't know who all else.

"Anyway, what I think is that Sandy found out about Jim Ed doing coke—and that's why they were fighting that night in the parking lot—and she was gonna tell you about it, and his parents too, maybe. I figure she was going to meet him that morning to try one more time to talk him into getting help, and he got zonked out before he got there. And when she confronted him, he killed her."

Charlie tapped a cigarette out of his pack and offered one to Elvis. Elvis took it, and Charlie lit it for him and then lit his own. He glanced at Tom.

"I'll quit again later."

"You know if Jim Ed has a gun?" Tom asked.

"I've never heard anything about it, but that doesn't mean he doesn't. Can't they figure out what gun fired the bullet and track the gun down that way?"

"They can if the gun is registered. Evidently this one wasn't."

"Oh."

"You ever think about becoming a cop, Elvis?"

"No."

"Well, you'd make a good one. You've got good instincts. That's a good theory. But consider this. What if it was Mr. Pratt that found out Sandy was gonna blow the whistle?"

Elvis's brow wrinkled in concentration; his eyes narrowed.

"How could he?"

"Maybe Sandy told him. Maybe she tried to talk him out of what he was doing and he refused. Maybe he just laughed at her. Or maybe he denied it, and she threatened to turn him in. Or maybe Jim Ed told Pratt that Sandy knew."

"Hmm. Possible, I guess. But I still think Jim Ed did it. I saw him slap her, and I saw what a temper he has. And if I'm right, I might also be right about him coming after me. But he won't do it alone. You see where I'm coming from now?"

Charlie nodded. "Yeah, I do."

Charlie ground out his cigarette in the ashtray.

"Elvis, did Sandy leave with you that night Jim Ed hit her?"

"No. She had her own car."

"Do you think Jim Ed knew y'all kept on seeing each other?"

"I don't see how he could have. He might have suspected it."

"Don't do anything stupid, Elvis," Tom said.

Elvis stood up.

"If I was going to do something stupid, I wouldn't have come here. I just wanted y'all to know what might come down. I hope it doesn't. But if it does, I'll be ready for it."

Elvis shook hands with Tom, and then he reached over the desk and shook with Charlie.

"Thanks for the Coke and for listening to me. I gotta get to work."

Tom and Charlie stood up and walked with Elvis down the hallway to the door that opened onto the sidewalk.

"If you need anything," Charlie said, "call me any time of the day or night." Charlie gave him a card with all his numbers. "Don't try anything alone."

"Oh, I'll call, all right, if there's time. I'm not looking to be some kind of hero, 'specially a dead one."

Tom slapped him on the shoulder.

"You're a good man, Elvis. Be careful."

"I intend to."

When he was gone, Tom looked at Charlie and said, "That's a damn fine kid. I never realized it."

"You believe him?"

"Why not? Don't you?"

"Well, his story rings truer than Jim Ed's. Elvis is no dummy. After listening to him talk, I'm beginning to wonder about this outcast act of his."

"Act?"

Charlie shrugged.

"Like I said, I'm too suspicious. If he's acting, he's been acting almost all his life. Still . . ."

"Still what?"

"Nothing. Are you ready to go pick up some trash?"

Tom smiled but his eyes showed no humor.

"I've been ready."

Chapter 20

Trying to remember what it was he'd forgotten, Leon Walker slid down into the big soft comfortable chair behind his desk.

He'd come in an hour ago and cleaned the top of every surface in his office except the floor, which he knew a custodian mopped every night. If by some freak chance his office was ever searched, no telltale trace of white powder would rear its pretty head and rat him out.

Walker stood up and began to pace, stopping to straighten and rearrange the stuff on the table where his coffee maker was set up, his desk, and the tops of his filing cabinets.

"There there, that looks good," he said to himself. "That looks natural."

He took the portrait of Christ off the wall and laid it face down on his desk. He pried the stiff cardboard backing off with a letter opener and removed a small white envelope, which he slipped into the inside pocket of his jacket, and then he replaced the backing and hung the portrait back on the wall.

He opened the envelope and took out a small plastic pouch. He walked to the back of his office and opened the door to his private bathroom where he flushed the pouch and its contents. Then he washed his hands with soap and water and wiped them dry with a hand towel that hung from a hook on the back of the door.

Walker sat down again. He leaned forward and propped his elbows on his desk and rested his forehead against his thumbs. The first few days of being clean might be a little tough, he thought, but not nearly as hard on him as they'd be for dear Jim. He, Walker, used sparingly, sometimes going two or three days without a line. Jim used daily and had for years.

He was grateful for the time he and Jim had spent in the hideout. No matter what came down, he had that to remember.

Despite being clean, Walker was worried. Ever since he'd gotten the call from his old army buddy, John Matthews, and had come here to this quiet country town, things had gone almost too good to be true. Here in Pinewood County, a high school principal stood right up there somewhere between a Baptist minister and God. In the past thirty years, Matthews had told him, only two Pinewood County teachers had been charged with unethical conduct—both of whom were exonerated—and the integrity of any principal had never even come into question.

Walker realized it wasn't his integrity being questioned that was worrying him. It was the nagging feeling he'd forgotten something. There was one more thing he'd intended to do, but he hadn't done it, and now he couldn't remember what it was. He hadn't dared write it down. He'd cleaned up so thoroughly, erased every trace of incriminating evidence. Or had he? No, there was something that—

A sudden rapping on his door startled Walker so that his hand clutched his heart as his body jerked back in his chair as if he'd been shot in the chest. He yelped as his door flew open and an ashen-faced Mrs. Johnson stood framed in the doorway.

"Damn!"

Walker's cry and sudden jump startled her. She gasped as her hand shot up to clamp over her mouth.

They looked directly at each other in silence for what seemed to Walker a full minute. Then his mouth began to move. "Wha . . . Wha . . . ?"

"Oh, I'm so sorry, Mr. Walker. I'm beside myself. I had to see if you'd heard. I just heard it on the radio."

Walker tried to stand up, but his legs were so wobbly he flopped back into his chair. Mrs. Johnson stood still in the doorway, her expression of horror equal to Walker's.

"I'm so sorry, sir. I—"

Walker opened his mouth to speak but could not find his voice. It was several moments before he could say anything.

"Mrs. Johnson, I believe you know you aren't supposed to enter my office like that. What is it so important you just barge in?"

Now tears were pooling in Mrs. Johnson's eyes and beginning to roll down her cheeks. "I'm sorry, Mr. Walker, but . . . Have you heard about Mr. Pratt?"

Walker wanted to stand up, but now he could not feel his legs at all. It wasn't as if they were wobbly or numb; it was as if they were not there. He laid his hands, palms down, flat on his desk to conceal the shaking.

He shook his head.

"I heard it on the radio just now on the way to school, Mr. Walker. Mr. Pratt has been arrested, sir. He's in jail!"

Walker's legs were gone, and now he had the eerie sensation that his upper body was the top half of one of those blow-up rubber dolls. An image came into his mind of someone pulling the plug, and he could hear the air come out of his lungs with a whoosh. The air in his office became thick, and he realized his hand had come up and his fingers were loosening his tie.

"Jim's in jail?"

"I heard it on the radio. Mr. Walker, this is just awful. It's must be a mistake, mustn't it?"

"Of course. I—"

"You know what he's charged with, sir?"

Walker shook his head.

"Possession of cocaine and—"

I told Jim *to get rid of it!*

"Sexual misconduct with a minor!"

I begged him *to leave the kids alone!*

Walker heard Mrs. Johnson calling his name. He blinked and saw she was staring at him. Had he been in a daze? How long? He mentally shook himself like a wet dog.

"Thank you, Mrs. Johnson," he said. "I—"

"It simply *must* be a mistake, mustn't it, Mr. Walker?"

Walker nodded his head.

"Yes. Of course. It has to be a mistake. Jim wouldn't do those things."

"No."

"Jim is a good man."

"Yes, he is."

A few moments of silence passed, and then Mrs. Johnson bowed slightly from the waist and began to back out of the doorway.

"Mrs. Johnson?"

She stopped.

"Yes, sir?"

"Call a sub, please. For Jim."

"Of course."

"And close the door."

Mrs. Johnson did that.

Walker stared at the closed door until it became a blur. A feeling descended upon him similar to the one he'd experienced in Vietnam the first time he'd gone into combat.

As if he were seeing it on film, a severed head came out of nowhere and thumped down upon his desk. In Nam, the head had fallen near his feet; it belonged to a soldier who, moments before, had stood beside him.

Walker did not want to look at the head, but he could not look away. The head winked at him, and then it began to grin. He felt the scream in his throat, and his hands clamped hard over his mouth to muffle it as the grinning, hideous head became his own.

*　　*　　*

Kara was eager to get out and do something. Maybe she'd go to school; maybe not. She'd let her car decide where she'd go. When she got on the road, she'd see which direction it headed. She'd give it its head, like a horse. As she headed for the door, the phone rang. She scrambled to grab it.

"Hello!"

"Hello, Kara."

The tone of Diana's voice made Kara want to hang up. She was feeling too good to be brought down by some sad sack.

"Hey, Diana. What's up?" she said, cheerily.

"I'm just calling to say good-bye, Kara. I—"

"Are you going somewhere?"

"Well, yes, I—"

"Diana, are you all right? You don't sound right. You sound sick. Are you sick?"

"Well, no. I mean, yes. I'm sick."

"Sick? What's wrong with you? Have you caught a cold? You don't sound like you've got a cold. You sound bummed out."

"Kara, please listen. I—"

"Diana. I gotta get on to school."

"All right," Diana said, her voice rising. "If you'll just let me talk, I'll tell you. I'm going away for a while, and I wanted to tell you good-bye, and I—"

"Where're you going?"

Kara heard a long, shuddering sigh.

"Oh, never mind, Kara. Listen, have you heard the news this morning?"

"No. Why?"

"Jim's in jail."

"What?"

"I heard it on the radio a few minutes ago."

A long silence settled over the line. When Kara spoke, her voice was cold. "Did you have anything to do with it, Diana?"

"What?"

"You heard me. Did you have anything to do with Jim getting arrested? I never did see why he chose you over me. I knew you'd make trouble for him sooner or later."

"Kara, listen, I—"

"You'll be sorry for this. I'll see to that. I promise you."

"I—"

Kara slammed down the phone. She took in a long, deep breath, and then another one. She walked to the door, squeezed the doorknob, and opened the door. She got into her car, started the engine, backed out of the driveway, put the transmission in drive, and gave the car its head.

* * *

Diana walked across the living room and looked out the window at the vast spread of lawn. Yesterday, after she'd come clean with Kitty and the cops, and later with her parents, she'd felt almost elated. But this morning, black rain started falling on her before she'd even gotten out of bed.

Well, I've got good reason to cry, she thought. *I've had an affair with a man old enough to be my father. I'm a cocaine addict. I have to go away for treatment, and I'll have to repeat at least one semester of my senior year of high school. My life will never be the same. Oh, I'd love to talk to Sandy. I miss you, Sandy. I wish I could bring you back. I love you more than anyone in the world except my father.*

"Diana?"

She turned to face her mother. As she came closer, Diana noted there was no smell of alcohol on her breath.

Mrs. Matthews put her arms around Diana and hugged her as she had not done in a long time.

"I'm sorry," she whispered.

Diana stepped back.

"You're sorry, Mother? I'm the one who's sorry. Just look at the mess I've made of things."

Shaking her head, Mrs. Matthews took Diana's hand and led her to the sofa. They sat down side by side, and Mrs. Matthews slid her arm around Diana's shoulder.

"Last night, after you went to bed, your father and I talked. You said you were sorry you'd made us ashamed of you. We're not ashamed of you, honey. We're ashamed of ourselves. Your father for being so wrapped up in work, and me for drinking all the time. Heck, I might need help myself. But anyway, we're going to try to change things and make it right."

"Mother, I—"

"Let me finish. Your father and I also realize how far we've grown from each other, as well as from you. It happened so subtly, we couldn't see it. We want us to go back to being the kind of family we used to be. After we take you to the center, we're going away for a while to try to find each other again. Then, when we all get back home, we're going to make things right with you—if you'll let us."

"If I'll let you?"

"Yes."

"That's all I've ever wanted, for us to be a family, like we used to be."

Mrs. Matthews held Diana in her arms and stroked her hair and whispered over and over, "Everything is going to be all right, darling. Everything is going to be all right."

*   *   *

Later, Linda Matthews went to Diana's room. Diana was sitting in a chair by the window, looking outside.

"Have you started packing, dear?"

Diana shook her head.

"Not yet. I wish we could leave today. I'm ready to get on with this thing."

"So am I. But your father said he had to have a day to get things in order. We'll leave before daylight tomorrow though."

"Mother, I've got to make a phone call. There's someone I want to see before we go."

"Kara?"

"No. I called Kara. She sounded weird, not too nice. I think she's off her meds again. You know how she gets. She's getting worse too."

"Who do you want to see?"

"Elvis."

"Elvis?"

"Since we're coming clean, I might as well tell you. Sandy was seeing him."

"Elvis? Sandy was seeing Elvis?"

"Yes."

"No."

"Yes."

"Sandy Carlton and *Elvis*? Roy Jenkins?"

"You don't mind if I call him, do you? He might not have left for school yet. He's late a lot."

"Uh, no. I don't mind."

Diana kissed her mother on the cheek and then put her arms around her and hugged her.

"I love you, Mother. Everything will be all right, won't it?"

"Yes, it will."

Mrs. Matthews could not make it compute, the image of Sandy and Elvis. Suddenly she wanted a drink. She realized with a shock that for everything to be all right again, a tremendous amount of courage and sacrifice would be demanded of all of them, maybe more than any of them possessed—except, perhaps, Diana.

While Diana was on the phone, it occurred to Mrs. Matthews that she could hurry into the kitchen and have a quick one, a slug of vodka straight from the bottle, and no one would know. She ran across the living room but just before she reached the kitchen, she heard Diana behind her.

"No! Mother, no!"

Mrs. Matthews stopped so fast she almost fell. She whirled around to face her daughter, but Diana was not there.

She collapsed into the nearest chair and began to tremble and then to cry huge tears she did not even try to wipe away.

Chapter 21

Elvis's father, Sam, hated new things in general, appliances in particular, and drip coffee machines specifically. He swore he'd never have one in his house, and up to this point, he hadn't. He declared that pouring water over cracked coffee beans and calling it coffee was no different than pouring hot water over a dead chicken and calling it chicken soup.

Sam's hands trembled as he fumbled with his twenty-two-year-old percolator. He got water in the pot without too much trouble and managed to get the filter in place. But the hand that spooned the coffee into the filter shook so that coffee scattered all across the counter top.

Of all times to be out of booze, Sam thought. Not even a beer in the house. He needed a drink not for fun, but as medicine to steady his nerves and make his hands quit shaking. Just one good guzzle of bourbon, Scotch, gin, or vodka. A beer would help some. Even Roy's aftershave might take the edge off if he could keep it down, but he knew he couldn't.

He finally got enough coffee in the filter to plug in the pot and congratulated himself on a job well done—except for the mess on the counter top, which Roy could clean up. Soon the percolator would gurgle, filling the house with that great coffee smell.

Sam wore old jeans he'd cut off above the knees and a T-shirt with a picture of the King shaking hands with President Nixon. On his feet was a pair of flip-flops that nearly tripped him as he staggered into the living room to flop down in his La-Z-Boy chair. He settled in to wait for the scent of the percolating coffee to begin to fill the room when the phone rang, startling him.

"Roy!" he bellowed. "Get out here and answer that damn phone!"

As he spoke, he looked toward Roy's room and then glanced back at the kitchen where the sun was shining in through the little window above the sink and splashing down on the pile of dirty dishes.

"And wash them dishes!"

"Daddy, I'm late already," Elvis said coming out of his bedroom. "I'll get the phone though."

He picked up the receiver.

"Hello."

"Elvis?"

"Yeah."

He recognized Diana's voice. He waited.

"Elvis, this is Diana. I'm going away for a while. Listen, I know how much you meant to Sandy and I—"

"Sandy told you about us?"

"She told me about the scene with Jim Ed in the parking lot, and I could see how happy she was. As well as I knew Sandy, it wasn't that hard to figure out."

"I don't guess it matters now."

"I'd like to see you, Elvis. Do you think we could meet somewhere after school?"

"Sure. Are you all right, Diana?"

"No. I'll explain later." She named a time and place to meet. "Is that okay?"

"I'll be there."

"Who was that?" Sam asked.

"Mr. Walker," Elvis said. "He said for me to get my ass on to school."

Sam pushed himself up out of his recliner. With his head bowed and his shoulders drooped, he took short, wobbly steps toward his son. It was hard for Elvis to look at him. In spite of all the heartache and embarrassment the old man had caused him, Elvis loved him. He remembered his father as he once was, healthy and strong, before the booze took over.

Elvis knew what was coming.

"Don't ask, Daddy," he said. "I can't do it. I'm late. I gotta hurry."

"Son, please," Sam whined. "It's my day off, and I want to do some work in the garage, and look—" He held out his hands. "My hands are shaking so bad it took me forever to fix that coffee pot, and I got coffee all over the counter. Run down to the County Line and get me a pint before you go to school. Just a pint, not enough to get drunk, just enough to stop these damn shakes. Please, son."

After his last DUI, Sam's license had been suspended for a year. When he got out of jail, sober, he had the good sense to sell his car before he got drunk and drove it without a license. Now every time he got drunk and wanted to drive, he cursed himself for having sold it.

Elvis looked at the floor and shook his head.

"Daddy, I can't. You know I can't. Listen, why don't you call one of those guys you used to go to meetings with? Any of 'em will be glad to talk to you. They can help you. They did before, and they can do it again."

"No. No, son. I can't. I've told you I can't. Don't nag me about it."

"I'm not nagging, Daddy. I love you, and I want you to get help."

"If you love me, go get me a pint, or a fifth. Can't you see the shape I'm in?"

Elvis looked at his watch.

"I'm sorry, Daddy. I can't do it. I won't. I've got to get to school."

Sam groaned and dropped to his knees. He stretched out his arms toward Elvis as if reaching for salvation. Elvis turned and ran to the door and slammed it behind him. He was backing out of the driveway when Sam burst through the door screaming his name.

$$* \quad * \quad *$$

Mrs. Johnson gave Elvis his tardy permit, and he hurried out of the office and ran to his first period class. He put the permit on the teacher's desk and went to the back of the room and slid into his seat behind his pal, Ira Shanks. Ira was a long-haired, scruffy-looking boy whose home life was worse than Elvis's: Ira's father was a mean drunk.

As the sub scribbled on the blackboard, Elvis leaned forward and whispered in Ira's ear, "Pratt's out again, huh?"

Ira turned halfway around and looked Elvis in the eye.

"Haven't you heard?"

"What?"

"Mr. Pratt's in jail."

"Jail!"

Half the class looked back and giggled. The sub, a blue-haired, retired classroom veteran of thirty-two years whirled around and glared at Elvis through thick glasses.

"Would you like to share with the class what's so funny, young man?"

"No, ma'am."

"Well, then, be quiet."

"Yes, ma'am."

"Humph! Please let's try to catch up and get these notes copied down."

"Yes, ma'am."

As the sub resumed her scribbling, keeping one eye on the board and the other on Elvis, he picked up his pencil and began to write. When he'd copied three pages, he realized he had no idea what he had written.

Throughout the rest of the morning, Elvis's body went through the motions of his usual routine, but he couldn't stop his mind from thinking about Diana's phone call.

She said she was going away. Where? Elvis had a hunch Diana had been seeing Pratt. Was she responsible for Pratt's arrest? Had she turned him in? Had they been caught together? Or did Pratt's arrest have nothing to do with Diana? Why did she want to see Elvis? Did she have some information about Sandy's murder? If so, why not go to the sheriff? Why come to him?

Lunchtime found Elvis and Ira eating hamburgers at a table in a rear corner of the big, noisy cafeteria. Most of the noise was chatter concerning Pratt's arrest. Nobody had any information—but everyone had a theory.

In the faculty section of the cafeteria, blissfully quiet behind its thick glass wall, Ms. Satterfield said to Mr. Smith, "I knew there was something fishy about that man. Any single man that young and handsome doesn't belong in a classroom with all those gullible young girls."

Ms. Jones leaned forward and whispered to Ms. Anderson, "You know what I heard? I heard he likes boys as well as girls!"

Old Ms. Wilkins, sitting next to Ms. Anderson, blushed and turned her head, pretending not to hear.

"I hear he got run out of California for messing around with his principal's wife," declared Mr. Tanner.

"Well," snorted Ms. Peyton, "I hear, and from a very reliable source, that he killed a girl in California. Raped her and choked her to death with his bare hands!"

Ms. Wilkins's gasp was audible.

*　　*　　*

In the corner across the cafeteria from the teachers, Jim Ed Pace and Martin Stanley eyed Elvis, waiting for the teachers to leave. They knew there usually was a gap of a minute or two between lunchroom duty shifts, and that was all the time the boys figured they'd need.

Just as the last teacher slipped her tray into the kitchen window, Elvis and Ira started to get up. But a hand clamped down on Elvis's shoulder like a vise and held him down. Elvis looked up and saw Jim Ed glaring at him. Beside Jim Ed stood Martin, his hands balled into fists, ready for a fight.

Here it is, Elvis thought.

He'd known it would come, as he'd told Charlie it would. He hadn't thought it would happen here at school though, especially in the crowded cafeteria. But this was good. How bad could it be with all the other kids around? And the teachers who'd be all over them in seconds? Elvis had believed Jim Ed might try to kill him because he thought he'd killed Sandy. Then again, this made more sense; Jim Ed would commit murder in secret, but he wanted to give Elvis a beating in public. He really had no reason to kill Elvis. He just wanted to hurt and embarrass him, as Elvis had embarrassed him in the parking lot.

Elvis was not worried about Jim Ed and Martin hurting him. He knew what they could do, and he knew what he could do. As the two bullies hovered over him, Elvis got a whiff of an acrid scent he knew to be marijuana. As they often did, the boys had gone off campus for lunch and smoked their dessert on the way back to school.

Elvis looked at them and smiled.

"Something stinks here, boys. I think maybe it's you."

"What's going on?" Ira said.

"Shut up," said Jim Ed. "Keep your mouth shut or you'll get some of what the hero here's about to get."

"Hero?"

"Shut up."

"You don't scare me."

"Hero, huh?" Elvis cut in. "Gosh, thanks, Jim Ed."

Jim Ed snatched an empty chair away from the next table and straddled it, facing Elvis. Martin yanked up a chair on Elvis's other side, mimicking Jim Ed.

Jim Ed looked into Elvis's dark eyes.

"Know what you are, Jenkins? You're a piece of shit, a low-class loser, white trash."

Elvis grinned. "Does this mean we're not friends anymore, Jim Ed?"

"I'm gonna fuck your smart-ass up, Jenkins."

Elvis saw Horace Willoughby enter the side door of the cafeteria. Half a dozen teachers would be behind him. Elvis looked at Jim Ed.

"No wonder Sandy dumped you. You're not only a bully, you're stupid."

Jim Ed's eyes darted around the room. Everyone within hearing range was watching. With the pot letting him down, Jim Ed was having second thoughts about this thing. He didn't doubt he could take Elvis, and he knew for sure he and Martin together could destroy him. What had him worried was that he'd suddenly remembered the automatic ten-day suspension for fighting at school. He could get kicked off the baseball team. His parents might take his car away.

But he knew it was too late to turn back now. He was in too deep. How could he ever hold his head up on campus again if word got around that he'd backed down from a fight with this prick, Roy Jenkins? He had a reputation to uphold.

No, there was no backing out now, no matter what the consequences. Besides, he really did want to fuck up this punk. Ever since Roy had slapped him in the parking lot in front of Sandy, he had hated Roy Jenkins with murderous fury that grew with each passing day. He'd fuck him up, all right, and gladly pay whatever price he had to pay.

With a move so sudden he surprised even himself, Jim Ed lunged forward to grab Elvis and pin him to the table. But the move was telegraphed, and Elvis saw it coming, and with a move his father had taught him, he spun his shoulders sideways and jerked his body backward. Jim Ed missed him and landed facedown on the table in a half-eaten hamburger. As he raised his head, with mustard smeared across his mouth, Elvis's hand shot out and grabbed a handful of hair and slammed his face down on the table. Jim Ed yelped and came up with both hands holding his nose; blood spurted through his fingers and poured down onto the front of his shirt.

"You broke it!" he screamed. "You broke my fuckin' nose!" He dashed for the door, kicked it open, and ran down the sidewalk toward the office.

Elvis looked to where Mr. Willoughby was yelling, "Hey! Hey!" and turned back just in time to see Martin draw back his fist. Elvis jabbed with his left, his knuckles slamming into Martin's mouth, splitting his upper lip and leaving his two front teeth loose and bloody. The boy gasped, took one wild swing, and ran.

With his hands at his side, Elvis bowed his head and waited as Mr. Willoughby and the other teachers descended upon him.

Chapter 22

Charlie got up off his hands and knees and stood up. He stretched and straightened himself to his full height. Wiping his brow with the back of his hand, he looked across the Peace River at a flock of wild turkeys that were feeding at the far end of a pasture near the edge of an orange grove.

"I don't think we're gonna find anything, Tom." He glanced at his watch. "We've been here three hours already."

"Crime scene was thorough, all right. I just thought we ought to look one more time."

Tom was still down on his knees, dragging his fingers through the grass near the edge of the river. He was near where Sandy's body had been found.

"We could've turned something up. You never know. It didn't cost us anything to look."

Charlie headed back to the car, but Tom lagged behind, zigzagging as he walked, his eyes scanning every inch of ground. He glanced over at Charlie, leaning on his car and smoking, and was ready to give it up and go on when he noticed something not quite right in the grass beneath the weeds. He squatted, spread the weeds with his hands, and that's when he saw the bent grass. Several leaves of the short brown grass close to the ground were bent as if someone had pinched them in half, or stepped on them.

Tom stood up and looked around. Not far from the riverbank, he saw near the end of the hammock a thicket of high weeds, dog fennels, palmettos, briars, myrtle bushes, tangled grapevines, and bougainvillea, surrounded and sheltered by live oaks and cabbage palms. Tom walked toward the thicket.

Several times, Tom knelt in the weeds and checked the grass. He knew the signs left by cattle, deer, raccoons, and wild hogs; the trail he was following was made by none of those. Once, he was able to make out the faint outline of a human shoe.

Now crawling on his hands and knees, he found more bent grass and more partial footprints. He inched onward until he saw what looked like a rotten board leaning up against a cabbage palm. He stood up, moved closer, shoved aside branches, weeds, and vines and saw what appeared to be the side of a shack. He called for Charlie as he found a door. There was no doorknob, so Tom pushed gently against the door, and it creaked open. As it gave, Charlie arrived. They went inside.

"I'd forgotten this place was here," Charlie said. "Actually, I thought it'd been torn down."

"What is it, Charlie?—rather, what *was* it?"

"A moonshiner named Cyrus Potter built this place years ago, when I was a boy. I'm surprised it's still standing."

Tom tapped one of the rotting walls with his knuckles.

"It just barely is."

"It's been used lately though. Look how the grass is mashed down. Look at that blanket over there, and those cigarette butts."

"Probably kids. This is a hell of a hideout. Somebody could walk right by it and not even know it was here."

"Yeah, we did it ourselves. Somebody has been very careful to make sure it stays well camouflaged. Would kids be that careful?"

"I doubt it."

Charlie went around the room tapping each board with his knuckles, inspecting the broken windows, reaching up and touching the roof. Cracks in the walls let in enough light to see and streaks of sunlight stabbed through the small holes in the roof like laser beams.

"That roof's got more holes in it than Grandma's pin cushion," Tom said.

"Yeah, but it's got to have been replaced, Tom. The original roof would have rotted away to nothing by now."

Charlie was crawling around on the ground on his hands and knees, brushing over the surface of the ground with his fingertips.

"What are you looking for?"

"I don't know, really. It just—" Charlie stopped talking, started to dig.

"What, Charlie?"

"There's something here. Well, what's this?" He was brushing loose dirt and grass off a little wooden door with a metal ring attached to one end.

"A trap door?"

Charlie hooked his finger in the metal ring, lifted up the wooden door, reached down into the hole, lined with plywood, and brought out a small metal box, seven or eight inches square, two or three inches deep. Holding it under a slash of light, he lifted the lid and ran his fingertips around the soft felt lining.

"Empty."

"May I see it?"

Taking the box from Charlie, Tom stepped out the door into the bright light and examined it closely, gently scraping the inside lining with his pocketknife. He went all over the sides and the bottom and then began to pick at the corners. The bottom on the lower right end slid upward a quarter inch.

Charlie had followed Tom outside and was watching.

"A false bottom?"

Nodding, Tom worked the point of his knife down under the thin felt-lined bottom, slid it up and out of the box, revealing a small cache of snapshots. As Tom flipped through them, the color drained from his face. He handed them to Charlie.

Charlie gasped.

"Good lord."

"I doubt the good Lord had much to do with this."

Charlie swallowed hard.

"I can't believe it."

Tom squeezed his eyes shut tight and shook his head, as if he could make the images on the snapshots go away.

"Pratt? Him I can believe. But Leon Walker? I had him figured for a lot of things, but not this. And these boys? My god!"

"What's this town coming to?"

"I think it's done gone, Charlie." Tom flipped through the pictures again. "You think Sandy found out about these?"

"If she did, there's motive for murder."

"Yep."

"Let's get out of here," Charlie said. "We need to go back to school."

As they walked through the brush and weeds toward the car, Tom said, "This is gonna be a real switch, Charlie."

"What?"

"Well, it used to be that when I went to the principal's office, *I* was the one in the hot seat."

Charlie couldn't help smiling in spite of the pictures hanging heavy in his pocket and on his heart.

* * *

"Come in and sit down," Leon Walker said to Elvis when Mrs. Johnson escorted him into the office. "Mrs. Johnson, close the door, please."

"Of course, sir."

Elvis remained standing, looked around the room.

"Nice art gallery, sir. That picture of Jesus is just like the one in the church I go to sometimes."

Walker studied the boy for several moments before he spoke.

"Thanks, but I didn't send for you to talk about art. You're in serious trouble, son. Those boys you hit had to be taken to the hospital. What do you have to say for yourself?"

"Nothing, sir."

"Nothing? Do you realize that not only will you be suspended from school for ten days, but there could also be criminal charges brought against you if those boys file charges, and I suspect they will."

"They came after me, Mr. Walker. I only defended myself. Plenty of kids saw it go down. They'll tell you Jim Ed and Martin jumped me."

"Why would they do that?"

"It's a long story, Mr. Walker."

Walker wished Elvis would sit down. It was he, the principal, who was supposed to do the intimidating. But with Elvis leaning nonchalantly against the wall, looking down, speaking politely with a soft voice that seemed to know a secret, it was he, Leon Walker, who felt intimidated.

And if Jim Ed and Martin had indeed jumped Elvis, instead of the other way around, why had they done it, especially in the cafeteria full of dozens of witnesses? Had Elvis found out something they didn't want anyone to know? Still, the *cafeteria*?

"Those paintings are really good, Mr. Walker. That one of you looks almost like a snapshot."

Snapshot?

"What did you say?"

"I said that portrait of you is so good it looks almost like a snapshot."

The snapshots!

The sudden remembrance of what it was he'd forgotten jolted Walker down to his toes.

The snapshots!

He'd been so consumed with erasing every speck of cocaine, he'd forgotten the snapshots. A colossal blunder! Maybe Jim had gotten rid of them. Or maybe Mr. Big had taken them. But Walker doubted it. Big was too smart. *Where the hell were they?*

The last time Walker had seen them, they'd been in the box in the hideout with the stash—but he had removed the stash yesterday, and the pictures weren't there. Or were they? Had Jim thought to look beneath the false bottom of the box? Walker had to find out fast. If they were still there, he had to destroy them, burn them. He hadn't wanted the damn things taken in the first place. That was Jim's bright idea. Sometimes when Jim got too high—

"Mr. Walker, are you all right?"

Elvis's words snatched Walker back from his thoughts. He cleared his throat, swallowed. "Uh, yes. I'm fine."

"You look sick, sir."

Damn this boy! Is he playing games? If he knows something, why doesn't he just come out and say it?

"Actually, I don't feel well, son. I think I'm catching a cold. Some nasty bug is going around, you know." He sniffled and wiped his nose with his handkerchief.

"Maybe you should see a doctor."

Damn him! He is playing games. He does know something. The boy is toying with me like a cat with a mouse.

Walker's throat began to close up, and he believed if he didn't get this devil-boy out of his office now, he'd suffocate.

He stood up, steadying himself by leaning against his desk. He stepped over to the door and opened it.

"I think maybe I will see a doctor, Roy. You go on home. Be in my office first thing in the morning, and we'll settle this thing. I want to see how bad those boys are hurt. And I want to talk to some of the witnesses."

"I hope you feel better, Mr. Walker."

Elvis walked out of the room.

Walker closed the door behind him. He sat down again and took several long, deep breaths. An image of a small bone-handled revolver he'd once owned flashed through his mind. He's sold it for peanuts to one of his teachers in California, a beautiful young woman who wanted it for protection, or so she said. He wished he still had it.

Walker stepped into the outer office, pretended not to hear Mrs. Johnson when she called his name, and hurried down the hall to the nurse's station.

Nurse Barbara was sitting at her desk doing paperwork. She looked up when Walker came into the room.

"How're Jim Ed and Martin?"

She shook her head. "They needed more attention than I was able to give them here. Jim Ed's nose is broken, and Martin's two front teeth are chipped and loose; he might lose them. They were bleeding all over the place."

Walker looked at the bloodstains on the floor and felt faint. He hurried out of the nurse's station and back to his office. He rushed through the outer office, ignoring Mrs. Johnson again. He entered his own office, and flopped down in his chair.

Having seen Walker's face, Mrs. Johnson tapped on his door, cracked it a quarter inch, and said, "Mr. Walker, are you all right?"

Walker wished she would just go away. The old busybody was always sticking her nose where it didn't belong. Why didn't she quit work and stay home and rock grandbabies?

But he said, "No, Mrs. Johnson, I'm not all right. I feel awful, actually. I think I'm coming down with the flu. I may go see a doctor."

"Oh, I think you should. There's something very nasty going around. Is there anything I can do for you?"

Yes, shut up!

"No."

He held his head in his hands. How'd it ever gotten this bad, he wondered? How had it happened? And happened so *fast*. Of course, he knew exactly why it happened and how it had happened: Jim Pratt.

Jim was bad luck. He had to admit it. Every time they got together, something went wrong. But they were so right together. Hadn't fate brought them together again? Or was it a dizzyingly improbable coincidence?

Walker felt sick. His head throbbed; he had a queasy feeling in the pit of his stomach like he used to get when he was a boy about to be caught in a lie. Oh, why had he ever let himself fall in love with Jim Pratt? He wished he'd never met him. He wished he still had the little bone-handled revolver.

The knock on the door startled him.

"What!"

The door opened slightly, and Mrs. Johnson peeked inside.

"Sheriff Morris and Deputy Wilson are here to see you again, sir. They say it's urgent."

Chapter 23

As Tom followed Charlie into Walker's office, the principal stood to greet them. His smile was strained, but he straightened his shoulders and stood tall. He told himself he was blowing everything out of proportion. After all, the odds of them having anything on him were slim. Unlike Jim, he'd been careful and selective in his conquests. He was 100 percent certain none of the boys he'd been involved with would ever talk. Their egos couldn't stand such stains on their carefully crafted macho images.

Jim had been a fool bringing those kids to his apartment. He'd done cocaine on a daily basis for years, along with weed, beer, and wine. His judgment had to have been warped. It was no wonder he got caught. The wonder was he hadn't been caught sooner. That Jim had been arrested didn't mean they had anything on him, Leon Walker.

Walker reached over his desk and shook hands.

"What a day," he said. "We had a fight in the lunch room. That Jenkins kid, Roy, the one they call Elvis, got into a fight with Jim Ed Pace and Martin Stanley. Roy worked them over pretty good. I wouldn't have thought it. We had to send both boys to the hospital. Pace got his nose broken, and Stanley looks like he might lose his two front teeth. It was a bloody mess."

"That's too bad," Charlie said. "How's Elvis?"

"Not a scratch on him."

Charlie smiled. "Where is he?"

"I sent him home for the rest of the day because I'm sick—coming down with the flu, I think—and I'm going home myself. I told Roy I'd deal with him tomorrow. I want to talk to the students who witnessed the fight. Jenkins swears the boys jumped him and he was just defending himself. Since I didn't see it, I don't want to mete out any punishment until I know the facts."

"Mighty noble of you."

Walker dodged the sarcasm in Charlie's tone and breathed in a lungful of air. "How is your investigation going, Sheriff? Turn up anything new?"

"Plenty."

Charlie reached into his pocket and brought out the snapshots. He slapped them down onto Walker's desk and spread them out about an inch apart.

"Ever see these, Leon?"

Charlie wondered if Walker realized this was the first time he'd called him Leon.

The reserve of strength that Walker had tapped into moments ago made a low whistling sound as it left him. It was a sound, Charlie thought, a man-sized rubber doll might make if stuck with a pin. What actually caused the whistling was the agonizing sigh as it escaped through Walker's teeth.

Walker slumped back into his chair. It was as if everything had gone out of him. He was deflated, defeated, ruined. He knew it. He knew it was all over but the crying. The jig was up. The well had gone dry. The fat lady had sung. He'd always known this day might come. As horrible as it was, it was not a total shock. He'd always known that one day his sins would catch up with him.

A numbing sensation swept through him. He thought he might be dying. *Yes*, he thought, *this must be how dying feels, or something like it. My life has just ended. Charlie Morris and Tom Wilson have killed me as surely as if they'd walked into my office and shot me. I'm a dead man walking. I think I feel a strange kind of relief. After all, what more can they do to a dead man?*

Charlie nudged Walker, pointed to the pictures again, and said, "Remember these, Leon?"

Walker felt his mouth move, and he heard a word emerge.

"Yes,"

Now the sheriff was speaking, his words sounding to Walker like an echo coming across a canyon.

"Did Sandy find out about these snapshots? Is that why you killed her, to keep her from talking?"

After the roaring in his brain settled down to a steady hum, the question began to sink in.

"I did not kill Sandy."

"Why should we believe you, Leon? All you've done is lie to us."

"I suppose if I were you, I wouldn't believe me either." Walker spoke with great weariness. "But it doesn't matter now. Nothing matters now. It's over for me. Everything is all over."

"It's over, all right," said Tom.

"If you didn't kill her," Charlie said, "you know who did. Was it one of these boys?" He pointed at the snapshots.

Walker shook his head. "I don't know who killed her. I only know I didn't. And I don't believe Jim did. If Sandy knew anything about these"—he waved a hand over the snapshots on the desk—"it's news to me."

Charlie leaned forward and looked into the principal's eyes. Their faces were so close their noses touched.

"I want you to explain something to me, Leon. Nothing Pratt has done surprises me. I wouldn't put anything past him. But I'll admit I was shocked seeing you in the, uh, condition you're in there, in those pictures. But after it sank in, I asked myself what I really knew about you. The answer was nothing. But what I can't understand is those boys. How did you get them to go along with this? No matter what I might think of them, I never in a million years would have suspected *this!*"

Walker shrugged. "I was against it from the beginning. It was Jim's idea. He always got off on that group stuff. It was Jim that got them into it."

"*How?*"

"I don't know. Jim has a way about him. He has some kind of almost supernatural charm. It's both a blessing and a curse, I suppose."

"Did you and Pratt know each other before he came here?"

"Oh yes. We lived together for two years in California. We knew each other for years before that. At one point, we discussed marriage. In San Francisco, lots of people are in same-sex marriages, and that's where we planned to go. But it didn't work out. I finally left because Jim was so promiscuous. It isn't his fault altogether. It isn't that he goes out and pursues partners—they pursue *him.* He's just so divinely handsome that women, and many men, can't resist him. Anyway, that's why I left. He was always bringing other partners home, even with me there. He wanted us to do the group stuff, but, as I said, I'm not into that. I guess I'm a little old-fashioned that way. I believe in loyalty and having only one partner at a time.

"Anyway, I hadn't seen or heard from Jim in a long time until he walked into my office one day, looking for a job. I was absolutely shocked speechless, and so was he. We believed that fate had brought us back together. But now, I don't know. After all that's happened, I wonder if—"

"Didn't you recognize his name on the application?"

"He didn't use his real name."

Tom said, "Well, you can call it fate. It sounds like bad luck to me."

Walker sat listlessly. He did not answer Tom.

"Tell me something else," Charlie said. "There you are, and Pratt, and the two kids. What I want to know is who took the pictures?"

Walker's mouth twitched.

"Nobody. We set the camera on ten-second delay and set it on a table."

"There's no table in that shack. Besides, unless that camera had wings and could fly, it couldn't have gotten all of these different angles."

Walker's words slurred, like a drunken man's, or a man suffering extreme exhaustion. "No one took them. We four were the only ones there."

"You're a liar," Tom said.

"Aside from all this sex stuff, I'm charging Pratt with possession of and dealing cocaine," Charlie said. "I think you're involved in that too. Do you have any idea how much trouble you're in?"

A grotesque smile moved across Walker's mouth. "Yes, I do, Sheriff. I know exactly how much trouble I'm in. I knew it would come down to this someday, and the thought scared me horribly, but not enough to make me stop. You know what's strange? Now that it's here, now that it has finally happened, I feel something almost like relief. I'm almost glad I got caught. I'm glad it's over. I'm glad I don't have to hide any more."

"You won't be glad when you're behind bars," said Tom. "I know. I've been there."

"I've been behind bars my whole life. But as for the bars you're speaking of, I'll never be behind those."

"We'll see about that. Tom, read him his rights."

*　　*　　*

Elvis drove straight home from school to check on his daddy. If Sam's shakes got too bad, Elvis might have to buy him some whisky to keep him from going to pieces. Once he'd gotten so bad, crying and screaming about spiders and snakes and people trying to kill him, that Elvis had rushed him to the emergency room at Pinewood County General Hospital. The doctor told Elvis that Sam was suffering from advanced delirium tremens. The incident had scared Elvis so badly that he'd done everything in his power to see it didn't happen again. So far, it hadn't. He wanted to keep it that way. So he drove home, parked in the front yard, jumped out of his car, and ran into the house.

Sam was gone. Maybe one of his drinking buddies, one with a few bucks in his pocket, had picked him up. Or maybe he'd walked to the nearest beer joint where he either cadged drinks or conned the bartender into giving him credit. Everyone knew that if Sam stayed on a binge for too long, lost his job and couldn't pay his tab, eventually Elvis would come along and clean up his mess. Elvis thought it was too much to hope that his father had taken his suggestion and called someone in the AA group.

Elvis washed the dishes, changed the sweat-soaked sheets on his father's bed, lay down on the sofa, and closed his eyes. When he opened them, he glanced at his watch and saw it was 3:45. He had fifteen minutes to make it to the park in Flowing Wells to meet Diana. He jumped up, raked back his hair with his fingers, ran to the bathroom and then to his car. At 3:58, he pulled into Pioneer Park.

He drove slowly down the winding road that ran parallel to the Peace River for three quarters of a mile to the boat landing. He parked, climbed out of his car, and walked the short distance to the launch area. Diana was not there.

He sat down on a weathered bench between two young cypress trees and began to toss acorns, one by one, into the water. He watched the patterns of the ripples on the water. He thought about his father.

It broke Elvis's heart to see him slipping farther and farther down into the dark despair of alcoholism, but what could he do? He'd done all he could. He realized his father would have to want to change before any change could happen, and for now, Sam seemed satisfied to commit that slow suicide. Even if Elvis could afford to send him away to a treatment center, it would do Sam no good in his present frame of mind.

Elvis was grateful that no matter how drunken Sam got, he was never mean. His daddy had never hit him. Elvis knew his father wasn't a bad person. He was sick. Elvis had read the "Big Book," *Alcoholics Anonymous*, revered by most recovering drunks almost as much as the Bible. He also read lots of other AA literature, and he understood that alcoholism was a progressive disease that affected the body, mind, and spirit. However, it was a disease that was treatable, provided the alcoholic wanted to get well. And there was the catch: Sam did not believe he was sick except on the mornings he suffered horrendous hangovers, which he forgot as soon as he began to feel better.

So if Daddy doesn't believe he's sick, why would he try to sober up and get well?

Roy wanted to help his father, but right now, he had problems of his own. If he got that ten-day suspension, he might fail the semester. He did not want that. Would Mr. Walker suspend him even after he'd explained that Pace and Stanley had come after him, and he was only defending himself? And what if they came for him again, off campus, carrying guns? If those two got high enough, Roy wouldn't put anything past them, not even murder.

The purr of an engine interrupted his thoughts. Turning his head, he saw Diana's Jaguar pull up and park behind his car. As she got out and came toward him, he thought she looked better than she had in a long time, even with her cropped hair. Her eyes were clear. She held her head higher than she had in months. He stood up to meet her, and they walked a few feet toward the river and sat down on a log.

They sat in silence for a while, watching the river and the squirrels playing in the oaks and cypress trees on the other side of the river. A breeze fanned their faces. It had the clean, sweet scent of country.

"It's pretty here," Diana said.

"Yeah. I come here a lot. I thought it was strange when you asked me to meet you here. Look over there." He pointed across the river to water oaks and cypress trees that stretched their branches out over the water. Cypress knees protruded up from the ground all along the bank. Cabbage palms and scrub pines grew among the live oak and cypress trees. Palmettos grew in waist-high clusters.

"We think it's pretty now, Diana, but I wonder what it was like a hundred years ago."

More silence.

"I'm going away for a while, Elvis. I just wanted to let you know, and say good-bye."

When Elvis didn't reply, Diana said, "I have a drug problem. I'm going away for help."

"Well, that's great. I wish I could get my daddy into some kind of treatment. But we couldn't afford it even if he'd go. No insurance. How long will you be gone?"

"A month. Six weeks, maybe. I don't know. As long as it takes, I guess. I probably won't come back to school until next year. I'm scared, Elvis."

"You might be scared, but you've got guts. I wish my daddy would get help for his drinking. You don't drink. Is it coke?"

"Yes."

"Lots of kids are getting hooked on it. Must be easy to get."

Diana nodded.

"Easy enough."

"Where'd you score?"

"Well, I don't think—"

"Mr. Pratt?"

Diana gasped.

"How'd you know that? Nobody could know that."

Elvis shrugged.

"You gotta know there's lots of talk about Mr. Pratt. I think he's supplying other kids too, not just you. No telling what kinds of other stuff he's into. Let's face it. Mr. Pratt's a weird dude. I heard he's gay."

"I can assure you, Elvis, you're wrong about that."

"Well, maybe he swings both ways. I'm beginning to wonder about Mr. Walker too, and Jim Ed and Martin—and a few others."

"Elvis, your imagination is running away with you. What do you mean you're beginning to wonder about them?"

"I don't know, exactly. Just a hunch I have, a feeling I get whenever I see any of them together. They kind of make my skin crawl, like they're looking at me in a weird way or something."

"No, you're wrong. You've got to be. Mr. Walker is a friend of my dad's. They were in Vietnam together. If Mr. Walker was like that, my dad would know it."

"Maybe he does."

"No. If he did, he wouldn't have anything to do with him. My dad's old-fashioned that way."

"Well, like I say, I'm just guessing. I could be all wrong."

"Have you told the sheriff or Tom Wilson what you suspect?"

"No. Actually, the idea didn't occur to me till this afternoon, after seeing Mr. Walker."

Diana made a face and shook her head. "I just can't believe what's going on right here in Flowing Wells. It's like something you see in the movies or read about in a book, not something that could happen here."

"Yeah, like *Peyton Place*, maybe. Ever read that? Listen, Diana, I wish you a lot of luck. I'm not much of a writer, but I'll write you while you're gone."

"I'll write you too if they'll let me. I hear some of those places are pretty strict."

"I'm proud of you for getting help."

Diana got very quiet. She reached out and touched Elvis's cheek, then pulled her hand away. "I have to tell you something."

"All right."

"Sandy was in love with you."

Elvis felt his throat tighten.

"We never used that word."

"She told me a few days before she was killed. Made me swear not to tell anyone. She said no one had any idea how special you are."

Elvis swallowed hard, but the lump in his throat would not go away. "We never talked about love. But I loved her. I did."

A racing engine stopped him. He looked around to see a green Camaro slide sideways to a stop ten feet behind them. Kara Mendel jumped out of her car. Her skirt flapped wildly as she ran toward them.

"That's mighty fancy driving, but you could have killed us, Kara."

Ignoring Elvis, Kara glared at Diana.

"You! I thought you were my friend."

"What are you talking about, Kara? I am your friend."

"Like hell you are! First you take Jim away from me, and then you turn him in to the cops!"

"What? No. I—"

Now Kara loomed over her.

"No, you listen. I'll get even with you if it's the last thing I ever do. I know who killed Sandy. I know lots of things nobody knows I know. I'm going to get even with you and a bunch more people too! I'm sick and tired of being treated like shit!" She whirled around and ran back to her car and sped away.

Diana was trembling. "I think she's getting worse, Elvis. She imagines things, or makes them up. You think she knows who killed Sandy?"

"If she did, she would have told somebody."

Diana leaned over and let her lips brush Elvis's cheek. "I have to go. Sandy was my best friend, and she was in love with you—so that makes you my friend. I just wanted to say good-bye."

Elvis looked at her, suddenly struck by her beauty. He looked off at the river.

"Write, if they'll let you."

"Elvis?"

He looked at her again.

"Yeah?"

"If this program works for me, and I get clean and can stay clean, you know what I want to do?"

Elvis shook his head.

"Well, I've heard lots of talk from older folks about your dad, and all I've ever heard is that before he got to drinking, he was a wonderful man. A good husband and father."

"He was."

Diana smiled. "Well, if I get clean, I intend to make it my mission to help other addicts and drunks. You know who I want to start with?"

Elvis looked at her but did not answer.

"Sam Jenkins. If you'll let me, Elvis—and if you'll help me—we'll get him sober."

"Diana, those places cost a lot of money. Like I said, we don't even have insurance."

She took his hand and held it in both of hers. "Elvis, Sandy loved you, and she would have wanted me to do this for you. And I want to do it, for Sandy. My daddy is rich. I won't have any trouble getting money from him for that. That small amount of money is nothing to him. Who knows? We might open a 'Diana Matthews Center.' Move over, Betty Ford!"

Elvis laughed. Then he looked into her eyes.

"I don't know what to say."

"You don't have to say anything. Maybe I've found my mission in life, helping people."

She put her arms around Elvis and hugged him.

"Take care of yourself till I get back."

"Sure."

Diana smiled and went to her car. Elvis walked with her and opened her door.

"Good luck."

"I'll try to write."

She started the engine.

Elvis touched her shoulder. "I see why you were Sandy's best friend. You're pretty special yourself."

"Sure. I'm a seventeen-year-old cocaine addict riding off into the sunset to some rehab center. I'm special, all right."

"Listen, I've done a lot of reading about alcoholism and addiction, and I can tell you it is not your fault. It's a disease. You are not a bad person,

Diana. You've been sick. But you've got the courage to fight it and get well. I'm not real good at praying, but I'll pray for you, if you don't mind."

She looked at Elvis and smiled.

"I don't mind at all."

*　　*　　*

As she drove away, Elvis sat down on the bench again and looked across the river and into the trees. He noticed his heart was beating fast, and he felt light headed. He thought again about what Diana had said about helping his father. He was glad no one was around to see him cry.

He also thought about Kara Mendel. How much did she know? Did she know who killed Sandy? He doubted it.

She'd sworn to "get even" with Diana.

How?

Elvis had dared to think he was close to having this thing figured out. But now a monkey wrench had been tossed into the machinery. Something was wrong; something did not fit. A piece of the puzzle was missing that suddenly threw the whole picture out of kilter.

He admitted to himself he could be wrong about the homosexual stuff between Walker and Pratt and Pace and Stanley. He had no real evidence of that, just a feeling he got whenever he saw any of them together. But the cocaine thing was almost a certainty. If either of those things were true, and if Sandy had found out, there was reason enough for any one of them to want her dead. Jim Ed Pace was the most likely suspect. It was Pace he'd seen slap her around. Of course, there was a big difference in slapping someone and killing them. But Elvis believed Pace was capable of killing. Of course, again, it was only a hunch. All of it was only his hunches.

The thing was Elvis had had hunches all his life, and more often than not, they'd proved to be true. But this could be one of those times he was wrong. Besides, now his hunch was no longer clear. Kara had cast a cloud over his intuition, and he knew that not until he found that missing piece of the puzzle would the cloud lift.

Before Kara's appearance a while ago, he had been ready to take his suspicions to the sheriff. But not now.

What was it? Something was right in front of his face, but he couldn't see it. Maybe if he talked to someone about it, maybe they could see what he was missing. Maybe if he talked to the sheriff or to Tom.

So Sandy had been in love with him? He'd prayed for her love every night after he'd talked to her in the parking lot. His prayer had been answered.

If she had lived and they had gotten together, wouldn't that have been a hoot to set tongues to wagging! Elvis grinned, but then a great sadness and sense of loss pierced his heart. For the first time since he'd heard of Sandy's death, Elvis stopped fighting them and let the great wracking sobs take him.

Chapter 24

The last cramp had been bad as it came around from Kitty's lower back to grip her stomach, but thank goodness it hadn't lasted long. This was exactly what the doctor had told her would happen. He said when it started, it would be a constant pain coming from the lower part of her back and wrapping around, and then it would get to be one pain after another that she could time. And before this last one had hit her, it had been thirty minutes since the previous one. So she had plenty of time. She was sure of that. The doctor had said to wait until they were three minutes apart before coming to the hospital. But she knew her time was near.

Now she lay back in Tom's big recliner, holding her stomach and breathing deeply, as they'd taught her in the Lamaze classes. When it quit, she'd get up and walk. They said that would help. Although she knew it wasn't quite her time yet, she wished Tom were home. She wanted him near. She wanted him to sit beside her and hold her hand. She'd called him not long ago. She knew all she had to do was dial the phone again and he would be here in minutes—but she didn't want to get him all excited and then turn out to be wrong. Anyway, she truly believed she had plenty of time.

When she heard a car crunch onto the driveway, she struggled up out of the chair and hurried to meet Tom at the door. She was anxious to see him, but hurrying was a struggle. She opened the door just as Elvis was about to knock; later they would joke about which one was more startled, him or her. Automatically Kitty's hand flew to her robe to hold it together even though it was buttoned almost to her throat. With the other hand, she smoothed the soft fabric over her bulging stomach.

"Oh! Elvis, I was expecting Tom. You startled me."

Elvis blushed. "I'm sorry, Mrs. Kitty. I didn't mean to scare you. I was just going to knock when—I'm sorry. Tell you the truth, when you opened that door so sudden, it scared me too. I nearly jumped right out of my skin."

Kitty smiled. "I guess we're just a couple of scaredy-cats. What were you wanting, Elvis?"

"I need to see Tom."

"I'm expecting him any minute. I thought you were him. That's why I yanked the door open like I did." She glanced down at her belly. "I'd ask you in, Elvis, but—"

"No, that's all right. I'll wait in my car, or come back later."

Kitty hesitated a moment, then said, "Oh, heck. It's okay, Elvis. Come on in and sit down."

"No, ma'am. I'll wait out here."

She took his arm and gently guided him inside the door. "That's not necessary, really. Have a seat there on the sofa. What can I get you to drink? I have soda, and there's coffee in the pot."

Elvis shrugged and sat down.

"I hate to impose."

"You're not. Soda or coffee?"

"Coffee, I guess. Black."

No sooner had Kitty stepped into the kitchen when another car pulled into the front yard. Elvis stood up and looked out the window to see Tom walk toward the front door.

"Howdy," he said as Tom came inside.

"Hey, Elvis. I thought that was your car. What's up?"

"Well, if you've got a minute, I need to talk to you."

Kitty came out of the kitchen with two mugs.

"Hi, honey. Good timing. You must've smelled the coffee."

She handed the steaming mugs to the men.

Tom gave her a quick kiss. "How're you doing?"

She looked down at her enormous stomach. "I have a feeling I'm on the home stretch."

Elvis said, "Tom, maybe this is a bad time. I can come back later."

"It's all right, Elvis," Kitty said. "You guys go ahead and talk. I'm going to lie down for a while."

"Sit down, Elvis." Tom sank down into his recliner.

"Listen, I didn't know Mrs. Kitty was so close. I can come back—"

Tom sipped his coffee, shook his head. "Tell me what's on your mind."

Suddenly Elvis felt unsure of himself. Who was he to bring his far-fetched theories to a professional who was paid to make his own theories?

"Well, I've been thinking, and I have some ideas, but—"

"But what?"

"Well, they seem silly now that I'm here. I mean, I don't have any proof or anything. Just hunches."

"Go ahead," Tom said. "I want to hear your hunches."

Elvis drank some of his coffee and set the mug on the coffee table between him and Tom. He leaned forward from his spot on the couch and began to speak, hesitantly at first, and then with conviction.

"Well, first of all, there's Mr. Pratt and Mr. Walker. I've seen them around campus a few times together, and I've seen them a few times off campus. And, well, I guess I've got too wild an imagination, but, if you ask me, those two are more than just friends. And then there's Jim Ed and Martin. They try to act tough and all, but whenever I'm around 'em and they don't know I'm watching, well, I don't know—I get this funny feeling like there's something creepy about them and, well, scary even. I feel like they're looking at me in a weird way. I know I probably sound nuts but . . ."

Tom listened quietly, amazed that this boy had surmised through instinct and observation what he and Charlie had stumbled upon accidentally by finding the snapshots.

"I think they're mixed up with cocaine too, Jim Ed and Martin. I don't know about Mr. Walker, but I wouldn't doubt it. I know for a fact Mr. Pratt is. He turned Diana on to it. She told me so, just a few minutes ago."

"You saw Diana?"

"Yes, sir. We met a while ago at the boat landing in Pioneer Park and . . ."

When Elvis finished his story, he and Tom sat in silence, drinking coffee. Tom said, "You know, I'm beginning to wonder if Kara plays a bigger part in this thing than I thought."

"I don't know, but after she said what she did and drove off, I got to wondering that too. Do you think Kara knows who killed Sandy?"

Tom shrugged. "Elvis, at one point I thought Kara did it. But I don't know what to think anymore. Only thing I know for sure is that every time Kara goes off her meds, her behavior gets more and more bizarre."

"And you think it got so strange that—"

"I don't know."

"She said soon everybody would know. She threatened to get even with Diana. She—"

The sudden ring of the phone stopped Elvis, and Tom reached over to the table at the end of the sofa and picked up the receiver.

"Yeah?" he said. "What?"

Elvis saw Tom's face go pale.

"No," Tom said.

Tom got quiet listening to the voice on the line.

"Okay," he said. "Yes. Now listen to this. Elvis is here. He just saw Diana a few minutes ago, and Kara. Diana called him this morning and . . ."

When Tom stopped, there was such a long silence he thought they'd been disconnected.

"You there, Charlie?"

"Yeah yeah, I'm here." Tom heard the excitement growing in Charlie's voice. "Why didn't I think of it sooner? Tom, can you be ready in thirty minutes?"

"Ready for what?"

"I want you to take a ride with me."

Tom grimaced.

"Charlie, I ought to stay home with Kitty."

"I know it. And you know if I didn't think this was important I wouldn't ask you to come with me. Can you be ready or not?"

Tom swallowed.

"Yeah."

He hung up the phone.

Elvis watched him.

"Probably none of my business, Tom, but—"

Tom stood up. He walked to the window and saw dark clouds forming above the horizon. He stood there for several moments, hands in his pockets, quiet as a corpse. He turned to Elvis.

"You'll know soon enough, anyway. Everybody will. Mr. Walker is dead."

"What?"

"I arrested him this afternoon. He's hung himself. Somehow managed to rip off a strip of seatbelt in back of the squad car and hung himself in the holding cell. He told me he'd never be behind bars. He was right."

Elvis sprang to his feet. "No *shit*! Tom, this must have to do with what Kara—"

"I don't see how."

"But, Tom—"

"Listen, Elvis, I appreciate you coming by, I really do. Thanks for telling me what you did. But this has been a damn long day already, and Charlie's picking me up in thirty minutes to go back out. I need a few minutes with Kitty."

"Sure, I'm gone. I gotta get back to the house to see if Daddy's home yet, anyway. No telling what kind of shape he'll be in."

"He's all right."

"I hope so."

Tom held out his hand. "Thanks, Elvis. I mean it. We'll talk again later."

They shook hands, and Elvis turned to leave.

"Elvis?"

He stopped and looked back.

"Yeah?"

"Charlie was right. You ought to think about going into law enforcement. You'd make a fine detective. We'll help you make the right connections if that's what you want to do."

The boy's heavy lips curled into his lopsided grin.

"Thanks, Tom."

*　　*　　*

When Elvis closed the door behind him, Tom had doubts. How could Elvis possibly know so much about Pratt, Walker, Pace, and Stanley? Was he really that smart, or did he have some other way of knowing? Could Elvis have taken the snapshots? *If that was so, why would he tell me what he suspects?* Tom wondered. *Is he playing some game? No, that's too far-fetched. Then again, everything about this case is far-fetched.* Every time Tom thought he had it figured out, there was another twist.

Pushing these thoughts out of his mind, he went into the cozy bedroom he shared with his wife and sat down on the edge of the bed beside her. Her eyes were closed. He reached out and touched her hand and she opened her eyes.

"Asleep?" he asked.

She smiled and squeezed his hand.

"Just resting."

He slid down beside her and put an arm around her and kissed her.

"Are you okay?"

She nodded.

"I'm okay. For now, anyway."

Tom put his hand on her belly, and they lay quietly for a few moments. Tom took in a deep breath and said softly, "Honey, I don't know if you heard me talking to Charlie on the phone, but some stuff has come up and I have to go back out. I—"

"Oh, sometimes I get so sick of . . . Tom, I need you. Listen, I've been timing the cramps, and they're thirty minutes apart now. When they're three minutes, I need to go to the hospital."

"I'll tell Charlie that. He'll see I'm back in time. You know he will. And if something comes up sooner, call my cell phone."

Minutes passed, and Kitty did not answer.

Tom said, "I know you get sick of my crazy hours, honey. Sometimes I get sick of this job myself. Sometimes I think about quitting, getting a job at the pepper plant or somewhere. And maybe I will. But right now, I have to go with Charlie. Bad things are happening. I think things are coming to a head. Another person is dead."

"Who?"

"Leon Walker."

"*What!*"

Tom explained about the snapshots, Walker's arrest and subsequent suicide, Elvis's meeting with Diana, the rude interruption by Kara Mendel.

"I don't know, honey," he said. "I never could have dreamed all that's happened in the past few days. It's come down so fast it's hard to believe."

"My god."

"When I told Charlie what Elvis said Kara told Diana, about getting even, he got real quiet, and then excited. That's when he told me to be ready in thirty minutes. I think he's on to something."

Kitty held his hand in both of hers, and they lay in silence.

"Tom, I'm sorry for being a nag sometimes. I just miss you so much and want you here with me, now especially—but I understand. Go on with Charlie and forget what I said. I'll be all right. I really don't think the baby's coming tonight. And I know all I have to do is call and you'll come, no matter what."

"I will, I promise. I love you, and I love our baby."

"I know you do. Go on now. But I'll tell you one thing. I'll be mighty happy when this is over, and our lives can get back to somewhere near normal."

"I will too. I meant what I said about getting out of this work. I'll mention it to Charlie as soon as I can."

Tom kissed her again and then pulled away and sat up on the side of the bed. "Charlie will be here any minute. Can I do anything for you before I go? Get you anything?"

"No, I'm all right, Tom. I don't need anything, but you."

A horn blasted in front of the house.

"Duty calls," Tom said.

"Please, be careful. And come home as soon as you can."

"You know I will. And if anything happens, call me."

"Sure."

He kissed her once more and, without looking back, hurried out of the bedroom and out of the house where he climbed into the car beside Charlie.

"This better be good."

"I'm sorry, Tom. I really am. Sally wasn't too happy with me either. She said she couldn't believe I was going back out, and she really couldn't believe that I'd ask you to leave Kitty right now." He spun his tires on the gravel as he backed out of the driveway. "If my hunch is right, after tonight, we can relax."

"Right," Tom said. "Listen, Charlie, if this cell phone rings, you have to bring me home fast. Kitty's timing her contractions. She doesn't think it's gonna be long now."

Charlie nodded, snapped on his turn signal, pulled out onto the highway, and sped northward.

"Where the hell are we going? Where's the fire?"

Charlie said nothing for a long time. When he finally spoke, his voice was icy.

"We're going after a killer."

Chapter 25

Tom turned his head to look at Charlie.

"Charlie, I must've missed something somewhere. Tell me what I've missed. What do you know that I don't? Do you know who killed Sandy?"

Charlie gripped the steering wheel so hard his knuckles turned white. His eyes, glazed with determination, stared straight ahead. "Maybe, maybe not—not sure."

Moments became minutes.

"Hey, Charlie, remember me? Tom Wilson? The ex-con you hired to work with you? He's been right by your side since the beginning of this case. Don't leave ol' Tom dangling in the breeze. Okay? Tell Tom what's going on."

"Just a little longer, Tom. I'm just not sure. I gotta be *sure*."

"Charlie, don't leave me out. You've never had to be 100 percent certain about something before you'd share your hunches—I thought that's what we did, shared our hunches."

Charlie sucked in a huge breath of air and sighed.

"You're right, Tom. I'm sorry. It occurred to me that maybe we've been so close to the forest we haven't been able to see the trees."

"That's cryptic, Charlie."

"Tom, right off the top of your head, who would you say is the main player in this mess?"

"Jim Pratt."

"All right. Who's second?"

"Leon Walker, I guess."

"Third?"

"Well, I guess we're getting down to kids now. Hard to say. Maybe Jim Ed or Martin. Or maybe Kara, or even Diana."

"I'm finding Kara is like a ghost, Tom. She's more an observer than a participant. A fly on the wall. She sneaks around and follows people. She looks and listens from behind cover. There's no telling what Kara knows that we don't. For a while, I sort of had the notion that Kara killed Sandy. Now I don't think that, but it wouldn't surprise me if she knows who did."

"But wouldn't she have told somebody? Kara and Sandy were friends."

"It depends on who the murderer is, Tom. It might be someone Kara doesn't want to see get in trouble."

"Someone kills her best friend, and she doesn't want them to get in trouble? I don't buy it."

"Tom, you gotta remember Kara doesn't always run on all six cylinders. I'm just not totally convinced that we can put complete credence in everything she tells us."

"All right," Tom said. "Go on."

"Well, after the kids, who would you think of next to go in our line of suspects?"

Tom thought about it.

"I don't know, Charlie."

"What about John Matthews?"

"What?"

"The whole time, Matthews has been right in the loop of all this, and we've never really looked at him for anything worse that cheating on his wife. But I'm beginning to wonder. He got rich so unbelievably fast. He's always taking these little jaunts down to Central America, says it's business, and never takes Linda with him."

"Charlie, are you saying you think Sandy found out Matthews is dirty and threatened to turn him in, and he killed her to keep her quiet?"

"All I'm saying is, Tom, I'm opening my eyes to new possibilities, ideas that hadn't occurred to me until now. Something is eating Matthews, Tom. Look at the weight he's lost in the past few months. Shoot, he's got darn near as skinny as Diana."

"I thought he'd just been working too hard, or maybe sick."

Tom thought for a moment.

"Charlie, if Matthews wanted someone hit, surely he wouldn't do it himself, would he? With his resources, wouldn't he hire someone?"

"Maybe, maybe not. Matthews is an arrogant man. I think he believes he's above the law. I really don't know what he might do."

"Damn," Tom said.

*   *   *

Over near the western horizon, the sun dipped behind a black wall of thunderheads. Shimmering streaks of red, purple, gold, orange, and green shot upward behind the clouds and shone with intense brilliance through cracks in the clouds. Charlie and Tom could smell the scent of approaching rain.

As Charlie pulled into the Mendel driveway, raindrops began to sprinkle the windshield. Turning off the engine, Charlie said, "Looks like it's gonna be a good one."

They got out of the car, walked to the house, and stood under the tin roof above the front porch as Charlie knocked on the door. The tin amplified the sound of the rain, and the patter of the drops seemed to tap out the rhythm to a song Charlie couldn't quite place. Lois Mendel opened the door and stood in the doorway, her face registering surprise at seeing them again.

The wind blew the rain up under the porch. Mrs. Mendel looked up at the sky. "Looks like the weatherman got it right for a change," she said. "Come on in before you get soaked." Her voice was flat, her eyes red.

The two men followed her into the warm, dry living room, where a light from a table lamp cast a soft glow across the room. The scent of a cake baking filled the men's nostrils.

Charlie said, "Lois, whatever you're baking smells some kind of good! Almost like a cake my mama used to bake when I was a boy. My god, that smell is bringing back memories."

Lois smiled weakly. "Thanks, Charlie. It's just a pound cake. Hang around long enough and you can have a piece hot out of the oven."

"Boy, I'd love to, Lois, with a slab of butter on it and three or four scoops of ice cream, but I don't think we'll be here that long." He glanced around the room. "Is Kara here? How's she doing?"

Lois avoided Charlie's eyes. "Yes, she's home, Charlie, but to be honest, I just don't know how she's doing. Even her doctors don't know for sure what's wrong with her. At first they thought she was schizophrenic, and they treated her for that. Then they decided she was bipolar. Now they say she also shows symptoms of obsessive-compulsive disorder—but that they've never heard of anyone having all three illnesses. And to confuse them even more, sometimes she seems as normal as you or I, *even when she's not taking her pills*. And, of course, since they don't know exactly what they're treating, they keep changing the damn meds!" She took a tissue from her pocket and blew her nose. "The doctors say mental illnesses don't always go by the book. I'm sorry, Charlie. This is just so hard on all of us."

"I know it is, Lois. Maybe she ought to be hospitalized again, so they can observe her more closely."

Mrs. Mendel nodded. "Just as soon as our insurance gives us the okay, we're admitting her—one way or the other. If she's in one of her psychotic states and throws a fit, we'll have her committed. It wouldn't be the first time."

"Well, I hope they get it right. How is she now? Think she'd talk to us? Think she's able?"

"She wouldn't take any meds at all for three days and got pretty wild. Yesterday I stayed on her a long time about taking them, and she finally did. I think she took them just to get me off her back. She was crying too, but she wouldn't let me touch her.

"All she said was, 'Oh, hell, what difference does it make now?' She doesn't usually swear, Charlie, at least not around me, but she did then. Then she went to her room and stayed there until dinner. She sat down to dinner, but she just picked at her food. Still she seemed all right, you know, not all wired up and mad like she gets. After dinner, she went back in her room, and she hasn't come out since. I knocked on her door this morning, but she just yelled at me to go away. It didn't sound like her mad voice though, so I didn't go in. I put my ear to her door later on, and I thought I heard her crying. You can go in and see her. Maybe she'll talk to someone besides me."

"You can come in with me, Lois, if you'd like," Charlie said.

"I'd better not. I'll just upset her. You won't be long, will you? And would you try to get her to come out of her room for a little while? Tell her I want to see her, and I won't say a word to her if she doesn't want me to."

"I have a few questions to ask her, Lois. I just need a few minutes. And I'll try to get her to come out and talk to you."

Lois walked into the hallway with Charlie and pointed to Kara's door. Then, crying, she walked back into the living room with Tom whom Charlie had asked to stay with her.

Charlie tapped on Kara's door.

"Go away!"

Charlie cracked the door and peeked in, then walked inside. Kara, fully dressed, was sitting on a chair. Her eyes were red, but she was not crying now. She seemed startled by Charlie's appearance. Charlie pulled up a chair beside her bed and sat down. Kara climbed back onto her bed, leaned back against the headboard, and pulled her knees tight against her body.

"How're ya doin', Kara?"

She shrugged. "Okay, I guess, for a nut case. That's what I am, you know, a nut case."

Charlie said, "Well, everybody I know is a little nutty, except Tom and me. And just between us"—he leaned closer and lowered his voice—"sometimes I'm not too sure about him!"

For a moment, Kara stared at him blankly, and then she threw her head back and laughed, a laugh that began as a chuckle and grew into a deep belly laugh that brought tears to her eyes.

"Darn!" she said. "That tickled my funny bone. I've haven't laughed like that in a long time."

Charlie grinned. "Well, they say laughter is the best medicine. That's why I watch *The Three Stooges* at least once a day."

Kara laughed again. "You're too much. Boy, I didn't realize how much I needed that. You really watch *The Three Stooges* every day?"

"Yep. I've got about a dozen videos and DVDs in case I can't catch 'em on the tube. I get kind of grumpy if I don't get my *Stooge* fix."

"May I borrow them sometime?"

"Sure, I'll be glad to share them with you. Do you feel like answering a few questions, Kara?"

"Well, a few minutes ago I wouldn't have, but now, well, sure. Payback for you making me laugh and offering to loan me your *Stooges*."

Kara wiped her eyes with a pillowcase. When she looked up and spoke again, her voice was serious. "Better make it fast though. You never know when I might zone out again."

"I hear you ran into Elvis and Diana today."

Kara sat up straight, her eyes opened wide; then she seemed to wilt.

"Oh no. I'd totally forgotten that. Oh my god, no wonder they think I'm crazy. I *am*!"

Charlie sat still watching Kara's fingertips press hard on the temples of her bowed head.

"Oh my god," she said, "I can't *believe* what I said to them. Oh, *shit*! They must *hate* me."

"No one hates you, Kara."

Now she held her head in her hands and rocked back and forth on the bed. Charlie could hear her soft sobs; he let some time go by before he spoke.

"Kara, Elvis says you told them you know who killed Sandy."

She locked her arms around her knees, pulling them tight to her chest and hanging her head down as if trying to draw herself up into a ball.

"Oh my god Oh my god." She said it over and over.

Charlie asked gently, "Were you in love with Jim Pratt, Kara?"

She lifted her tear-streaked face to look at Charlie. Her mouth moved, trying to make words, but all she got out was "Oh my god."

"Were you?"

"Oh my god."

"Kara, lots is going down in this town, stuff that a few months ago I'd never have believed. Nothing is ever going to be the same. Why don't you just come on and tell me what you know? I'll find out anyway. You can save me some time and trouble and help keep anyone else from getting hurt."

Kara shook her head, slowly, back and forth, back and forth. Finally, she let her eyes meet Charlie's. "You're wasting your talent wearing that badge, sir. You ought to be a shrink."

Charlie shrugged. "I'm just an ol' country boy. I never even went to college."

Still shaking her head she said, "You've got something, though, that I don't think they teach in college."

"Tell me about Mr. Pratt."

Kara stood up and looked up into Charlie's face.

"Yes, I was in love with him. I still am."

"You told Diana she stole him from you, and that you were going to 'get even'?"

Eyes downcast, she nodded.

"Yes, I said that."

"What'd you mean, Kara? That you were going kill Diana?"

"*No!*" She screamed the word, then took a breath and said almost in a whisper, "I might be crazy, but I'm not *that* crazy. I could never *kill* anybody."

Kara looked frightened. Her eyes darted around the room.

"Can you keep going, Kara?" Charlie asked. "You're doing great. But if this is too hard on you, if you want to stop—"

"I—I don't know."

"It's up to you, Kara."

"I just can't believe . . . I mean, so much has happened. It seems impossible that—"

"Take a deep breath," Charlie told her. "Then tell me what you know."

Kara took some tissue from the box on her bedside table, turned her back to Charlie, and blew her nose. Then she faced him again, pulled in a long breath, and shuddered as she let it out.

"Like I already told you, before Sandy left here Saturday morning, she said she was going to meet somebody before she went to see you. It was killing me to know who it was so I followed her—"

"You followed her?"

"Yes. I was already dressed, so I just went and jumped in my car and took out after her—Mama and Daddy were still in bed, or they would've stopped me. I stayed far enough behind her that she didn't see me, and I followed her way out past an orange grove and across a cow pasture to a place near the river. Only I didn't go all the way across the pasture because I was afraid she might see me, so about halfway across, I parked behind some myrtle bushes. Sandy drove all the way across the pasture and into an oak hammock. I ran into the hammock, and there was her car. I couldn't see her, but I heard her walking, and I followed her footsteps."

"What happened then?"

"Well, I hid behind some palmettos and watched Sandy walk on down to the river. She was a good ways off, but I could see her standing there, looking around, like maybe she was looking for somebody. She just stood there for a long time, and I was getting real tired of crouching down behind those palmettos, so I decided to go on back to my car and get back home before Mama and Daddy got up and found me gone. Finding out who she was meeting didn't matter enough for me to squat out there in the woods all day getting eaten up by bugs."

"Think you could find that place again?"

Kara thought before answering.

"Well, if I was *there*, I'm pretty sure I'd recognize it—but I don't know if I could find my way back to it. I was just following Sandy, not really paying that much attention."

"All right."

"Well, just about the time I was getting ready to leave, I saw this person walk toward Sandy from the other direction. They were a good ways off under a big cypress tree, and I couldn't tell if it was a man or woman. I thought it was a man because they had on pants and short hair, but I'm not sure. They talked for a few minutes—I couldn't hear a word—and then that person pushed Sandy."

"Pushed her?"

"Yes, they just hauled off and pushed her, hard."

"Did she fall down?"

"No, but she staggered back and almost did."

"You still didn't recognize who it was?"

"No. It was real overcast and dark that morning. It was so dark I couldn't even tell if it was a man or woman, but like I said, I think it was a man because of the short hair."

"Well, go on."

"When he pushed her, she stumbled back and almost fell. But she stayed on her feet, and I thought they were going to fight, even though I couldn't imagine Sandy fighting. She's never been in a fight in her life that I know of. Anyway, all of a sudden, Sandy backed away and ran toward the river and just stood there, staring across it. I thought she might have been waving at someone, but I never saw anybody. Then the one that pushed her walked up behind her and shot her in the back of the head!" Kara began to tremble; tears rolled down her cheeks, and she took more tissue from the box and wiped them away. She swallowed hard.

"It sounded like a cap pistol, didn't hardly sound like a real gun at all. But Sandy dropped to the ground like a sack of sugar—she didn't fall over, she just *dropped*. It was *awful*. I ran back to my car and got out of there as fast as I could. I had to be careful because I was scared the killer might hear my car and come after *me*."

Again Kara turned her back to Charlie and began to sob. She sat down on the edge of her bed. Her face was pale, her eyes, haunted.

Outside Charlie heard thunder rumble. Lightning followed quickly with a blinding white flash through the bedroom. The rain came harder, blowing against the bedroom window. Charlie thought of the pound cake baking and of being safely inside his childhood home on rainy days.

"You never saw who Sandy was looking at across the river?"

Kara shook her head. "No. I don't think there was anybody. I think she was just standing there thinking, or wondering what to do."

"The guy with the gun solved that problem for her, didn't he?"

Kara sobbed and held her face in her hands.

Charlie sighed. "We're almost through, Kara. Listen, I want you to think before you answer. The hammock you were in is at least a hundred yards from where Sandy was shot. It was early morning and, as you said, overcast, and visibility wasn't good. I know you say you couldn't see the shooter well enough even to tell if it was a man or woman, but—please think—was there anything familiar about him? The way he stood, walked, anything at all?"

Kara began to shake harder. "Oh my god," she moaned. "How can this be happening? I can't believe—"

Charlie patted her shoulder.

"There was, wasn't there? You know who the shooter was, don't you, Kara?"

Her nod was so slight Charlie wasn't sure it was a nod. She said, "I'm not sure, but I think—I mean, it looked like . . ."

Charlie leaned over and whispered, "Tell me, Kara. Please. Tell me who you *think* you saw shoot Sandy."

Charlie put his ear close to her mouth. Another clap of thunder rumbled through the house, lightning lit up the room. Charlie heard Kara's sharp intake of breath, and he felt her breath on his skin when she whispered a name into his ear.

Charlie stood up so fast he could have been yanked by a pulley. Kara raised her swollen eyes to look at him. His face was a mask of confusion.

"You think I'm lying, don't you?"

"No no. I don't think that. But are you *sure* that's who you saw?"

"No. I *told* you I'm not sure. You asked me who I *thought* it was, and I told you. You made me tell you. I didn't want to because I wasn't sure, and I'm still not sure."

"Okay," Charlie said. "And you never did see who it was that Sandy was looking at across the river?"

"I don't think she was looking at anyone. I did at first, but now I think Sandy knew she was in danger and the waving was a trick. Or, maybe she wasn't waving at all. It just might've looked like it from where I was. Like I said, maybe she was just standing there thinking."

"Hmm," said Charlie. "It could be." He paused a moment, then sighed. "But if she did wave, and it was a trick, the trick didn't work, did it?"

Kara did not reply. She flung herself facedown on her bed and buried her face into her pillow.

Charlie left the room. He walked down the hallway to the living room where Tom and Lois were drinking coffee, Tom on the sofa and Lois in a chair by the window. When she saw Charlie, Lois stood up so fast coffee slopped from her cup.

"How is she, Charlie? Is she all right? Is she coming out?"

"I think she'll come out after a while," Charlie said.

"Is she all right?"

"Yes, I think she is."

"Did she tell you anything?"

"She was very helpful. Listen, we have to go. Say hi to Dick for me."

"Got time for some cake?"

"Wish I did. We really have to go; next time, maybe." He was already heading for the door, Tom right behind him. Outside they ran to their car ignoring the pounding rain.

Lois yelled from the door, "You'll get soaked! Wait! Let me get you an umbrella!"

Before she finished her sentence, Charlie was spinning his wheels as he backed out of the driveway.

Chapter 26

Before his car came to a complete stop, Charlie ground the transmission into drive and aimed his vehicle on down the highway.

"Did you call Kitty, Tom?"

"She says the cramps have stopped. Another false alarm, she thinks."

Charlie briefed Tom on his talk with Kara. Tom said nothing and stared straight ahead through the windshield.

They rode in silence through the rain.

"Well, I'll be damned," Tom said.

Even with his wipers swiping furiously, the raindrops blurred Charlie's vision so he had to squint and lean forward over the steering wheel to see the road. He said to Tom, "I could get out and *walk* faster than this."

"I wouldn't try it," Tom replied.

Charlie squeezed the steering wheel until his knuckles were white again as he scowled over the steering wheel trying to see the road.

"I'm not looking forward to this, Charlie," Tom said. "Slow down even more and it'll be fine with me. I don't think I've been around long enough to confront a man like John Matthews."

"You think *I'm* looking forward to it, Tom? If I'm wrong, we might both be looking for jobs."

"Well, I hear the pepper plant is hiring. Whatever jobs we get would have to be less stressful than this."

"I can't argue with that."

Charlie crept along the highway and then turned onto the long, winding driveway that led up an incline to the Matthews mansion. Charlie stopped in front of the house and cut his engine. He and Tom sat in the car for a few minutes, watching the house. Now and then, a silhouette passed behind a lighted window. The garage door was closed; a thin strip of light shone through the crack at the bottom.

"Well, Tom, you ready?"

"Ready as I'll ever be, I reckon."

They hopped out of the car, slammed their doors behind them, and sprinted through the rain to the house and up the steps onto the long porch that stretched halfway around the house. Tom pressed the doorbell.

Diana answered the door dressed in jeans, a white T-shirt, white socks, and sneakers. With her soft, short hair, she looked like a beautiful young boy. Perhaps, Charlie thought, the way Jim Pratt had once looked—minus the breasts, of course. When Diana recognized who it was standing in the doorway, her eyes went wide, but she rallied fast and motioned them in.

"You're soaked," she said. "We haven't had a storm like this in a long time."

"Mighty early in the year for one too," said Tom.

"It's coming down," Charlie offered.

Diana led them into the living room. "I'm glad we didn't leave tonight, in this weather. We're leaving early in the morning though. The weatherman says it ought to be over by then. I'm going to a treatment center in California. After Mama and Daddy leave me there, they're going on a *vacation*, the first one they've been on in years." She turned to Tom. "I'm *so* glad I got up the nerve to go talk to Kitty. I've known, sort of, what was happening to me for a long time, but I didn't have the courage to admit it, or to try to do anything about it. Now I'm going to try."

Tom's eyes moved away from her to the logs flickering in the fireplace. "I'm very happy to hear that, Diana."

"Is your daddy here?" Charlie asked.

"He just took a load of stuff to the car, in the garage. Mama's upstairs, still packing, I think."

"We need to talk to your daddy," Tom said.

"Is anything wrong?"

"We just want to ask him a few questions before y'all leave," Charlie said.

"Oh. Well, I'll go look—"

A man's voice rang out from an adjoining room. "Di, honey, I can't find that Polaroid anywhere. Any idea where—"

John Matthews walked into the room. When he saw Charlie and Tom, he stopped so suddenly he almost tripped, but he stayed on his feet, smiled, and turned on the charm.

"Well, I'll be darned! What in thunder brings you guys out here on a night a fish wouldn't go out in? I know you didn't drive through this storm just to say good-bye."

"Maybe we did," Charlie said. "We're gonna miss y'all. Where you headed, John?"

"Linda and I are going on vacation," Matthews said, grinning big. "We're long overdue for one."

"Well, I know you're busy getting packed up and all, but we need to talk to you."

"Well, I—"

"It won't take long."

"Well, okay. Sure. Let's go back to my den."

Leaving Diana in the living room, they followed Matthews down a hallway to his den. In the spacious room, a picture window faced the front lawn. A cherry wood and bronze-handled refrigerator decorated one corner. A plush sofa ran halfway around the room. An aquarium, full of exotic, colorful fish, gurgled along one wall. Bookshelves filled with leather-bound books and artifacts lined a second wall. The third was adorned with paintings, including one of Christ that was the exact match to Pratt's and Walker's. Charlie and Tom flicked a glance at each other when they saw it. Matthews's mahogany desk with his huge leather chair behind it stood near the bookshelves.

Matthews held out a gold embossed cigarette case.

"Smoke?"

"I quit," said Tom.

"And I'm trying to," Charlie said.

Matthews, Charlie knew, had been born and raised in Ybor City and had graduated from the University of South Florida with marketing and business degrees. In his senior year, he'd met Linda Bevins, and after graduation, they'd married and moved to Linda's hometown, Flowing Wells. During the first year of their marriage, Linda taught first-grade school while John worked at the bank.

Matthews's meteoric advancement in the bank had been astonishing, but the speed with which he accumulated a fortune was even more amazing. Soon after he and Linda had purchased their first home, Matthews had bought one thousand acres of seemingly worthless land in Polk County. Within a year, Simon-Simms Phosphate Industry moved into the area and gave Matthews twenty times what he had paid for the land. Immediately he reinvested in other enterprises, all of which made him more money. Townspeople called Matthews "Mr. Midas" since everything he touched turned to gold. But it remained a mystery where he got the money for the original one thousand acres in Polk County. He didn't borrow it, and it was rumored he'd paid cash. But his fortune was amassed so quickly, everyone quit wondering about that initial purchase and eventually forgot it altogether. Everyone, that is, but Charlie Morris.

Matthews looked over his desk at Tom and Charlie. He said solemnly, "I can't thank y'all enough for what you've done for Diana, for this family. I've been so wrapped up in business the past few years, I lost track of what's really important—my family. But now we're making a new start. Diana's going for treatment for her drug problem, and Linda and I are going on vacation, just the two of us. It looks like things are finally coming together for us, and we owe that to y'all. And I'm glad that I'm in a position to show you just how grateful I am—if you know what I mean." He leaned forward in his chair and patted his wallet. "But tell me what brings you out in this storm. Is Diana in some other kind of trouble? Is there something I don't know about?"

"This has to do with you, John, not Diana," Charlie told him.

"Me?"

Matthews lit up a cigarette.

"Yes, you." Charlie leaned forward. "May I tell you a little story, John?"

Matthews tapped his ashes into the ashtray, sank back into his chair, and sighed. "I'm a busy man, Charlie. I don't have time for stories. If I had time for stories, I'd read books."

"You've got time for this one," Tom said. "And if I were you, I'd listen."

"Once upon a time, there was this little country town that was pretty quiet and peaceful for the most part," Charlie began. "Then one day, a tall, handsome stranger marries a local gal and comes to live there and goes to work in the bank. He rockets right to the top of the banking business in no time. He's also a magician. He pulls a big wad of cash out of his hat and buys a bunch of land. Pretty soon, he sells it and makes a killing. From then on, everything he touches turns to gold, and he's the richest man in the county in no time—one of the richest men in the whole darn state, in fact!

"Well, about this time, there's a drug epidemic all over the state, mainly in the big cities at first, but gradually it creeps into small towns, including the town in my story. The sheriff tries to find out how the stuff is coming in but has no luck.

"Time passes, and the rich banker gets richer and richer. More and more drugs, mainly cocaine, keep coming in too. But what upsets the townspeople and the sheriff the most is when this pretty little high school girl, who has everything in the world to live for, is found murdered, with a bullet hole in the back of her head."

Charlie paused, took a cigarette out of his own pack, and lit it. Out of the corner of his eye, he saw Matthews watching him. Charlie scooted his chair closer to the desk.

"Well, of course, everybody in town was outraged. The girl's parents were devastated. The question on everyone's lips was: why? Why would anyone kill this sweet, innocent, lovely girl? Why?"

"Any ideas, John?"

Matthews crushed out his cigarette, lit another. "It's your fairy tale, Charlie. But as I said, I'm a busy man, and I'm in a hurry. Can you speed it up a little?"

"Fairy tale? Sure, but it didn't seem like a fairy tale to the girl's parents. Anyway, the sheriff was stumped. What was missing was motive. It always came back to that question everyone was asking. Why? Why on earth would anyone kill a sixteen-year-old girl everybody loved?"

"Maybe some nut," Matthews suggested. "Maybe some bum passing through."

Charlie scratched his head. He stood up and moved to the side of the desk. Looking down on Matthews, he said, "Yeah, maybe. The sheriff thought of that, but somehow it didn't fit. Why would some bum, someone who knew nothing about the town or the people, be prowling around that far from town, way out in that deserted stretch along the river where old Cyrus Potter built that little shack years ago?"

Neither Tom nor Charlie missed the twitch of Matthews's mouth at the mention of the shack.

"By the way, Mr. Matthews," Tom said, "you are familiar with that little shack, aren't you?"

"No."

"Not many people are," Charlie said. "Shoot, you could put a half dozen shacks the size of that one in this den. It's all covered up with trees and weeds and brush and vines and stuff. It was pure luck Tom found it. Anyway, on with my fairy tale.

"The sheriff thought and thought about the case, but nothing seemed to make sense. The only possible explanation for the murder was that the girl had found out something that someone didn't want her to know, something that would be so bad for him if it came out that he had to kill her to be sure it never got out.

"Well, the sheriff and his men started peeking into closets and turning over rocks, looking for any kind of clue they could find. Finally, they caught a break. Where? Why, right in that little shack I was telling you about. They found some snapshots."

Charlie stepped to the window and looked out just as a flash of lightning lit up the lawn. The rain beat down, streaming down the outside of the large window.

"Mighty unusual," Charlie said, "a storm like this so early in the year."

"Lots of unusual stuff going on," Tom said, keeping his eyes on Matthews.

Charlie walked away from the window and went back to Matthews. "Now, John, I'm telling you those snapshots were some kind of filth. Sick stuff. Not man and woman stuff, mind you, but man and man, and man and boy stuff. My god, it makes my skin crawl just to think about it. I tell you it was stomach-turning."

Charlie put his hands on the desk, leaned over it close to Matthews's face. He lowered his voice and spoke as though he were confiding a secret to a friend. "And you know what, John? You won't believe this. One of the men in those pictures was the principal of the local high school! You know what else? The other man in the pictures was a teacher, and the two boys were his students! Now is that weird, John, or what? And Lord have mercy, you should have seen the stuff they were doing. Why, it'd make you puke all over the place."

Charlie shook his head as if he were in disbelief that such behavior could occur anywhere on earth, much less in his own little town.

"Now the sheriff figured one of those four . . . But let me back up a little. This thing just gets crazier, John. You're not going to believe it."

"Probably not," Matthews said. "Are you anywhere near the end of this tall tale? You know, Charlie, I don't want to hurt your feelings or anything, but this story of yours just doesn't interest me."

"Well, I apologize if I'm boring you. Just wait, it gets better. It turns out that the teacher in these pictures had been selling cocaine to his students. He wasn't the head honcho in the coke business, but he had connections. One of the girls he turned on got into bed with him. So there he was, screwing one of his students, who happened to be the daughter of the rich man!"

Matthews winced and started to stand up, but then flopped back down into his chair. He tried to light another cigarette but gave up when he couldn't control his trembling hands. His face flushed as he fought to keep it expressionless.

"So," Charlie went on, "it seemed to the sheriff that the principal, knowing the teacher so, uh, intimately, must've also known about the cocaine racket. In fact, he was probably mixed up in it himself.

"Well, by now, the teacher had been arrested and put in jail. The principal got arrested too, on the evidence of the pictures, and he also got locked in the slammer. But not wanting to face what he knows lies ahead, he hangs himself."

Matthews's mouth twitched, but again he forced himself to sit still. He reached for another cigarette but threw it down on his desk when his hand shook so he couldn't light it.

"Another question besides 'Who did it?' and 'Why?' that kept bothering the sheriff and his deputy was 'Who took those pictures'? The camera didn't fly around inside that little shack and take those photos on its own. So before they arrested the principal, they asked him that question. He claimed they had set the camera on a table and set it on a ten-second delay. Those pictures were taken from too many different angles for the principal's claim to be true. Somebody else had to have been there to take them. But the principal wouldn't budge from his story, even though it had to be a lie. The sheriff was sure the principal was protecting someone.

"Now in this same town, there's another very pretty little girl, who's sweet as pie most of the time, but she has a problem with her mind. As long as she takes her medicine as prescribed, she's okay, most of the time, but when she quits taking it, her mind plays tricks on her, and sometimes she has trouble knowing what's real from what's only in her head. Now this little gal—let's call her Kara—was a good friend of the girl who was murdered. Let's call her Sandy. In fact, Sandy went by Kara's house early in the morning on the day Sandy was killed."

Matthews sat up straight and said in his authoritative boss's voice, "I don't want to hear any more of this shit."

Charlie stepped closer to Matthews and signaled Tom to get up too. Flanked by the two big men, Matthews sat still, looked down at his desk. He crossed his arms across his chest.

"I don't blame you, John," Charlie said. "If I were in your shoes, I wouldn't want to hear any more either. But hold on. I'm almost to the end. You wouldn't want to miss the most interesting part. It happened that the sheriff and his deputy, on a dark and stormy night, a night a lot like tonight, went to see the girl called Kara. The sheriff had begun to believe that Kara committed the murder. Kara was in love with the slime ball teacher, and she might've thought Sandy was planning to turn him in for selling cocaine to students. I told you this thing was crazy, John. It gets even crazier. So the sheriff went to see Kara, who just happened to be her normal self that day. And you know what she told him?" Charlie lowered his voice dramatically. "Kara said that when Sandy left her house the morning of the murder, she followed her and she saw who killed Sandy!"

Matthews tried to shrink, to sink deeper down into the folds of his chair until he disappeared. Finally he spoke through clenched teeth. "Even if that girl did see something, which I doubt, no court would believe the word of an idiot."

"Oh, she's no idiot, but there's more. It wasn't, you see, until the sheriff was driving through the storm to the suspect's house that he understood what happened. He finally figured out the truth. Or more like it, the truth just sort of came to him, in a flash, so to speak. Want to hear it?"

"No. I want you to get the hell out of my house. I'm leaving early in the morning, and I've got a lot to do. I told you I—"

"Oh, come on, John. Take it easy. I won't be but a couple more minutes. You gotta hear this. When Kara whispered the name of the killer to the sheriff, he was stunned. He couldn't believe it. It was too far-fetched. It made no sense. Kara had to be lying or covering up for someone.

"So as the sheriff drove on through the rain, the words *cover-up cover-up cover-up* kept bouncing around inside his head.

"Then, like a flash of the lightning striking all around, the answer came. The sheriff knew. At last he knew!"

Chapter 27

Not more than an hour after Jim Pratt's arrest, a car with Tampa plates pulled into the parking lot of Uncle Buck's Blue Duck Café. A tall, well-built dark-complexioned man of about thirty got out, crushed a cigarette under his heel, and with slow, deliberate moves, lit another. A kid who bore an amazing resemblance to the young Elvis Presley walked past him, without looking at him, on the way to his car. He'd spoken to the boy once, and now he made a mental note to do so again if the opportunity arose. The boy climbed into a car with an old man in the passenger seat, and drove away. The tall, well-built man smoked half the cigarette, flipped it away from him, and went inside.

The man, whose name was Zeke, known professionally as the Zebra, took a booth facing Highway 17. A few feet on the other side of the Zebra, a young cop sat at the counter, drinking coffee and talking to a pretty waitress whom he called Wanda. The Zebra did not want to draw attention to himself by calling for a waitress, so he lit another cigarette and waited.

"I was such a fool," Zebra heard the waitress tell the cop. "I don't know what got into me. Do you think you can ever forgive me, Mike? Can it ever be like it used to be with us?"

"I forgive you, Wanda. You know I do, and I still love you too—but I reckon it'll take some time for things to get back like they used to be—as far as the trust goes, I mean."

"I really am so sorry, Mike. I can't begin to tell you how sorry I am. I—"
She suddenly noticed the tall man in the booth for the first time. "Excuse me," she said to Mike. "Be right back."

Wanda walked around the counter and went over to the man.

"I'm sorry, sir, I was talking to my boyfriend and didn't see you come in. What can I get you? The meatloaf is good today and—"

"Just coffee," the man said. He smiled a smile that was all teeth and charm. "And I don't mind the little wait. It was worth it to hear young love getting back on the right track."

Wanda felt her face flush and knew she was blushing.

"Oh," she said. "Were we talking that loud? I'm so sorry, sir. I—"

He held up his hand. "Don't apologize. It gives me hope there still might be a chance for me and my ex-wife. I pray every day she'll take me back. Fool that I am, I cheated on her—only one time!—and she found out about it, and she's having a hard time dealing with it."

Wanda was quiet for a moment, looking at the floor.

"I hope it works out for you, sir, like it has for us. I'll get your coffee."

When she set the coffee down in front of the Zebra, he said, "Maybe you can help me out."

"Well, sure, I'll try," Wanda replied. "What is it?"

"An old buddy of mine, Jim Pratt, called me the other day and said he was teaching school here in Flowing Wells and said if I was ever through here to look him up. I'm in sales, on the road a lot. You know Mr. Pratt?"

Wanda stared at the man with her eyes wide for several moments.

"What?" the man said. "I say something wrong?"

"Oh no. I'm sorry. There were some other guys in here the other day looking for Mr. Pratt. Their names were Ed—"

"Eddie and Bruce! Well, I'll be darned! It is indeed a small world. We all used to hang out in California, back in the day. What the heck were those guys doing here?"

"On their way to the Keys, they said."

"Well, I'd like to see those guys too. It's funny how you can be so close to people and then just lose touch. It's sad, really. Anyway, what about Jim Pratt?"

"Well, I hate to tell you this, sir, but, uh, Mr. Pratt has been arrested."

"What?"

"Yes, sir, less than an hour ago. Everybody who comes in here is talking about it."

"Jim arrested? I can't believe it. What for?"

"Well, of course I don't know for sure, but what I hear is he was selling drugs and messing around with some of the high school students."

The Zebra shook his head. "I told Jim to leave the young girls alone. I'm a little bit surprised about the drugs though."

"I'm very sorry about your friend, sir. Can I get you anything else?"

"No, thank you," the man said, a look of deep sorrow settling over him that made Wanda look away.

"Let me know if I can get you anything else," Wanda said and went back behind the counter and put on a fresh pot of coffee.

"Who was that?" Mike asked. "He looks familiar."

"Friend of Jim Pratt's. Looked pretty torn up when I told him he'd been arrested."

Mike looked around to see a five dollar bill beside an untouched cup of coffee and an empty booth. The man was gone.

* * *

Jim Pratt sat on the edge of his cot in his shitty little cell, holding his head in his hands, wanting a beer. He wanted a beer bad. And he wanted a line. Two lines. Hell, he wanted a fucking mountain.

He still could not believe this had happened. He kept thinking maybe he was dreaming. He'd had dreams before that seemed so real he'd wake up surprised it was only a dream. Maybe this was one of those.

He hoped so. If it wasn't, it was unquestionably the absolute worst day of his entire miserable life.

Pratt had no way of knowing that this was the luckiest day of his life. If Charlie had held off with his arrest for another hour, by now the Zebra would be showing him what a really bad day was all about.

* * *

The Zebra was pissed not for the loss of the ten thousand dollars cash, which he'd probably be paid anyway—it wasn't his fault the prick had gotten arrested—but for the loss of the job itself. This was the kind of work he liked and excelled in. The kind that required all his precision instruments, the skills he had acquired in using them, and all day to do the job well.

He swore aloud as he drove the backcountry roads through Pinecrest, Fort Lonesome, and Wimauma on his return trip to Tampa. His 150-mile round trip had been a total waste of time and gasoline. The man whom he had been hired to make sorry he had ever been born was safe and snug inside the Pinewood County Jail.

Zebra had had a premonition that something was going to go wrong on this job. The call had come in on his untraceable cell phone, and the robotic, mechanical sounding voice had given detailed instructions and named a price that suited Zebra fine.

If the job had been a simple hit, Zebra would have demanded more money. But judging from the instructions he received on the phone, this job was ideal for his special skills. This was a job that was meant to send a message to every enemy of his employer in the country—hell, the *world*.

Whether his employer knew it or not, he had chosen the right man for the job. His employer's name had not been mentioned, but Zebra knew who he was. He'd met him once when he'd been on an assignment in Los Angeles. They had been introduced in the lobby of a hotel and immediately recognized each other's names and exchanged nods of mutual respect. The meeting was brief, but before Zebra departed, he slipped Scarletti his business card and told him if he ever needed any work done to give him a call. Scarletti said he would keep him in mind.

Now, two years later, the call had finally come, and Zebra had been unable to perform the service. Zebra was known internationally for his reliability, and he wanted no stain on his perfect record. But no one would expect anyone, not even a talented guy like himself, to break into a jail, do the kind of slow, delicate work the contract called for, and then break out without being caught. It couldn't be done.

What gave Zebra an eerie feeling about going to Flowing Wells was that he'd done a few jobs for a man who lived there, a guy named John Matthews. He'd never killed anybody for Matthews, just scared them badly enough to convince them which way to lean in some business deal Matthews was involved in. It had turned out to be fun, really, because the Zebra borrowed a few lines from his favorite movie, *The Godfather*. When Mathews's contact person asked Zebra how it went, Zebra had answered, "Oh, it went fine. He saw it our way fast. Tell Matthews I made him an offer he couldn't refuse."

It was while Zebra was working for Matthews that he'd met that kid outside The Blue Duck, the handsome boy resembling the young Presley whom Zebra believed was a piece of work with potential aplenty. With some coaxing, and proper coaching . . . Well, who knew?

But Zebra was confused about the contract on Pratt. Obviously he couldn't do the kind of work on Pratt that was called for while the man was in jail. And when, or if, he got out, would Scarletti still want the job done—or by then would things have changed so much that he would call off the contract? From all Zebra had heard about Scarletti—that he was an honorable man and an honest man—he felt sure he would get his money, or at least half of it, even if the contract was cancelled. Of course, with a job like this, the money wasn't the main thing. The attention to details and keeping the subject alive and conscious until the last possible moment was the main thing. Simply killing a man, or woman, to get him or her out of the way was one thing; doing the job so as to send a message to Scarletti's enemies all over the world was another. And at that, Zebra was the best. He knew it and took great pride in it.

Zebra drove on through the piney woods on County Road 62 and headed north on U.S. 301. Within a few miles, he could see the lights of Tampa. After being so primed and excited about doing the job for Mr. Scarletti, he hated the thought of going back to his boring house to watch television. He needed action. He felt it in his loins and all over his body, the way most men feel the sex urge. Just thinking about his work tools in the trunk and what he had planned for this Pratt fellow gave him a rocklike hard on.

Maybe he'd cruise Dale Mabry Boulevard and pick up one of the street whores that propositioned men at red lights. Maybe he'd even find that hot little redhead who'd given it to him for free. She didn't know it, of course, but her decision not to charge the Zebra was what saved her life that night. *Sure, baby, hop right in, baby.* One thing was for sure; whoever he picked up, it would be a night she would never forget—if, that is, he let her live to remember it. No one could ever accuse the Zebra of not being a merciful man!

He laughed as he sped down the road, unbuckling his belt and unzipping his zipper. He wouldn't reach a climax, but why not allow himself a little foreplay before he picked up his date for the night? Thanks to his many disguises, he had no fear of ever being identified.

But first, he had to go home and make some phone calls. He doubted he could reach Scarletti directly, but he could call some of his people and leave word for Scarletti to call him, and he was sure Scarletti would.

Sure enough, fifteen minutes after he made his first call, Scarletti called him back. Zebra told him Pratt was in jail so he couldn't get to him. Scarletti told him exactly what he had hoped to hear. Keep the ten thousand, which would arrive tomorrow, and put Pratt on hold. Scarletti said he'd put a man in Flowing Wells to give him a daily report. Whether or not Scarletti would need Zebra's services regarding Pratt later on would depend on what the system did with him. A few years in prison for a pretty boy like Pratt might be punishment enough. Thanks to prison guards on Scarletti's payroll in almost every prison across the country, he could get day-by-day reports on any prisoner.

If the little bastard survived, Scarletti might call for Zebra's services when he was released. Of course, it was possible that by then, Scarletti might decide Pratt had paid enough and let him go. But any way you looked at it, Zebra couldn't lose. He had his money, and if later Scarletti told him to finish the job he'd hired him to do, hell, it would be icing on the cake.

Zebra turned into the parking lot of an all-night diner. In the dim light, he put on a mustache and beard and changed his eye color with contact lenses. In twenty minutes, he'd be cruising Dale Mabry Boulevard, ready to offer some lovely lady a night to remember. *If I allow her to live to remember it!* Having the power of life and death at his fingertips made the Zebra feel like God. He smiled. He was in control, nothing like the hoards of dumb suckers out there punching time clocks and working their miserable lives away for peanuts.

Chapter 28

John Matthews ground his teeth and pushed back hard against his chair. He clenched his hands into fists, ready to slam anyone who tried to stop him from getting away.

"Goddamn it!" he yelled. "If you've got something to say to me, say it! Why the hell don't you cut through this bullshit and just say what you've got to say?"

"I am saying it, John," Charlie said. "If you've got ears, open them up and listen. The sheriff knew that as far as the drug thing was concerned, the teacher and the principal, who hung himself, were small potatoes. There had to be a main man, a head honcho. This big guy, whoever he was, had to have money and power and contacts all over the place."

"Bullshit." Matthews smirked. "You're crazy, Morris. I'll have your job for this."

"Maybe, but once you get it, you won't want it. Anyway, I grant you all this was the sheriff's two-and-two together, but his speculation was grounded on solid intuition he'd developed over long years of police work. And, it was *fact* that the murdered girl, Sandy, had a good friend whose father was just like the big guy would have to be—we'll call Sandy's friend Diana."

Matthews's lips pressed together so tightly they made his mouth look like a line a fine-tipped marker had drawn underneath his nose. The line split and came apart for him to speak.

"Damn you, Charlie Morris, you son of a bitch, you leave my daughter out of this."

"Take it easy, John. Remember your blood pressure. Your face looks like a ripe strawberry. Everybody in town knew that the rich banker was a philanderer. He wasn't nearly as discreet about his affair with a gal we'll call Shirley as he was about certain other areas of his private life. But you know how rumors spread in small towns.

"The sheriff heard whispers on the wind of another rumor about the banker that blew his mind. Want to know what the wind whispered to the sheriff, John? No? I don't blame you. But I'll tell you, anyway. The whispers said the big banker liked men, and boys, as well as women!"

Charlie lit a cigarette and took a couple of long, leisurely puffs.

The anger went out of Matthews as if someone had pulled a plug. It was replaced by paralyzing fear such as he'd not known since his first combat mission in Vietnam. How had this hick bastard of a sheriff found out? It was impossible. He'd been so careful. Morris wasn't that smart. Matthews drew in several deep breaths, fighting for the control he'd had so for long.

"You're full of shit, Charlie. You're fishing without any bait." But he heard the tremor in his voice, felt the fear seeping from his pores, a putrid stench near to that of death itself. He knew Charlie heard the tremor too, and that Charlie smelled his fear. His control was gone.

"Maybe so," Charlie said, "but the hole I'm fishing in is boiling with big 'uns, just like Tom's catfish hole!" He glanced at Tom and winked. "You see, John, nosey as our sheriff is, he sniffed out some other stuff. Proving the rich man was the person who took those pictures was easy. All he had to do was to borrow the banker's Polaroid camera, snap some pictures, and have a chemist compare them with those masterpieces found in the shack. You know, don't you, John, it's as easy to prove pictures were taken by the same camera as it is to match bullets fired from the same gun, or letters typed from the same typewriter?"

"No judge will admit those pictures, not taken from a camera you stole from my house."

"Oh, we didn't steal it, John. Tom came by yesterday and borrowed it from Linda to take some shots of Kitty. It was all on the up and up. You know I wouldn't do anything underhanded or go above the law."

"You son of a bitch."

Charlie lowered his head solemnly and drew on his cigarette. A brilliant flash of lightning lit up the den and the yard, followed by an ear-shattering explosion of thunder.

Matthews made a sound in his throat like the growl of a mad dog. When he spoke, his words were small, pointed slivers of ice, sharp in their extreme coldness.

"You'll pay for this, Morris, you motherfucker. I'll have your badge. And your balls too. And his." He cast a withering look at Tom. "Do you have any idea who I am, who you're fucking with?"

Charlie went on as if the banker had not spoken.

"Finally, the rich man in our story got a little too confident, too complacent. When he started thinking he was so mighty on his high horse that no one could touch him, he made himself vulnerable. He got clumsy. Taking those pictures with his own camera was stupid. By the way, John, where is your Polaroid?"

"I guess you know, you miserable cocksucker."

"Not me. I wasn't in any of those photos."

Matthews slid further down into his chair, looking to Charlie like he wanted to crawl under it and hide.

"Any of five people could have had motive to kill Sandy," Charlie said. "But there was one thing that still bothered the sheriff. One thing still didn't fit. Sandy didn't *know* about the sick sex stuff the boys were up to. So if she wasn't killed to keep that hush-hush, then there had to be another motive. But what? So the sheriff was stumped again. And it wasn't until that dark and stormy night, when he was creeping along through hard rain that lightning struck inside his head and showed him the truth."

"The truth?" Matthews's voice was so shaky Tom and Charlie could barely understand him.

"Yes, John, the truth. Do you know the meaning of that word? All of a sudden, all the pieces fit. The puzzle came together. The cocaine kingpin was none other than the rich banker himself! And somehow, his daughter, Diana, had found out about it. By now, she was hooked on the stuff, which she got from her teacher, who got it from her father!"

Matthews groaned.

"Now let's remember that Sandy was Diana's best friend. Sandy surely knew that Diana was hooked. What I figure is, Diana confided in Sandy about her father's drug dealing. Sandy, tough nut that she was, confronted the rich banker about it—confronted you, John! That's why you had to kill her."

"No no, wait a minute, wait a goddamn minute! I didn't know Sandy knew, if she knew. So why would I kill her?"

"You had to assume Diana told her. You couldn't take the chance."

"No, you're wrong about that, Charlie. I swear it."

A sudden movement and the blink of an eye drew Charlie's attention to the door of the den that was now partly open. The eye watching from the dimly lit hallway blinked again. Charlie's stomach flipped. Kara? What if he had been wrong? What if the eye belonged to Kara, the ghost-girl who knew all and saw all? What if Charlie had been right at first and Kara had killed Sandy?

The entire case could suddenly flip.

Charlie noticed that Tom had also seen whoever was standing behind the door.

Lightning flashed again so brightly that it startled everyone when the door was shoved wide open and Diana ran into the room.

"I love you, Daddy!" she screamed. "I did it for you! Don't let them hurt me, Daddy!" She whirled around to face Charlie. "Leave my daddy alone!"

Matthews's mouth worked soundlessly. Tom turned his back and punched a number into his cell phone, spoke softly, and hooked the phone back on to his belt.

"I did it for you, Daddy," Diana repeated. "I didn't want to, but I had to because I couldn't let her tell on you. I just couldn't. I tried to talk her out of it, but she wouldn't listen."

Matthews emitted a sound that began as a low gurgle deep in his throat and emerged from his mouth a high-pitched, mournful wail.

""Who else would have done for you what I did, Daddy? Now you've got to know how much I love you, and you've got to love me again too. I'm your little girl."

Charlie heard sirens in the distance as he cuffed Diana and began to recite her rights. "You have the right to . . ."

"Fuck you!" she screamed. "I had to kill her! Can't you see that? She was going to put my daddy in *jail*."

"And if you can't afford an attorney, one will be appointed by the court."

Tears were rolling down Diana's face and dripping off her chin. "Daddy," she cried, "don't let them do this to me, I'm your little girl. I did it for *you*!"

"Good god," Matthews gasped. "Good god almighty."

The room was quiet. Outside, the thunder rumbled, distant; lightning flashed farther away, with less brilliance. The sirens were closer, and the blue lights of the state police cars flashed across the yard and through the house.

Diana looked pleadingly into her father's face. The angry, confrontational voice was gone, replaced by that of a terrified child. "I really did do it for you, Daddy. You believe that, don't you? Now you know how much I love you, don't you, Daddy? You know I'd do anything for you."

Tears blinding him, Matthews got up to go to his daughter. Tom stepped between them.

"What the fuck?" Matthews said. "I want to hold my daughter."

"Sorry, John."

"What the fuck?"

"Regulations, John," Charlie said. "Be cool."

"Be cool, your big ass! You're arresting my Diana for murder, and you expect me to be cool?"

Two state police officers entered the room then, went straight to Matthews, cuffed him, and read him his rights. Matthews held his head high and did not speak as he was led out of the room.

Another officer escorted Diana out behind them.

Tom looked at the floor and shook his head.

"This is a nasty business we're in, isn't it, Charlie?"

Charlie lit up and did not answer.

Tom looked around. "Matthews had so much. He could have gotten out of the coke racket years ago, got away clean. Why'd he stay in?"

"Greed."

"How long have you known, Charlie?"

"Not till a few minutes ago, Tom. I had it so set in my head that John killed Sandy; when Kara told me she saw Diana do it, I thought she must have imagined it or somehow Diana, with her short hair, resembled her daddy. If Diana hadn't come through that door when she did, I might never have known the truth."

"What was that about me borrowing Matthews's Polaroid?"

"I've played a little poker."

"Well, you could have let me in on it."

"No time."

Just then, Linda Matthews called from upstairs, "Okay, John! That's it. That's the last—"

When she saw Charlie and Tom, she started down the stairs.

"I didn't know y'all were here. I've been packing. Can't hear anything upstairs, especially with the storm and the music blasting. We're leaving early in the morning and I don't want to forget anything. It's good to see y'all, but what . . ."

The looks on their faces stopped her. She said, "Is anything wrong? What's the matter? You both look like your favorite dog just died. Where's John and Diana?"

Charlie nodding toward the front door and the spinning blue lights. He said, "I'm sorry, Mrs. Matthews."

"Sorry about what? What are you talking about? What's the matter?" She hurried to the bottom of the stairs and ran past them toward the door.

"Come on, Tom," Charlie said.

They walked out onto the front porch. Charlie said through a cloud of smoke, "I'm gonna quit again, you know, now that this case is over."

Rain was still falling, but softly. The freshly washed air felt cool and clean. Tom breathed in deeply.

"That job at the pepper plant is looking better and better, Charlie."

Linda Matthews came back up the steps onto the porch, stopped just long enough to give Charlie and Tom a murderous look. Then she walked on into the big living room and went straight to the marble and onyx trimmed bar where she poured herself a glass of vodka and lit a cigarette.

"It's a nasty business," Tom said.

Turning so Tom couldn't see his face, Charlie snuffed out his cigarette in the soil of a potted plant, stood to his full height, straightened his wide shoulders, and turned to go back inside.

Chapter 29

Every Saturday for a month following the arrests, Charlie and Tom tried to make up the fishing trip that had been cancelled because of Jumbo Jones's telephone call announcing Sandy's murder; but each time something interfered with their plans. The Saturday of the fifth week looked promising, but Kitty decided that would be the perfect day for a party to celebrate the baptism of their son, Charles Thomas Wilson. When Tom told Charlie about the name, the sheriff was speechless.

"Nice name," he finally managed around a lump in his throat.

Tom and Kitty decided to have the celebration in their backyard. As he set up picnic tables in the shade of a sprawling live oak, Tom said to Kitty, "About that job at the pepper plant . . ."

Kitty snuggled little Charles Thomas to her breast.

"What about it?" she asked.

"Well, I've been thinking about it. I know the hours would be better, unless I got stuck on the graveyard shift, but—"

"You're not ready to give up police work, are you, Tom?"

"Well, I know there're things about it aggravating as all get out, but"—he looked at the baby on his wife's breast—"I want him to be proud of me."

"He'll be proud of you no matter what you do, Tom. I am too. Don't leave the department until you're sure that's what you want. You're a good cop. Charlie brags on you like crazy—behind your back, of course."

Charlie and Tom grilled hotdogs and hamburgers. Charlie's wife, Sally, made bowls of potato salad and coleslaw. Wanda Dunn brought a pot of baked beans from The Blue Duck, compliments of Uncle Buck.

In the backyard under the oak tree were the picnic tables and folding chairs that Tom had borrowed from the nearby Flowing Wells Elementary School, which he knew little Charlie would attend in a few years. The tables were set with paper plates and cups; plastic forks, knives, and spoons; catsup and mustard and mayonnaise; sliced tomatoes and onions, lettuce, and pickles. Bags of chips. A chocolate cake mysteriously appeared.

There were gallon jugs of tea, sweetened and unsweetened. On the ground at that end of the tables were coolers full of ice, soda, bottled water, and beer.

Adults sat in the shade of the oak as children ran and played in the yard. As Tom held his infant son in his arms and stared into the small face, he felt a tiny hand grasp his finger. Charlie chuckled. "Reminds me of me when Peg was a baby."

Unable to tear his eyes away from his boy's face, Tom said, "You know, it's like a miracle. When I look into those little eyes I . . ."

"It is a miracle," Charlie said. "Anybody that can hold one of those little angels in his arms and not believe in miracles has no soul."

Sally tossed her head to throw back her hair. "Our big tough guys have a soft spot."

"They do," Kitty agreed.

Tom looked at Charlie who was grinning

A car door slammed in front of the house. Mike Evers walked around the house to the backyard. Wanda ran to meet him, kissed his cheek, took his hand and guided him toward the baby.

"Look Mike," she said. "Isn't he precious?"

"Uh, yeah."

Wanda squeezed his hand. "Want to hold him for a minute, Mike?"

"Well, sure, I guess so. I don't know much about holding babies though. What if I drop it?"

"Where's Plumber, Mike?" Charlie asked.

"He stayed at the station. Wants me to bring him a couple of hot dogs. He's talking to Garcia."

"Garcia's here?"

"He was passing through, he said, and stopped in to congratulate us on a job well done. You know, he's not quite the jerk I thought he was."

"He can be," Charlie said. "But he's a good cop."

"Why didn't you invite him over, Mike?" Tom asked.

"I did. He said he had to hurry, but he'd take a rain check, and to tell everybody hello and congratulations. Oh, he also told me to ask you if you got the cake."

Mike fixed himself a plate of food and sat down by Charlie. "That Plumber is a real pain," he whispered "Him and his meetings!"

"Sam Jenkins started going again."

"Yeah?"

"Elvis called this morning to tell me about it. He wanted to be here today, but he said he was taking his daddy to a 'meeting marathon' in Tampa."

"Hey, what're you guys whispering about?" Sally asked. "No secrets!"

Charlie winked at Mike.

"Sorry, honey. Police stuff."

"I hear Linda Matthews is selling the mansion and moving to California," Tom said.

"It's true," Charlie confirmed. "She claims she's going to start a 'Diana Matthews Center.' Says it'll be relatively small, and no one over twenty-one will be admitted. When they both get clean and sober, they plan to run it together—when Diana is released."

"That might be a while," said Tom.

"I know John will be happy to hear about it," Kitty said. "What's going to happen to him, Charlie?"

"He'll do time."

As shadows lengthened and color spotted the western sky, everyone had gone home except Charlie, Sally, and Peg. Tom and Charlie cleaned up and put everything away. Tom's backyard was now just a backyard again.

"You got a good man here, Kitty," Sally said. "You better keep a close eye on him or some shameless hussy will try to steal him right out from under your nose."

Kitty smiled.

*   *   *

Tom suggested they drive to the boat landing in Pioneer Park on the Peace River to watch the sunset. Tom sat in the passenger seat of Charlie's car with little Charlie in his arms. Kitty drove. Peg leaned over into the front seat looking at the baby.

"Connie and David have got to be going through pure hell," Tom said.

"It's too awful even to think about," Kitty said. "Let's not talk about it. Charlie, do you think Diana will be in that place a long time?"

Charlie shrugged. "She's in the system now. It's up to her shrinks, and the court. I don't know what will happen. She did commit cold-blooded murder. Killed her best friend."

"I'm sorry for Linda," Sally said. "She was more or less just caught in the middle. I don't think she had clue what was going on around her."

"I don't think she wanted to know," Charlie said. "It was easier hiding in a liquor bottle than facing the truth of what was happening."

Kitty sighed.

"I'm just glad it's over. Maybe now things can get back to normal—or as close to normal as a cop's life can be—and I'll have my husband back again."

Charlie parked in the grassy area by the boat ramp. They got out of the car and walked down to the edge of the river. The current was slow; the smooth water mirrored the oak and cypress trees on the other side.

The sun was dipping down behind the trees. Charlie took his namesake out of Tom's arms.

"Charles Thomas Wilson," he said, "I promise to make sure you get a good education, and some religion. I will also help teach you how to throw a ball, hit a homerun, and I'll show you where to catch the big ones in this river."

The baby stared at Charlie and then burped. Everyone laughed as the first rays of sunset tinged the water pink.

Chapter 30

Elvis knew the back roads to Tampa well. He found the church hosting the AA meeting marathon with no problem, walked Sam inside, found him a seat, and brought him a coffee.

He looked around the room at the crowd of recovering alcoholics and realized he'd achieved his goal of getting his father some help, saving his life.

He whispered, "I'm out of cigarettes, Daddy. I'm gonna take a break and buy a pack. Be back in an hour or so."

"Don't forget me."

Elvis laughed.

"Not likely."

*   *   *

Elvis drove a few blocks and turned onto the shell driveway of a modest house shaded with oak and elm trees. *Perfect cover*, he thought as he got out of his car and walked to the door and knocked.

The door opened, and a tall, well-built dark-complexioned man filled the doorway.

"Elvis?"

A touch of surprise tinged his voice.

"You said come see you sometime."
"Yes, I did."
"May I come in?"
"Sure," said the tall man, closing the door behind them.

The End

Leland Durrance (Chip) Ballard was born and raised in rural central Florida. He earned an AA degree at South Florida Junior College, and graduated with honors from the University of South Florida, with a BA in English.

His weekly newspaper column, "Inside Out," has run in *The Bradenton Herald*, *The Herald Advocate*, *The Franklin Chronicle*, *Highlands Today*, *The Polk County Democrat*, *The Charlotte Sun* and *The Fort Meade Leader*.

His short stories have won local, state and national awards and have been published in magazines including *The State Street Review*, *Fiction Quarterly*, *The Tampa Bay Review*, *The Pentangle*, *Land & Living in Southwest Florida*, *Florida Living*, *Spectrum Magazine* and *The Garden Doctor*.

Peace River is his first published novel.

Made in the USA
Lexington, KY
09 December 2011